WEST OF WEST

Jim Taylor

authorHOUSE®

AuthorHouse™
1663 Liberty Drive, Suite 200
Bloomington, IN 47403
www.authorhouse.com
Phone: 1-800-839-8640

First published by AuthorHouse 7/26/2007

ISBN: 978-1-4343-1446-8 (sc)

Library of Congress Control Number: 2007903832

*Printed in the United States of America
Bloomington, Indiana*

This book is printed on acid-free paper.

To Shirley, my wife, and the many other people who helped and encouraged me.

PROLOGUE

In the middle of the street the huge man known as Bear Beaumont stood in front of Josh Collins' team that was hitched to the wagon. In his huge, hairy fist he was holding the bridle reins to prevent the wagon from moving. His deep gravelly voice matched his imposing size.

"Collins, they say you are the best fighter this little pissant town has to offer. But you won't fight me because you got a wedding planned for tomorrow. I told those folks standing there you'd fight me today, and they put money up against that happening."

From the wagon seat, tall and slender Josh looked at his friends, about eight men, some standing and some sitting on the porch of the saloon. It was obvious to all he was not pleased with the situation they had put him in. He had been told that a prizefighter was coming to town looking for a fight, and he had let everyone know he was not available.

Josh turned to Bear Beaumont. "Mr. Whoever You Are, you are going to lose the bet, because I don't plan to fight you or anyone else today. Now turn loose those bridles, and I'll be on my way."

The bear of a man directed his voice at Josh as he smiled and glared at the beautiful lady on the wagon seat next to Josh. "That ugly thing on your wagon seat the one you plan to wed tomorrow? Or just one you're using today?"

Aware that the professional fighter intended to provoke him, the farmer remained still and did not respond. But he was thinking about stepping from the wagon onto the back of the bay mare. He knew she was gentle and would not bolt out from under him if he used her broad back to launch himself onto the loud bear of a man. However, he rejected the idea quickly, because he did not wish to fight, and he knew if he got close enough for this man to wrap his arms around him, the monster would break his back or collapse his rib cage. Neither of these events appealed to the slim farmer.

Tired of waiting for a response, Bear Beaumont growled, "You know she ain't nothing but a slut, and most of the men there have had her."

The men standing and watching knew that the things just said about the lovely bride-to-be, Carol, were not true. As Josh stepped down from the wagon and started walking toward Bear Beaumont, they also knew they were about to lose their bet with the prizefighter.

Bear Beaumont turned loose the bridle reins and stepped to meet Josh.

He didn't see the blow coming, but he felt the pain as his nose began spurting blood. With his eyes watering badly, it was suddenly difficult to see. He realized that the farmer who did not wish to fight was lightning fast and had a powerful punch. Within seconds, Beaumont was wishing he had never heard the name, Josh Collins.

CHAPTER 1

(Seven years later)

Race to sorrow
Or to some fun —
Too soon,
The race we run.

The hilly land around West, Mississippi, was not part of the rich Mississippi Delta. In fact, it in no way resembled the rich, flat delta land.

Most people living in these hills had never seen a plantation. The people, white and black, all worked hard to survive, living in small, unpainted houses.

Most of the topsoil had been washed downstream to enrich the delta area hundreds or thousands of years ago. Making a living on this land was not easy. Almost every farmer found a way to supplement his income. Those who held on year after year had to. Some made whiskey; others made molasses.

Thirty-year-old Josh Collins had struggled all his adult life to survive and provide for his family. Some of his neighbors lived and farmed on bottomland along the Big Black River and fared a little better. However, the rich bottomland didn't extend far from the muddy river, and when the river flooded it would sometimes wash their crops and houses away. So life was often a struggle for them as well.

The year 1886 was a little better than most. Rain had come at the right time to make a better corn and cotton crop than in recent years. Farmers who lived in the Mississippi Delta would not have considered it a good crop, but for the area around West, 1886 was as good as it could get.

That year, Joey Collins was one year old, Dan was five, and their sister, Betty Sue, was two. Their mother, twenty-five year old Carol Collins, worked hard taking care of the three children, the chickens and the garden, while doing her part in the fields as well. It was understood in that part of the world that when the cotton needed chopping or picking, all the women donned their bonnets and helped.

She was a pretty, medium-sized lady with blue eyes and blonde hair, but not as healthy as others in the family. It seemed as though she caught every sickness that was going around.

She had a ready smile that puzzled those who bothered to pay attention. But there was a reserve in her smile, as if smiling caused a little pain.

Horses and mules were necessary, but they were also a big problem, because they ate. They were needed to farm the land, pull the wagons and for personal transportation. In the spring, they were necessary to break the ground, to plow and plant, and you could get good money for a horse or mule come spring. But in the winter months, they died, or farmers sold them to keep from dying themselves. After the crops were in each fall, most people didn't have enough feed to keep their animals in good condition through the winter.

Josh had observed this cycle. He began to grow less cotton and more corn.

He also bought some land that everyone said was good for nothing, because cotton had been grown on it for so many years it would no longer produce cotton, corn, or any other crop. He started buying a few horses and mules each fall, holding them on the land that others considered worthless, feeding them a little corn to keep them in shape and selling them in the late winter or spring. This work brought in much-needed extra cash.

Josh agonized over telling Carol his new plan, because he knew she would be upset. Now time had run out, and he could delay no longer.

CHAPTER 2

When loved ones are apart
Fear of the unknown
Rests heavy
On the heart.

"I need to take a trip to Fort Worth, Texas," Josh said to Carol. "We've been making more money with a few horses and mules each year than others around here have with cotton. In the spring, we can sell all the horses we can find. I've been hearing about how many horses they have out there, and I want to find a way to get more horses to sell next spring."

"Josh, have you got enough money to buy more than five or six horses?" Carol asked him.

"No, not at the prices I pay for horses here. But I've been told that horses are cheap in Texas. I've got enough money to go find out what the situation is and get back home. It may work out that I'll buy a few horses and lead them home. We may not be able to make any deals this year. But I'll at least know what the possibilities are. I really don't know how many I can buy, or how I can get them home. I just know I've got to go find out."

Since getting married seven years ago, they had not spent one night apart. She had watched him figure out how to make a little better living than their neighbors. She had confidence in him. But even so, her thoughts frightened her. What if something happened to him? What if he never returned? What if something went wrong while he was gone? She kept these terrifying thoughts to herself, knowing that she would cry herself to sleep every night until he returned.

He went to the kitchen and got himself a drink of whiskey from the jug he kept there. She went outside, looked up at the stars, and she said a prayer to summon her courage.

The next morning she was up before daylight, cooking biscuits, ham and eggs. Josh would eat his fill of these, along with some molasses, and carry some biscuits and ham along to eat on the journey.

"If anything happens, send for Dave," he told her as he sat down to his breakfast. "I talked to him yesterday, and he will be here each day to make sure you and the children are okay and to take care of anything you need. You know you can count on him and Nor to help handle anything that comes up."

Dave was a black man who came to work on the Collins' farm almost every day, and he never needed to be told what to do. He and Josh had worked side by side since they were young boys.

"Dan's only five years old," Josh said, "but he knows the way to Dave's place, and he knows the way to town. Just put a bridle on the bay mare — he doesn't need a saddle. But make sure the boy has his shoes on, so the mare can feel him kicking. Put him up there, and he'll get the job done. I've never seen a young boy try so hard to get things right. We can be mighty proud of that boy."

He walked over to her and held her soft cheek in his rough hand.

"And I'm mighty proud of my lovely wife, too," he told her.

Somehow, she managed to hold back the tears and hoped the fear didn't show in her eyes.

"I'll ride the brown horse up to Memphis," Josh continued, "and leave him at the livery until I get back.

"I understand you can get on the train there and go all the way to Fort Worth without getting off. I don't know what you do about going to the outhouse or eating, but I guess I'll find out. It'll take two or three days to get to Memphis — I don't know how long to get to Fort Worth. I don't know how long it'll take to learn what I need to know. I think I should be back in two to three weeks. But I don't know. So don't look for me till you see me."

The uncertainty of all this didn't console Carol, who was determined to pinch back her tears until her tall husband was gone. But her determination wasn't enough, and her tears spilled out.

She knew he was a good fighter. Even as he held her in his arms, she could feel the gun under his jacket. But what if a gang attacked him — or what if he tried to rescue someone else from harm and ended up injured, or worse?

They wrapped their arms around each other. She sobbed as he fought to make sure his own tears didn't show.

Neither of them could imagine the great changes that were about to take place in their lives.

CHAPTER 3

A man can make new friends
Away from home
And still be
So alone.

As Josh rode into Memphis three days later, cold and tired, he saw a skinny boy leading a milk cow that really needed milking, and he considered talking to him about taking care of the brown horse. On second thought, he could see the boy had his hands full trying to lead the reluctant Jersey. Josh rode on to the livery.

Once there, staying in the saddle, he said, "Howdy."

The big blacksmith just grunted.

Josh took that for a howdy. "How much to have you take care of this horse for a couple weeks?" he asked.

"I'll put him in the lot over there on the east side with those others. I give them some hay each day for one dollar a week. Or I put him in the pen on the west side, and he'll get hay and corn each day for two dollars a week. If I can rent him out, I'll take some off," the big man replied, without taking his eyes off the red-hot horseshoe he was pounding.

Josh noticed that neither bunch of horses looked well fed. The thought of the brown gelding being rented out to just anyone gave him a sick feeling. He suspected this big man was going to rent his horse out to others, whether he agreed to allow it or not. He nodded and said, "Reckon I'll think on it," then rode off.

He rode back to where he had seen the boy with the cow and found their tracks were easy to follow in the soft ground. The tracks led him to an overworked-looking woman wearing a bonnet. She was milking the cow that was tied in the corner of a pen made from old sawmill slats. The boy was on the other side of the fence, holding the cow's tail. Apparently his job was to keep the cow from kicking, and if she did kick, to pull her by the tail, throwing her off balance at the right time to prevent her hoof from making contact with the woman or the milk bucket. Judging from the spilled milk on the ground, they hadn't been entirely successful. Josh guessed the lady and the boy had some bruises that just didn't show as well as that spilled milk.

Josh waited, sitting quietly on his horse until they were finished, when he was surprised to see that the bucket was almost full. Then he said to the woman, "Excuse me, Ma'am. Would it be all right if I talk to this boy about taking care of my horse for a couple of weeks?"

"May I ask why you need him to take care of your horse?" she asked, after looking Josh and the brown gelding over carefully. "Looks like to me you're doing a good job."

"I need to take a business trip to Fort Worth, Texas, on the train. I'll be gone for a week or two."

"He's out of school for Christmas," she said, "but he has chores to do. As long as it don't interfere with his getting his chores done, he can do it. Is that horse likely to hurt him?"

"No, Ma'am. He's nice and gentle. If the boy handles him right, they should get along." Then Josh looked at the skinny boy who was about to jump out of his skin with excitement. "Son, my name is Josh Collins. What's yours?"

"Thomas, sir. My name is Thomas Calcoat."

"Thomas, I'll be gone a week, maybe two, I think. If I am gone longer, I'll pay for the extra time. I'll pay you a dollar a week when I get back. I'll give you two dollars now to buy corn. I want him to have six ears of corn each day if the ears are big, or eight if they're small. If they're just nubbins, give him ten or twelve. Grass every day and plenty of water."

The boy's blue eyes looked as big as saucers when he told Josh, "I never had two dollars. I never had *one* dollar."

"Well, you do a good job for me, and you'll have a few dollars. Oh, by the way, will you exercise him each day, if I give you an extra dollar when I get back?"

"Sure! I'll lead him around for a good while every day."

"Well, I guess I can settle for that, but I was hoping you'd ride him some each day. You ever ride a horse?"

"Yes sir, I rode some. But I ain't never rode one with a saddle. I ain't never been paid to ride one either."

Josh smiled, thinking he had brought his horse to the right place. "Just make sure his back and girth are clean before you put the blanket and saddle on," he told the boy. "And walk and trot him some each day."

Knowing a little about boys, Josh figured the brown horse would probably get plenty of galloping. But he hoped that by asking Thomas to only walk and trot, he wouldn't gallop the brown gelding until the horse was exhausted.

"Here's the money for corn. I expect to find my horse in good shape when I return. Good day to you, Ma'am." He put two dollars in the boy's dirty right hand, the bridle reins in the left, untied his bag from behind the saddle and headed toward the railroad station. As he looked back, he saw Thomas standing there not knowing whether to look at the money or the horse. Josh smiled, pleased that he had not left the brown gelding at the livery.

***

When he got off at the depot in Fort Worth, he was disappointed to find that he was several miles from the stockyard. It was early morning, and he knew that walking would help warm him up. He got directions from the train conductor and started out. Just about sunrise, as he came over a hill, he looked up and held his breath for a long minute. He was shocked at the size of the massive operation before him. He was looking at hundreds or maybe thousands of cattle.

Men on horses were driving some toward the railroad pens and others toward buildings much bigger than any he had ever seen. At first he thought the large buildings were on fire. Then he realized that these were bigger versions of the slaughterhouse he had seen in Memphis, and the white cloud was steam, not smoke.

There was no grass, and in the early morning stillness the dust was terrible. He had seen a lot of cattle and a lot of dust back home. He had handled cattle all his life. But he had never seen so many cattle and so much dust. It hovered like a giant bird that covered the world before him. He even had the thought that he would like to go back to town and wait for the dust to settle. After standing there a few minutes he realized it wasn't going to settle anytime soon, and the men working on horseback and on foot were not dying and didn't seem to be suffering. They were just going about their work, though some of them did have handkerchiefs covering mouth and nose.

From his advantage on the ridge, he studied the best way to get to what he thought might be the railroad loading pens. He decided to stay to his right, close to the slaughterhouses, because there were walkways up over the pens near the steam monsters. As he moved forward, he looked with amazement at several train cars loaded with hides. Another was being loaded as fast as six men could work. He couldn't even guess how many hides were in each car.

He walked across a bridge and up on the walkways that led to the railroad pens. He moved on to the far side of the pens to make sure he didn't get trampled. After he came down from the overhead walkway and passed between two buildings, he had another surprise: the area in front of him looked like a town. Restaurants, bars and office buildings lined the street. There was even a bank.

Thinking that some coffee and breakfast would be wonderful, he headed for the nearest café sign. Starting into the street, he had to jump back to avoid being run down by a herd of cattle running down the street, driven by men on horseback. After they passed, he caught his breath and looked both ways before stepping out to cross the street that was now choked with dust.

Though it was early, the waitress looked like she had been working for quite a while. She poured him coffee without asking if he wanted it. He ordered two eggs, bacon and biscuits with butter and molasses. He was hungry but glad he had waited for lower prices than those he had found on the train.

Two men came in while he was waiting for his food. One was short, unshaven, stocky, dressed like a cowboy and covered with dirt. The other looked like a cross between a cowboy and a banker. He had a small notebook and several pencils in his clean shirt pocket. They sat down at a table near Josh. He could hear that they were having a heated argument.

CHAPTER 4

We make new friends
Out west of West.
We make enemies, too.
Every task is a test.

The dirty cowboy's face was flush with anger. "God dammit, Walter," he was saying, "you told me that if I'd bring them mules up here, you'd buy 'em!"

"What I told you was, if you would get those mules up here the first week in December, I would buy them. You are over a week late, and my customer has bought some from one of my competitors. He's mad at me because I didn't get the mules to him like I said I would. The reason I didn't is because *you're* late getting here. A man's word is most important in this business, and you made me look bad. Not only will I not buy your mules, I'll never buy horses or mules from you again. Don't bother to contact me next time you have livestock to sell."

"Are you calling me a liar?" It was obvious the dirty cowboy was getting hotter.

"No, I'm just saying you are too late to do business with me," the man named Walter answered. "There are quite a few men around here who may buy your mules. If you ask around, you may still be able to get rid of them. And I'm also telling you to be careful what you accuse me of."

The stocky cowboy stomped out without saying another word.

The waitress came over and filled Walter's coffee cup, without asking him if he wanted it filled, and asked him if he was ready for some breakfast. He smiled at her and nodded, and she disappeared into the kitchen like she already knew what he wanted for breakfast.

Josh realized his food was in front of him. He had been concentrating on the argument the two were having so much that he hadn't realized the tired waitress had served him. He hoped that the man with the pencils in his shirt pocket had not noticed how intently he'd been listening.

Josh ate without paying much attention to what he was eating, but he couldn't help noticing that

Walter's breakfast resembled nothing Josh had ever seen. It looked like eggs with a lot of stuff on top, like tomatoes and peppers. These were things Josh had never seen placed on top of eggs.

"Looks mighty good, Judy!" Walter told the waitress as he crumbled a biscuit on top of that strange sight in his plate.

When Josh thought Walter had finished his breakfast — by mopping up the remains of it with a second biscuit — he stood and walked over to his table.

"Excuse me, Mister," Josh said politely. "May I have a word with you?"

"Sure can," came the friendly answer. "I just hope you're not as fired up as the last man who had a few words with me. Have a seat, and let's see if we can get Judy to bring us some more coffee." He thrust his hand toward Josh and said with a friendly smile, "I'm Walter Ragsdale."

"I'm pleased to know you, Mr. Ragsdale," Josh said as they shook hands. "I'm Josh Collins."

Not knowing where to start the conversation, Josh was thankful for the delay as they waited for coffee. It was on its way when he managed to say, "I live near West, Mississippi."

"Mr. Collins, I hear there is sure a lot of good farm land in that delta in west Mississippi."

Relaxing a little because his new acquaintance was so at ease, Josh smiled. "Yes, there sure is, but that's not where I live. West, Mississippi, is a small town about a hundred and fifty miles south of Memphis. Our land is not as rich as the delta. It has a lot more hills and gullies."

"Well, I'll be damned," Walter said. "I guess they name a town like that to confuse people like me. There's a town called West, Texas, about eighty miles south of here. Of course, at one time that was the western-most part of Texas. I guess they didn't know back then, there'd be a lot more Texas west of West.

"What did you want to talk about, Mr. Collins?"

"Mr. Ragsdale, where I live, along about February, March and April, there's always a good market for horses and mules. Most folks who want mules get them from Missouri, Arkansas or Tennessee. And folks back home who breed mares usually breed them to a jack.

"What I'm trying to say is, there's a better market for horses than mules. For several years I've been buying horses, after crops are brought in during the fall, and holding them through the winter. I do pretty good on most of them when I sell in the spring. But I

20

could sell more, if I had more to sell. From what I hear there never is a shortage of horses around here."

"That's interesting, Josh," said Walter. "Why don't I call you Josh, and you call me Walter?"

Without waiting for an answer he asked another question. "These buyers, do they want broke horses?"

"That's the other part of the story," Josh explained. "They'll pay more for a horse that is broke to do the work of three horses. They like to use a horse to plow, pull a wagon, work a cow and then ride to town. The horses I've been buying are mostly broke to plow. We break them to ride too, and that makes them worth more. Then I can ask for a little more when I sell."

"Who breaks these horses to ride?" Walter asked, taking a sip of coffee.

"I got a darkie that works for me by the name of Dave who's good at it. Dave and I do all the work. I got me a son by the name of Dan, but he's just five years old. His younger brother Joey is just a yearling."

"Always good to have some boys coming along," said Walter, studying and stirring his coffee even though he'd not added any cream or sugar. Then he looked up at Josh to ask, "So what you are looking for is someone who can sell you some horses that you can break and make some money on?"

"That's right. But I need to buy cheap. Corn or grass is usually scarce where I come from. That's why people don't want horses in the fall. They don't want to carry them through winter. But they can't do without them, come spring.

"I couldn't keep from hearing your conversation with the man with the mules," Josh went on. "It made me reckon that you might be in the horse business. I've bought some land with a little grazing and switched to mostly growing corn instead of cotton. I was hoping you might know where I could get some horses."

"I do know where you can get some horses," Walter told him, taking the pad and a pencil from his shirt pocket. "Do you have a banking affiliation that you might use for a reference?"

"Yes Sir, I do," Josh answered. "I've been doing business with The West Bank ever since Mr. Durant first opened it up. Mr. Durant is a good man."

"Josh, I have an account here at the restaurant and breakfast is on me. I have a meeting coming up pretty quick. Please stay and drink all of this bad coffee you can hold. Can you meet me here tomorrow morning at about the same time?"

"Walter, I'll be pleased to buy breakfast, but I need to tell you something else."

"I apologize," Walter said quickly, "but we'll have to talk more tomorrow. I've got to hurry on. I make it a point never to be late for a meeting."

He reached for his hat and extended his hand, which Josh shook.

"Judy, breakfast is on me!" he shouted, hurrying out the front door, leaving Josh somewhat bewildered.

As Judy approached, carrying the coffeepot like it was filled with lead, Josh realized how weary he was. "I don't think I can handle any more coffee, thank you, Ma'am."

"Is there a hotel close by?" he thought to ask. "I haven't had much rest in the last few days."

"Don't talk to me about rest," she answered, with a forced smile. "I came to work yesterday. But to answer your question, there's a hotel two blocks down on the right. If you go around the corner just past that one, you will find another one that's not so expensive."

"Thank you, Ma'am," he said. Then he headed for the door.

He hoped to get a room at the cheaper hotel. Along the way he observed that this stockyard area, even without the giant slaughterhouses, was much larger, and the commercial activity was much greater, than that of the entire town of West, Mississippi.

But his mind kept going back to Walter Ragsdale. He regretted that he'd not told him up front that he didn't have money to buy more than three or four horses, depending on the price. His fear was that the man with the pencils in his pocket would think he'd been trying to deceive him.

CHAPTER 5

Out west of West,
Man to man
Sometimes words,
Sometimes gun or hand.

In what Judy had told him was the cheaper hotel, he was surprised to find — along with a full size bed — a pitcher of water, a wash basin, mirror, clean towel, spittoon and chamber pot. He had expected only the bed. Wondering what the more expensive hotel would furnish that this one did not, he fell across the bed and almost at the same time fell asleep. It was late afternoon before he opened his eyes.

Looking in the mirror he realized it had been several days since he'd shaved. He opened his bag, retrieved his razor, soap and brush, and went to work. When he'd finished, he poured the soapy water into the chamber pot, poured some clean water in the wash basin, and rinsed his face. Out of habit, he left the rinse water in the basin to use for wash water later. Josh locked his room, walked slowly down the hall and down the stairs.

This building was three stories high with who knew how many rooms. He'd seen buildings larger than this, but he had never before been inside one.

It was late afternoon, so the hotel bar was open and doing a lively business. A first drink of whiskey felt good going down, so he had another.

Several hours later, he'd walked every street in the stockyard area and had begun to feel more comfortable. Most of the folks he met on the streets were quite friendly, even the policemen who were carrying large clubs.

The amazing thing was how many people there were busy on the streets of the stockyard area. These were the most crowded streets he had ever seen.

It was obvious that some of the women on the streets made their living with their bodies, and they were standing in front of what had to be whorehouses. He tried to imagine what difficulties in their lives had caused them to end up in this profession. As he walked by, he touched the brim of his hat and greeted them with respect. He took solace in the knowledge that he had a lovely wife at home and would not let himself be tempted by the ladies of the night.

It was getting dark and cold. He decided he should have supper in a different place, so he carefully read the signs. The one where he'd eaten breakfast had a sign that read, "café." All the others had signs that read, "restaurant." He didn't remember anyone telling him, but he felt sure that a restaurant would be more expensive than a café. As usual, Josh chose practical over different.

The café was more crowded than it had been in the morning. He found a table near the kitchen door. He liked it because he could see almost all the other people.

Just as he was settling into the cane bottom chair, Judy came out of the kitchen carrying more plates of food than it seemed one person could possibly carry. She delivered this load of food to a table with three men who looked like cowboys. One of them was dressed a lot like Walter Ragsdale, down to the pad and pencils in his shirt pocket.

Before he could figure this out, Judy was at his table asking for his order. He could tell she was hurrying to keep up with the crowd. "Howdy, Ma'am. I figured you would be home resting about now."

"Here's your menu," she said back to him. "I just live around the block. I've been home resting, and I'm ready to be here all night again. Want some coffee?"

"No thanks. I'll have a beer though," he said, and before he could tell her what he wanted for supper, she was gone. When she returned with his glass of beer, he ordered a steak with gravy and cornbread.

As he ate his good supper, he decided he was right to come back to the café. Those restaurants couldn't be much better than this.

It was noisy, so he couldn't hear all that the men at the next table were saying. But from what he could hear, the man with the pencils in his pocket was giving instructions about moving some cattle.

When they left, and another man came to sit at that table, Josh sure could hear what *he* was saying. It was the dirty cowboy who'd been sitting with Walter Ragsdale that morning. When Judy came close to get his order, he asked her in a drunken voice, "That lyin' no good son of a bitch Ragsdale been in here tonight?"

"I don't know who you're referring to. I only know one man named Ragsdale, and he never lies," she said, looking him straight in the eyes.

This stocky man was as hot as he had been this morning, only now there was whiskey added.

"Don't get sassy with me, you goddamn bitch," he snorted — as he grabbed Judy by the arm and started twisting.

Before he could break it, and he was certainly strong enough to do just that, Josh hit him in the side of his head with his right fist. The loud, dirty man was obviously stunned. Before he could recover his senses, the same right hand landed square on his chin. To others in the room, the blow sounded like someone had slammed a door shut. He grabbed a chair as he was going down and ended up stretched out cold, with the cane bottom chair on top of him.

When Josh looked at Judy, he saw she was standing with feet wide apart and a steak knife in her hand. She looked like she hoped the unconscious man would get up, so she could use it.

By that time, several men rushed to her aid, and someone just outside the door shouted.

Josh was not sure if he should apologize or not. He had been taught that when in doubt, go ahead and apologize. He said, "Miss, I sure am sorry this…."

Two policemen coming through the front door interrupted him. They didn't stop running until they were next to Judy. One of the policemen placed the end of his club on Josh's chest and told him in a firm voice to step back. The other one told Judy to put the knife on the table. They both did as they were told. The policeman who had spoken to Judy looked around and asked, "Who saw what happened here?"

About ten men started trying to explain what they had seen. When the policeman held up his hands and said, "Quiet," another man dressed about like Walter stepped forward.

"Officer, the man sprawled out on the floor there, he verbally attacked Judy. He cussed her, then grabbed her by the arm and started twisting it. Before the rest of us could come to her aid, this gentleman cold-cocked him with two rights."

"You saying that he just hit this big boy on the floor with his fist?" the policeman asked. He looked surprised.

About ten men answered, all at the same time. The policeman smiled and started to say something when he realized that the man on the floor was coming around. He raised his club while the other policeman brought the big man's hands behind his back and clamped handcuffs on his beefy wrists.

Then the policeman turned to Josh with "What's your name, and where are you staying?"

"My name's Josh Collins, and I'm staying at the hotel two blocks down and around the corner."

"Let me see your room key," the policeman demanded.

Josh pulled it out and handed it to the policeman. After the policeman looked it over and handed it back, he was ready to leave the scene. But on his way out, he said to Josh, "If you're looking for a job, I'm sure the chief would like to talk."

Judy came over and said, "Mister Collins, I have seen a few fist fights, but I've never seen anyone hit that hard. I want to thank you for coming to my rescue. Your supper is on the house. Thank you again."

"Miss Judy," he told her, "you don't owe me anything. I'm just glad I could help. I'll pay for my supper."

"Mister Collins, I'm witness to the fact that you can hit like a mule kicks," she said with a chuckle and a smile. "But I've got more than one steak knife, and you don't want to cross me. I repeat, I'm buying your supper." With that, she leaned over to kiss him on his receding forehead. Then she headed for the kitchen.

CHAPTER 6

Out west of West
Lightning and thunder roll.
Will the rain that follows
Cleanse my soul?

As he entered the hotel he was drawn to the smoky bar, where he had two drinks of whiskey before going up to his room. In his room, he noticed that the chamber pot and washbasin had been emptied, and the pitcher was filled with clean water. He went to sleep worrying about the meeting the next morning.

He woke up before dawn with a sore right wrist. He washed his face and hands and hurried to the café for his meeting with the man who'd said he tried never to be late for a meeting. Not being as hungry as yesterday, Josh ordered biscuits and sausage with butter and molasses.

Judy looked even more tired than she did yesterday. And it was obvious that using her arm the drunk had twisted last night was painful.

Before Josh finished the first biscuit, Walter showed up wearing fresh clean clothes exactly like the ones he had on yesterday, with the pad and pencils in his shirt pocket. He said, "Howdy, Josh. How's the town hero?"

"I don't know, Walter. I don't think I've met him yet."

"Well, if you looked in the mirror this morning, you saw him," Walter said back.

"I don't see how that could be," said Josh, puzzled.

Walter placed his well-worn hat on an empty chair and sat across from Josh. "You see, Josh," he explained, "a large majority of the men in this town are in love with Judy. The rest of them admire her. You rescued her from that scoundrel last night. They wish they could have done what you did. That makes you the town hero."

"I sure don't agree with that conclusion. But I can see why everyone thinks so highly of Judy. It's none of my business, but I think whoever owns this café needs to give her some time off. She looks awful tired."

"Your observation is correct," said Walter, "and I have talked to the owner about that many times, with no results."

Walter smiled at Judy as she brought him that same strange breakfast she'd served him yesterday. His smile faded as he said, "Judy, Mr. Collins has observed that you look tired, that you may need more rest than you're getting."

"After what Mr. Collins did last night, he has a right to express his opinion. But that doesn't mean I have to listen to yours, Walter Ragsdale," she said.

Both men watched her backside as she strolled into the kitchen. Obviously, the subject of her fatigue was a source of friction between Walter and Judy.

"I guess I had better tell you the whole story," Walter said to him. "Two years ago the owner that was running this restaurant went bust. Judy was working for him as a waitress at the time. She went to the bank and made arrangements to buy this joint. She cleaned it up, started serving the best food in town, and made it the most popular eating-place around these parts. She comes to work about five o'clock each afternoon. Works all night through breakfast, goes home to catch a few hours of sleep and comes back. I don't think she has missed a day, or night, since she took over."

Josh frowned and said, "I can understand someone working that hard. What I can't figure out is why in the world does a café need to stay open all night?"

"This place never shuts down," said Walter. "Some people claim those two slaughterhouses are the two largest in the world. There are probably some folks in Chicago and maybe Kansas City who would argue that point. But we can agree they are huge, and they operate around the clock." It was obvious that he liked this Fort Worth Stockyard area where he spent his days.

"In addition to the trains hauling meat and hides," Walter went on, "there are thousands of live cattle shipped out of here, each week, to other parts of the world. Add to that the horse and mule business, and you have trains arriving and leaving at all hours. Just like you arrived here hungry yesterday morning, many people do night and day. With the people who come to do business, and those who live and work here, you can understand why we need a good all night café."

As soon as they both finished breakfast, Josh started the conversation he had been dreading. "Walter, I didn't have a chance to tell you something yesterday that I need to make sure you understand. Fact is, I only have enough money to buy a few horses, depending on the price. My reason for coming out here is to find out what I *could* do, if I had some money. I guess I just feel a need to know what's possible. I wanted to tell you that yesterday, so you wouldn't think I'd misled you."

Walter stirred his coffee. "I suppose the reason you didn't tell me yesterday was my fault. I'm the one that cut our conversation short. Thanks for telling me as soon as you could. Yesterday morning I sent a telegram to your banker, Mr. Durant. In the return telegram, he spoke most highly of your conduct. I find the most valuable asset in doing business is a good name. It's even more valuable than money. And we both know it's not easy to maintain a good name. There are always scoundrels, like the one you took care of last night, who are trying to pull you down to their level. And there's always temptation to make a short-term gain by telling people what they want to hear. It looks to me like you know the proper way to handle either of these."

Josh was relieved to know that Walter was not angry because he hadn't told him earlier about his financial situation.

He noticed that Judy never let Walter's coffee cup get more than half empty without being there to fill it. Walter took a sip of the hot coffee, set the cup down and said, "Josh, I've two horses hitched to a buggy outside and a place a few miles northwest of here where I hold livestock. I think it would be a good idea if you and I ride up there and look at some horses. If we leave right away, we should be back in time for supper."

It was a longer ride than Josh expected. He admired the two sorrel horses, but he couldn't figure out why people used buggies. He would not spend money on one because he found riding a buggy more uncomfortable than riding a horse. A horse moves with rhythm, but you couldn't know from one second to the next which way a buggy seat was going to bounce. Besides, there was not enough room to haul anything that amounted to anything.

After several hours he knew why Walter had two horses hitched to this buggy. The terrain got hilly, and the sorrels had to work.

To his surprise there were no trees on the hills. Aside from the occasional cornfield, the hills were covered with grass, tanned by winter. Along the streams in the bottoms, there were oak trees and, to his surprise, green grass. Where he came from there was no green grass in December. And back there, hills that weren't used as fields were covered with brush and trees, unlike this beautiful grass covered country.

When they pulled up in front of a gate, he knew it was the passenger's job to jump down and open it. It was another mile, at least, before they began to see horses — and even then, no stallions.

"Walter, I haven't seen any stallions," he said soon. "Are they all mares and geldings?"

"Yes, most of the horses I sell get hauled on railroad stock cars. In such tight quarters, stallions fight and you end up with too many crippled horses. Besides, I sell mostly to the army. Sometimes they will buy mares, but for the most part, a few years back, they stopped buying anything but geldings. That's why most of the horses you see here are mares. I can sell you mares a little cheaper than geldings."

There were cattle and mules in other pastures on Walter's property, but they came here to look at horses. The idea of buying mostly mares sounded good to Josh, who knew his buyers usually wanted mares.

"Walter, how much would a few of these mares cost?"

"I'm not interested in selling a few," Walter told him, "unless you call a car load a few. I can sell a carload for twenty dollars a head. It will cost about fifty dollars for you to rent a railroad car from Fort Worth to Memphis."

Josh was thinking that about all he could handle was the railroad fee. With the vision of an empty railroad car, which would do him no good, he asked, "How many do you usually ship in one railroad car?"

Walter motioned up and north. With urgency in his voice he said, "Look at that dark north sky. That blue norther is gonna have us cold as two icicles before we get back to Fort Worth. I just hope the rain holds off." Before he'd even finished the statement, Walter had turned the buggy around to head for the gate.

With the buggy horses in a high trot, conversation was over for now. Just after they passed through the gate, the north wind overtook them, and that alone was loud enough to stop all conversation. The lightning and thunder rolled in as fierce as any Josh had ever experienced. They passed over two of the rolling hills before the rain came. Walter hollered as loudly as he could, "In the box behind the seat, there's some slickers."

When Josh turned away from the box with the slickers, Walter shouted, "Put one on and take the lines while I put on the other one." They were both thankful that after the rain came, the lightning and thunder were not as fierce.

When the two men entered the café and took the slickers off, they were wet and shivering cold. Both hats were soaked, and the brims were drooping low. Judy had seen them coming and without saying hello she'd headed for the kitchen. She came back with two cups of coffee and left them on the table. Walter looked at Josh and put his finger to his lips telling Josh to be quiet. After Josh took a sip of coffee, he knew why. There was no whisky on the menu. A sign on the wall opposite the front door read, "No Whiskey Allowed." But their coffee cups were half-filled with whiskey. The combination of hot coffee and whiskey helped warm the two men's bodies from the inside out.

Walter leaned toward Josh with a laugh. Then in a whisper he said, "Better make it last. It will be a long time before you get any more from that woman."

"Before we order supper," Josh said, "I want it understood that I'm paying. I find myself beginning to feel like a bum, because I've been here the best part of two days and have not paid for a bite of food."

Walter smiled. He liked his new friend from Mississippi.

"Well, we can't have you feeling like a bum," he said. "Since you're buying, I'm going to do my part to help you get over feeling like a bum. I'll order myself the biggest steak on the menu."

Walter said, after they'd ordered, "I couldn't help but notice, it appears that you are left- handed. But I understand that you rescued Judy with two rights. Are you saving your left for more serious opponents?"

"I'll answer that question," said Josh, "but like this coffee we're enjoying, it would be a good idea not to spread the word around.

"When I was a youngster, I got my hands on a book about a prizefighter. This book made the life of a prizefighter sound quite exciting. And it reported prizefighting to be one place where being left-handed was an advantage. Naturally, I decided to become a great prizefighter. I got me a tow sack, filled it with sand and hung it from a rafter in the barn. I didn't do much damage to the sack of sand for quite some time. Finally, though, I started breaking tow sacks. I realized that I'd learned to hit pretty hard.

"In the next few years I got in fights with several local bullies and came out on top. The day before my wedding to Carol, a professional prizefighter came to town, went by the name of Bear Beaumont. He provoked me to fight him by insulting my bride-to-be.

"He was bigger, stronger and more experienced than me. I was younger, faster and had longer arms, so I managed to see that he didn't land a solid blow or get me in his grip. I admit to being both pleased and surprised when I took him down quickly. You can imagine that after whipping tow sacks, bullies and an old washed up prizefighter, I thought I could whip the world.

"Well, not long after my marriage, I was hitching a mule to a plow, when he kicked me. I walked around to the other end of the mule and hit him with a left, right between the eyes. I didn't see any sign that he even felt my best punch. I sure felt it, because it broke several bones in my left hand. After it healed, it was okay for most jobs, but I don't dare hit anything with it. I doubt if I could kill a fly with my best left hook. That's how my career as a prizefighter ended before it started. Probably a good thing, all in all."

"Yeah, probably a good thing it ended that career," Walter said, already laughing. He had trouble stopping.

"What makes it so funny is not your misfortune," he finally managed to say, "but knowing that all us boys have hit a horse or mule, with a fist, in anger. Like you, we learned that it was a bad idea, and promised ourselves never to do that again. Most of us just couldn't hit as hard as you, so we learned the lesson without breaking anything."

Judy brought each of them one of the biggest steaks Josh had ever seen. After he'd eaten every bite, he pushed back and mentioned a little thing that had been on his mind. "Walter," he asked, "how is it that you and some others around here dress so much alike, down to the pad and pencils in your shirt pocket?"

"I guess it's just clothes that fit the job. If a man is a broker, or order buyer, he's going to be in and out of the bank, business offices, meeting people for a meal, or going to receive, ship, or move livestock. So, we come to work prepared to be a cattleman *or* businessman. As for the pad and pencils, we count livestock every day, make offers to buy and get offers to sell. Taking notes is a necessary part of the job. We need to keep up with the numbers. Aside from that, we mostly all buy our clothes from the one store in the stockyard area that sells clothes. So, I suppose that's how the uniform comes to be."

"By the way, I never did answer your question about the number of horses in one carload. There's anywhere from thirty-five to forty-five. I usually like to keep the number down, then we have fewer injuries. Also, it makes a difference how long the trip is going to take."

CHAPTER 7

Judge a man by
Color of his skin, you'll
Cause great pain.
No one will win.

Riding back home on the brown gelding, Josh thought he must have been feeling a lot like the boy, Thomas. Thomas was most excited when he saw the two dollars he was paid for taking care of the horse, plus two more Josh gave him for doing such a good job. Thomas *had* taken good care of the horse.

"The next time I'm in this town and need some dependable help, I'll come to you, Thomas," Josh told him.

"Mr. Collins I hope you come back real soon," said this skinny boy with big blue eyes.

Josh was going to get home less than two weeks after he'd left. His trip had been successful beyond his wildest dreams.

He had a train carload of horses coming next month. He had to keep reminding himself of the agreement with Walter Ragsdale, not to tell anyone about the business arrangement they'd agreed on. Walter had said that like the extra strong coffee and Josh's left hook, they should keep it just between them.

His most immediate worry was the bad cough he had. Getting wet and cold had resulted in both him and Walter getting bad colds. He wasn't worried about himself. For him, living through such conditions was just part of life. But when anyone else had a cold, Carol always picked it up, and then she'd have a rough time with it. He knew it was not likely she could avoid it this time.

He had a picture of her smiling face in his mind, and it caused him to push the brown gelding a little harder. Her unique smile was a mixture of happiness and pain. It was as if her lips smiled, but her eyes knew a different story. The picture in his mind of her and her smile was precious to Josh.

***

It was a good Christmas. The hope and optimism Josh had was contagious. Unfortunately, the bad cold he had picked up in Texas was also. Both Carol and Joey were miserable.

Josh tried to help as much as he could. He tried unsuccessfully to get Carol to take a drink of whiskey for her cough. He would sometimes put some on a rag and put it near Joey's mouth for him to suck on. The boy sometimes went to sleep afterwards. This was all the proof Josh needed that whiskey was a good remedy. He would never be able to convince Carol.

During this Christmas season, he and Dave were busy getting ready for the load of horses. They built some new pens and fixed the old ones. They had a crib full of corn, but not enough to keep so many horses in good shape. Most of Josh's working money went to buy lumber for the pens and a second corncrib, along with corn to fill it.

Each morning, when daylight was just a shadow, Josh and Dave started working. They worked until they could not see, because darkness had moved across the land. Then they went home to take care of chores that had to be done. They were quite an efficient team. Most of their lives they had worked this hard, side by side.

As the January date for the delivery of the horses got closer, the daunting task of driving them from Memphis to the farm near West demanded attention. Fortunately, this time of year it was easy to hire help, because farming activity was minimal. Most people spent time hunting, as well as cutting and stacking a year's supply of wood for the fireplace and the cook stove. After plowing and planting started, there would be no time for such activity. With so many people hunting this time of year, squirrels, possums, coons, quail, wild hogs, wild turkey and deer were not safe. Also, it was the time to slaughter domestic hogs and hang them in the smokehouse.

Josh and Walter had talked about the drive. Walter agreed he would do his best to send horses that looked to have had experienced being driven on trail. They'd decided that at least four men on horseback would be needed, and six would be much better. Josh liked the economy of four and hired two men to help him and Dave.

He thought about taking young Dan. He could ride drag and keep the heard moving along. This was usually a simple job that mostly required eating a lot of dust. After some consideration, he decided he wanted Dan to take care of chores at home and be there if Carol needed him.

Jeremy Lane, Lyle Slaughter and Josh met at Josh's house before daylight for breakfast.

After a good breakfast by lamplight, they all got some corn bread and ham from Carol, to eat on the trail, and they headed for Memphis.

Dave's house was on the way, and he joined them as they rode by. This fit the general understanding of how things should be. In this part of the world, you would not have a black man sit at the table to share a meal with white men.

With some excitement and anticipation of a new experience, they made good time the first day. They camped close to a spring of fresh water and talked about the idea that this would be a good place to rest the herd on the return trip.

There were towns along the way, but one of the things they were trying to do was find a trail to use that did not go through towns. Josh would drive through a town if he had to, but he didn't want to, if it could be avoided. He had started this search for the right trail on his first trip.

About noon the second day, he was considering the option of going through the town of Batesville or through a large field west of town. Of course, this time of the year there were no crops growing in fields, so most farmers wouldn't mind. A house west of the field looked as if it would be the home of the owner.

Josh instructed the men to wait while he rode over to the house.

The gentleman who came out onto the porch of the house introduced himself as Harvey Wesfall. When Josh explained his situation, Harvey was fascinated with the enterprise. He not only agreed to allow the herd to cross his field, but he insisted the crew of four have lunch with him and his wife.

Josh explained, "One of my hands is a darkie, and it would probably be best if we ride on."

"We can all sit around on the back porch and have lunch," Harvey said, "and no one will object. I insist."

Harvey and his wife were delightful hosts. The hungry men enjoyed pork roast, collard greens, corn bread, apple pie and hot coffee.

"How do you plan to handle these horses?" Harvey asked, as they were finishing the meal. "I think keeping them from scattering will be difficult."

"I think most of these horses have been trailed before," Josh explained, "so I hope they won't be too big a problem. I figure Dave will ride in front and lead the way. I'll ride drag and keep them pushed up, and Jeremy and Lyle will each have a side to keep gathered up. Of course, with horses, unexpected problems always come up. Dave is better at dealing with horse problems than anyone I know. To make sure we don't have a misunderstanding, when problems do come up Dave will be in charge, and we'll all take orders from him."

Harvey rubbed his chin, obviously studying Josh's plan. "Sounds like you have thought this out quite well," he said. "I believe it should work."

But Jeremy jumped to his feet, saying, "No, it damn sure won't work. It's bad enough I have to ride with a nigger, sleep with a nigger, and eat with a nigger, now you want me to take orders from a nigger! I'll be goddamn if I'll put up with such shit. I sure don't intend to do any such thing."

Before Jeremy was finished with this tirade, Josh was standing in front of him blocking his way. With his face just inches from Jeremy's, Josh said, "You don't have to do any of these things, because you don't work for me any longer. You can turn around and go home, or anywhere else you want to go. I'll settle up with you when I get back to West. But before you take another step, you are going to apologize to Mrs. Wesfall for cussing in front of her."

Jeremy had heard about Josh being in a few fights, but he'd never heard about him losing one. It was well known around West that if there was a fight involving Josh, and if his right hand made contact, the fight was over.

"I apologize, Ma'am," Jeremy muttered as he stepped back out of Josh's reach. Without another word, he got up on his horse and galloped south.

"Mrs. Wesfall, Mr. Wesfall, I wouldn't have brought that man to your house if I'd any idea he would behave so badly," Josh told them sincerely. "You've been so kind to us, and for him to act so uncivilized is a great embarrassment to me. I don't know how to apologize."

Mrs. Wesfall spoke up to say, "There's been enough apologizing. Would any of you like some more pie or coffee?"

Harvey said, "I like the way you handle things, Josh. When you come back through here with your Texas horses, plan on resting your horses in my field, and you and your men having supper with us."

"I appreciate the offer, I surely do. You have been so kind, I just couldn't impose on your hospitality."

Harvey came back with, "Well then, I guess you'll have to find another trail to drive your horses on. Part of the deal is, if you cross my field, you have to eat my wife's cooking,"

"Harvey, I've heard of paying a toll. I just never dreamed it could be enjoyable. If we can get them horses headed in the right direction, you can count on us showing up right back here in two or three days."

"What do you intend to do about being short handed," Harvey asked, a worried look on his face. "I'd love to go along and help, but I have some neighbors coming over tomorrow to kill hogs. We all take turns helping each other. The good news is, the smokehouse will be full when you come back through."

"Well, most everything we do, we do shorthanded," said Josh. "It doesn't look like this job of driving horses is going to be any different." He was thinking how glad he was he had stopped at this house.

Mrs. Wesfall, who had disappeared into the house, came out with a flour sack about half full of food. Dave was closest, so she shoved it into his hand as she said, "That ought to get you to Memphis."

Dave smiled as he held the sack out in front of himself and moved it up and down a little, as if weighing it. He said, "I should think so. I don't know where it is, and I don't think I want to go there, but this much food might just last long enough for us to get to New York City."

As they rode away from the Wesfall house, headed north, Josh said, "Dave, I am truly sorry for what happened back there."

There was a long period of silence until Dave replied, "That's the way it is."

CHAPTER 8

When a man's work
Is done,
He is a man
And a boy in one.

They arrived in Memphis in the afternoon. While the others looked for the best place to camp for the night, Josh went to the railroad office to make sure everything was in order. On leaving the office, he figured it must be about milking time. Sure enough, he found the lady wearing her bonnet milking the cow. The cow was more content than the last time Josh had witnessed the milking operation. Thomas was squatting on the ground, actually sitting on his heels, like only a skinny person can, watching intently. Apparently the cow had learned that getting milked wasn't so bad. Thomas didn't need to hold her tail.

When Thomas saw Josh, his big blue eyes got bigger. "Hello, Mr. Collins!" the boy said.

"Hello, Thomas. Howdy, Ma'am." He tipped his hat to the lady, who didn't stop milking.

Thomas came over to the side of the pen, and Josh extended his hand to shake hands. Reluctantly the boy placed his bony right hand into Josh's big right hand.

"Need me to take care of your horse, Mr. Collins?" he asked Josh.

"No, not this time. How are things going in school, Thomas?"

Thomas hung his head down and kicked the ground with his worn brogans. "Not so well, Mr. Collins. I quit going to school. Didn't go back after Christmas. I know how to read and write, and I can do numbers, some. I need to get a job, so I can be more help to my momma. Not been able to find one yet. But when folks start plowing and planting, I bet I can get one."

"Thomas, it sounds like we may be able to help each other again. Do you have chores around here?"

"Yes sir, I bring in the eggs, feed the chickens, slop the hog and take the cow over near the river to graze."

"Your paw around?" Josh already knew the answer to the question he was asking.

Again Thomas kicked the ground and looked down. "Ain't got no paw," he said.

"Howdy, Mr. Collins," said the lady in the bonnet, getting up from the milking stool. " I hope you need this boy to work some more."

"I do," said Josh. Then he added, as he removed his hat, "I apologize, Ma'am. I didn't find out what your name was the last time I came through."

"Susan. We are Susan and Thomas Calcoat. You need Thomas to take care of your horse again?"

"Well, it's a little more complicated this time. We are going to receive a railroad stock carload of horses from Texas tomorrow. Then we have to drive them about a hundred and fifty miles south of here. I need another hand for the drive. I was just talking to Thomas about his chores."

It was obvious Susan Calcoat was bewildered. "Thomas is just 10 years old! We sell eggs, milk and butter to survive. I don't know how I could get along without him helping with the cow. I could take care of the other chores, but the cow needs to graze every day. Besides, my Thomas is just too young for such a job." She turned and carried her bucket of milk into the rundown house, with visions of her son leaving, never to return.

Josh looked at Thomas. He was puzzled about what to do next. He said, "Thomas, there *would* be problems. You'd need to be gone for more than a week. Perhaps this is *not* a good idea. I reckon we should both think on it. I'll come back and talk with you and your maw tomorrow morning. We don't want to do anything that will cause hardship for you and your maw."

The next morning, he showed up riding the brown gelding and leading a bay gelding. There were two sacks of feed tied to the saddle on the bay gelding. Susan Calcoat came out of the back door of her house, and Thomas came from the hog pen, carrying an empty slop bucket.

Josh had his presentation ready. "I hope what I am about to propose is beneficial to the three of us," he began. "If it's not, and either one of you don't agree, then I'll leave and there will be no hard feelings. I need to hire Thomas, but if I do, he'll be gone from home for more than a week. I've hired someone to bring a wagon full of hay and leave it beside this pen. Your cow will have to stay in the pen and eat hay instead of grass. There's a sack of cottonseed hulls and a sack of cottonseed meal tied to this horse's saddle. You can put it in the shed over there, have plenty to feed the cow each time you milk her. This bay horse is rented from the livery. Thomas can use him on the drive and return him to the livery when he returns home. I'll pay Thomas six dollars for the work, and I'll feed him. If both of you agree on his going with me, he needs to be at the railroad loading pens by noon. By the way, he'll need a blanket, because we'll be sleeping outside — if we sleep. If it's decided that he does not go with us, then the feed, hay and use of this horse for a week is paid for. You're welcome to it. Just make sure the horse is returned to the livery within one week."

After saying all this, he rode over to Thomas and handed him the bridle reins with the bay gelding on the other end. He touched the brim of his hat to Susan as he turned and rode away.

The clerk from the railroad office was there at noon, along with Dave, Lyle Slaughter and Josh. The three had been talking. They decided that if Thomas didn't show up, Josh and Lyle would keep moving from behind the herd to the side and back behind again, as needed, to try to keep the herd from scattering.

Lyle was worried. "Please go find someone else," he asked.

"Don't worry, Thomas will be here," Josh told him.

"How can you be so sure?" Lyle queried.

"Because he's a boy, and boys are predictable."

"What do you mean by that?" Lyle asked, a puzzled expression on his face.

"I mean, under the circumstances, a boy is going to try to do the same thing you or I would've done, when we were boys. When you were a boy, would you have passed on an opportunity to ride with men on a drive like this? He'll be here directly."

Josh's answer was validated when a skinny boy on a bay gelding came around the side of the loading pens. It was obvious his mother had put some clothes on him that didn't fit. He looked a lot like a scarecrow.

Josh introduced him. Then he told him how to ride drag and keep the horses pushed up, but not to push them too hard.

"How will I know when to push and when not to push, Mr. Collins?"

"You keep looking up and checking with Dave. He's the best man I know with horses, and the best one I know with boys. We all take our directions from him."

About that time, Dave moved closer to Thomas and the others and started demonstrating the signals he would use to let them know what to do. He explained, "These horses are fresh and nervous. They'll run a little faster than we want them to when we leave the alley. Not too much we can do about it. Don't worry about the speed. Just try to keep them gathered up. When they get to the river, they'll stop to eat and drink, and we can get control of them.

"If one gets away, don't leave the herd to go get him. He'll most likely come back to join up with the others. Generally, horses don't like to be by they self. If he doesn't come back, we can go after him while the others are eating and drinking. Most important, don't let several horses get away from the herd. They'll have their own small herd and just keep on going, God knows where."

As he rode back up to the west end of the alley to open the gate and let the horses out, there was no doubt in the mind of the others about his knowledge of the subject. He swung the gate open and calmly walked his horse toward the river.

Josh and Lyle rode through the open gate and took their positions on each side. The herd didn't move. Thomas didn't know whether to push them or not. Then he remembered the instructions and looked up at Dave. Dave was riding away without looking back, but he was signaling to take it slow.

"Slow, hell!" Thomas thought. "They're stopped! How much slower can you get?"

About that time a gray mare moved up the alley and out of the gate. Others began to follow. As more horses passed through the gate, they picked up speed. By the time the last one cleared the gate, they were all running. The gray mare was running with her head up high, looking back at the others to make sure she didn't get passed up as she made a run — straight for the river.

Dave took off as fast as his horse could run, not for the river, but for a point southeast of where the horses were heading.

Lyle and Josh had to spank their ponies to keep position on each side. As the herd ran faster, they both knew to move out away from the herd. If they were too close and some horses tried to leave the herd, there wouldn't be much they could do about it. If they were out away from the herd, they could move and crack their whips, hopefully convincing the horses they were better off staying together.

Thomas had seen this much dust before, but he could not remember being in the middle of what looked like a dust storm. His duty of keeping the horses pushed up was no problem. His problem was keeping up. Dave, the man he was told to look to for instructions, was out of sight. Josh and Lyle were riding along the side of the herd, cracking their whips and paying no attention to him.

When he'd rode away from his house he'd told himself that *he may have become a man*. Now in the noise and dust, he knew he was a frightened ten-year-old boy. He tried to keep himself from thinking of his mother and his home. It was impossible. He had no spurs, so he kicked the livery horse with his brogan shoes as hard as he could, trying to keep up.

It was about a mile from the pens to the river bottom and about another two hundred yards to the river. This was not enough running to take the edge off fresh horses. When the lead horses plunged into the river, they stopped to drink. The others ran down-river from the leaders. Some were obviously going to keep running south along the riverbank. Then, up ahead of the running horses, the black man on the bay gelding stepped out from behind a big sweet gum tree. His whip cracked, and the southbound horses stopped. They looked at him and the bay gelding for a minute, then they calmly walked into the river to drink.

Like a summer storm that blows in suddenly with clouds, wind, lightning, thunder and rain, to then have sudden sunshine and calm, this storm was over, as quickly as it had come.

The men and the boy backed off, to let the herd drink and eat grass. They spread out with the herd between them and the river, got off their horses and held them while they grazed. They were ready to jump into their saddles to take whatever action was needed. They never took their eyes off the Texas horses.

After they'd let the horses graze about three hours, they were ready to head south. Before they could get them gathered into a tighter herd and moving, the gray mare had moved up front and assumed her lead position. The bay gelding with the cowboy on top was the only horse that dared to take a position in front of her. It was plain to see that without the cowboy, the gray mare would not have granted the gelding such a privilege.

It was almost dark before they reached the spring, where they planned to spend the night. Josh had selected a flat area with gently sloping hills on three sides, because horses have a fear of being closed in and are more comfortable in an open area.

During the night, after grazing and resting, the horses might become nervous. But now, still full of water from the visit to the river, they weren't going to make any trouble. Again, the riders got off their own horses and held them while they grazed.

Each hand had been given a post to watch from. Josh rode from one to the other, passing out biscuits filled with ham. When supper was taken care of, Josh walked, leading his horse, to the spot that had been assigned to Thomas. "Thomas," he told the boy, "get your blanket out and get some sleep."

Thomas objected, as Josh knew he would. Boys didn't like to go to sleep that early. "We're going to need you later in the night," he explained, "and you better get some rest."

Thomas untied a heavy large wool coat from the back of his saddle. He spread it on the ground and curled up inside of it, like anyone else would use a blanket. He was asleep almost immediately.

The three men would get no sleep tonight.

After about three hours, the horses began to drop to the ground to rest. Dave, leading his horse, keeping both eyes on the herd, walked over to Josh. "If these horses get too much rest, we are likely to have troubles," he told Josh.

"What do you reckon we should do?"

"I reckon we ought to think on moving out. There's enough light from the moon and stars. About an hour before day, the moon will go down. With the light from the stars and a little luck, we should be okay."

"Head on out, Dave," Josh told him. "We'll be right behind you."

"I'll go tell Lyle the plan," said Dave, turning his horse away. He looked back over his shoulder and added with a big smile, "Don't forget the coat."

CHAPTER 9

Slaughter a hog.
Life is pain.
You may never
Be the same.

Mid-afternoon found them in Wesfall's field. Keeping the horses moving, not letting them rest, had been a good idea. Now it was the cowboys and saddle horses who were exhausted.

Leaving the herd, Josh rode up to the Wesfall house. He didn't know why, but he had a feeling something was wrong. He sat on his horse near the front porch until Mrs. Wesfall came out. It was obvious she'd been crying. He jumped off the horse, took off his hat, and approached her, asking, "What in the world is wrong, Mrs. Wesfall?"

She still needed a few moments to compose herself to answer. Then she told him, "Harvey lost his arm."

Josh was ashamed that he'd been feeling sorry for himself for being so tired. "I'm so sorry," he said. "What can I do to help?"

"I saw you drive them horses into the field and told Harvey. He's quite weak, but he wants to talk to you."

Josh followed her inside the house. As he entered, hat in hand, he could smell the antiseptic and whiskey.

Harvey, with his wife's help, explained the accident. It was common practice to put a hog that was about to be slaughtered in a small pen, more like a cage. Before that, the cage would have been placed on a ground slide. A ground slide is two skids, made from heavy timber, with boards across the top, making a platform about five feet by five feet — just inches, the thickness of the skids, off the ground. Chains connected the skids to a singletree. Trace chains from the harness, which is on a horse or mule, connect the pulling animal to the singletree.

The driver sometimes would ride, or if the slide were loaded, he would walk beside the ground slide. The ground slide was used to transport the hog from his pen to the place of slaughter. There he would be killed and hoisted up using a block and tackle attached to his hind legs. One of the neighbors used a ground slide for transportation to the Wesfalls'. With this mule and slide so handy, Harvey decided not to bother putting a harness on his mule and hitching it to his own ground slide.

After putting the cage, with hog, on the neighbor's slide, Harvey hurried to make sure things were ready at the location of the slaughter. The hoist was hanging from the limb of a big oak. The fire was hot, and the water in the large wash pot was boiling. The women folk were getting ready to stuff sausage and make hog headcheese. This was all a great deal of work, but it was also an opportunity to visit with neighbors.

He called for the men to bring the hog. When the slide moved forward the hog squealed. The squealing hog frightened the young mule. The mule took off pulling the slide at a fast pace. The driver tripped and fell, losing control of the lines, leaving the runaway mule to gain speed as he headed for the table — where the women were waiting.

Harvey jumped in front of the mule and waved his hands. The mule jumped to one side, causing the heavy ground slide to become airborne and slam into the side of the smokehouse. The only thing between the ground slide and the smokehouse was Harvey's right arm.

After two days, the doctor and his wife convinced him that even if the mangled arm didn't kill him, it would still never be of any use. Harvey let it be removed, just below the shoulder.

Harvey insisted it was his decision not to hitch his older mule. He wanted no blame placed on his good neighbor.

"Josh, I could always do the work of two men. Now I guess I'll only be able to do the work of one and a half."

Not in the mood for Harvey's humor, Josh asked, "What can I do to help?"

"Take care of yourself and hurry back," Harvey told him.

Mrs. Wesfall came into the room carrying a flour sack almost full of food. "Another thing you can do is help with this food. Our neighbors have been bringing food — more than any ten men could eat! If someone doesn't eat it, it'll spoil. I'm sure more will come in tomorrow. Take this to your men."

"I wouldn't feel right taking food your neighbors brought. I should be bringing food, not taking food."

"Josh, I'm not *asking* you to take this food. I'm *telling* you to take it. You look exhausted. Take this to your men and get some rest."

"I don't want to add to your burden. We have a ten-year-old boy with us. After we finish the drive, he'll be going back to his home in Memphis alone. His name is Thomas. Will it be all right with you, if I tell him he can stop here on his way back?"

Mrs. Wesfall stepped closer to Josh to tell him, "No! Don't you dare tell him he *can* stop here. You tell him he *must* stop here. I'll be worried sick about him. If he don't stop, I'll likely worry myself to death."

The trip from Batesville to the farm near West was uneventful. The gray mare was in the lead and had made Dave's task much easier. All he had to do was show her the way. Thomas found his job getting harder and harder. As the horses became tired and hungry, they required more pushing. Earlier in the trip, Dave kept signaling him to slow down. Now he continually signaled him to push on. The last time they stopped, Dave cut Thomas a good switch from a persimmon tree. "Keep your horse pushed along," he told the boy as he handed him the switch.

Sometimes the boy was frustrated. Josh would fall back, when he could, to help. Thomas, like any youngster, sometimes tried to talk like he had heard adults talk. On one of the occasions when Josh was helping him, Thomas said, "Can't please that damn nigger."

Josh rode over, placed his hand on the neck of Thomas' horse, and looked the boy directly in the eye. "That man's name is Dave," he told him. " Don't you forget that. All he expects from you is that you do your best. Don't you forget that."

After the drive was over, Dave came over to the two of them standing together. "I ain't never seen a ten-year-old take on such a hard task and do such a good job," he said to Josh but loudly enough for Thomas to hear. "I had some doubts when we started out. I should have known you know a good hand when you see one." Dave's words caused Thomas to be more proud of himself than he had ever been in his short life.

Josh put his hand on Dave's shoulder to steer him away from the ten-year-old. He didn't want Thomas to hear. "I'm a little worried about him making the trip back by himself," he told Dave.

Dave smiled. "I reckon it's not the trip you should be worried about," he said. "Remember, he's been living in Memphis. You need to worry about him foundering when Mrs. Wesfall sees how skinny he is. She's likely to put more food in him than he can handle."

CHAPTER 10

Years go by.
Tears of joy and
Tears of sadness
Fill the eye.

Most of the horses from Texas were not beautiful or well bred. They were mostly mustangs. Some were the results of a cross between a mustang mare and a draft horse or an army remount stud. These crossbred horses were usually easier to break and train, and they would bring a little more money, too. Josh and Dave were most pleased when one turned out to be already broke and trained, either to pull a plow or to ride. The large majority had never been introduced to saddle or harness. They worked those that had some training and put them on the market to be sold quickly. This not only saved on feed, it made their job a little easier.

Dave worked out a plan. The horses were divided into groups of eight. Eight head would be ridden and hooked up to pull each day for about two weeks. These were ready to be sold even though their training was not finished. Most of the customers had been handling horses all their lives and could take over the training now that they were broke.

The biggest surprise was the market. Josh had envisioned taking these broke horses to town each Saturday until he finally found buyers. This is how he and others had been selling horses for years. As it turned out, the news of his train carload of horses spread quickly, and folks took time out from hunting and chopping wood to come see them. He didn't have to go looking for buyers. They, along with curious onlookers, came to his place. Often he had to talk with them when he wished he could be working with the horses.

Each morning before working with the horses, Dave would plow the field adjacent the horse lot with a turning plow. The ground would be plowed so deep it was difficult to walk across. They would rope a horse and pull him up to the snubbing post in the horse lot. Next they would sideline him by using a rope to raise one foot off the ground, put a saddle on, cinch it tight, then turn him loose and let him try to buck the saddle off. When he stopped bucking, they would continue to run him around and around in the lot until he was too tired to worry about the saddle. Next, they roped him again and snubbed him up, this time to a trained horse. They would lead him to the plowed field where one of them would climb into the saddle from a third horse. After the rider had a good seat, he would nod to the one holding the mustang, who would turn the horse loose. A horse can't buck very hard or long in deep plowed ground, especially one tired from his experience in the horse lot. Seldom did Dave or Josh get thrown. If they did, they would land on soft plowed ground. After doing this for a few days, it was just a matter of spending time with the horse, teaching him to respond properly. Buyers came, horses left, and the word spread. By mid-March all the Texas horses had been sold except for the gray mare and a roan mare. Josh wanted to keep these two.

It was a little late to plant corn, but Josh planted most of his fields in corn anyway. It was unheard of for a farmer in Mississippi not to have some cotton. So, he planted some cotton. After a few years of refining the operation and receiving a carload of horses each year, Josh was doing as well as those of his neighbors who had river bottomland.

The arrangement with Walter Ragsdale changed. Now Josh delivered two drafts to the railroad office when he picked up a load. One was for rental of the railroad car, and the railroad company delivered the other one to Walter.

Folks around West were amazed that he had been able to come up with enough capital to get this enterprise started. Of course, they believed he was making a huge profit on each horse and had no doubt he could continue.

Along with these rumors came respect. Everyone liked to claim they had visited or had a drink with Josh Collins. Though he enjoyed his position in the community, he didn't change his habit of working from before daybreak until after sundown.

He was proud of his wife, his two sons, and his daughter. Carol was showing her age more than Josh. Life was hard on women, and it showed. She still had her beautiful but sad smile. She worked hard taking care of her family.

Dan, the oldest, with dark hair and eyes, was quiet, somewhat like his mother. It was known around the neighborhood that he was a hard working youngster who accepted responsibility in a manner that would be expected of an adult. At the end of his fifth year in school, he graduated from the eighth grade. The school in West only had eight grades. He made his first trip to Memphis to help bring back horses when he was just eight years old. He learned fast. He tried hard to do things right. When possible, Josh had him work beside Dave. Dave's talent for working with boys equaled his talent working with horses. He seldom gave them direct answers or instructions. Instead, he helped them figure things out.

The lovely Betty Sue was one of those girls too pretty for her own good. Although it was not easy, Carol did a good job of teaching her to respect others. There was always a look in Betty Sue's eyes that said, "You don't know what I am going to do next." One problem was that her father couldn't say no to her. If she heard "No," it came from her mother or one of her brothers.

As the youngest, Joey was in a position to enjoy life. Unlike his sister or his brother, he had blond hair and blue eyes. He was at his best when smiling or daydreaming. He was good at these two things. To get his attention you usually had to speak to him twice, because he was dreaming of horses, or hunting, or just running across an open field. Josh or Dave only had to give Dan instructions one time, and the job would be done correctly. They had to repeat instructions several times for Joey. And even then, it was unlikely he would remember very long.

CHAPTER 11

In the Mississippi hills,
Hard we try.
Together we live.
Together we die.

Life changed for the Collins family when Dan was twelve years old, Betty Sue nine and Joey seven. It was a hot humid summer. One day some clouds appeared, and a little later it started to rain. The clouds stayed all day. All night the rain and wind would come and go.

Josh worried, because the rain was too late to help the corn crop and more than the cotton crop could use. The ground became soaked. The wind uprooted trees and blew corn flat down on the ground. Streams and gullies ran full. Josh knew that the folks who lived on the river were getting flooded out. Their livestock, crops, homes — and probably some of their bodies — were floating down the Big Black River.

Most of the fields in this area were on hillsides, including those on the Collins' farm. This much rain resulted in crops being washed away as the topsoil had been years ago. It was one of those storms that occasionally came up from the coast. The West newspaper told a story of many lives lost and untold damage on the coast. For the area around West, Mississippi, the worst was yet to come.

With water and mud everywhere and the hot summer sun coming down, the heat and humidity were brutal. After several days, people started getting ill.

No one knew what to do. Everyone said, "The fever is going around." It was too wet to plow and work in the fields, so neighbors visited and talked about how bad the storm had been and how bad the fever was. They didn't know these visits were spreading sickness and death.

Carol was not the first one in the community to come down with it, but when she did, it was bad. Most people who caught the fever were very sick for a week. After about a week, some would get better, but some would die. After Carol came down, she only lasted three days. Her sad smile was no more.

She died in the middle of the night. Josh sat by her body, drinking whiskey, until daylight. At daybreak, he didn't see Joey go to the outhouse. Joey watched, from the cracks in the walls of the outhouse, as his drunken father saddled his brown gelding and rode away, his bottle of whisky in one hand. That was the last time anyone saw Josh Collins alive.

Dave found him later that day. There was a low area in one of the fields holding about three feet of water. Josh was floating face down. His favorite horse was grazing close by. Josh was a good swimmer who'd made a point of taking his children to the stock pond to teach them how to swim. No one will ever know if he intended to commit suicide, or if he just fell off his favorite old horse, too drunk to stand. They wrote in the local newspaper, "Carol Collins Dies From Fever. Josh Collins Drowns In Accident."

Because of the fear of fever spreading, bodies were buried quickly. The day after Josh was found in the water, he and Carol were buried in the cemetery, beside the little church in West. During the funeral, Joey's mind kept reviewing the scene of his drunken father saddling the brown gelding and riding away. Because his young eyes had seen that, and then, soon after, he'd found out about his mother's death, his young mind became convinced that his mother died because his father rode off. This would shape his opinion of the man he called Paw for years to come. Today his tears were for the loss of his mother, not his father.

Friends and neighbors came. They scrubbed the house, brought food and helped take care of the livestock. Many families wanted to take the two boys home with them — some out of compassion, some because of the work boys could perform, some for both reasons. Two or three families wanted to adopt the little green-eyed girl.

The awesome decisions to be made concerning the lives of the Collins children and the estate were in the hands of Judge McCool. Judge McCool and Josh had been friends all their lives. They had grown up together, and the McCool family lived only a few miles from the Collins' house. Though it had probably never been expressed, they loved and respected each other.

The only close living relative was Josh's sister, Teresa. When she was sixteen, she had married a peddler, twice her age, and moved to his home in New Orleans. Occasionally, the peddler, Lance DeVeau, would stop by and stay overnight. He was a fun-loving man, fluent in French as well as English. He always brought candy for the kids and good whiskey for Josh. Teresa had never returned to her childhood home. Judge McCool sent two telegrams to her.

After a week with no answer, he stopped trying to communicate with her.

But he had no way of knowing how much trouble would soon come from New Orleans.

CHAPTER 12

When we lose
Precious life,
Those left behind
Must pay the price.

One hot afternoon, Dan entered Judge McCool's office. "I didn't know whether to come to your office or your home, Judge," he said.

"Dan, you come to either my office or my home any time you wish. What's on your mind?"

Dan was fighting back tears. He felt that if ever in his life he must be a man and not show any tears it was now. "Judge McCool," Dan said, "it's all this talk about splitting up what's left of our family."

"I know it's hard," the judge said to Dan, "but the law doesn't give us any choice in the matter. The only hope is for someone to take you all in and become the guardian of all three. You are all minors. So far, no one has come forward with such an offer."

"But Judge, we have a farm!" Dan said. "I know how to farm, and I have Dave to help. Why can't I adopt or become the guardian of my sister and brother? We have a house to live in, and I know we can make it. Please."

"Dan, I want to commend you for coming here with such an idea," Judge McCool said kindly. "The answer to your question, why can't you do it, is that you are a minor."

There was a long pause. Dan's head was hanging low. The judge, grieving the loss of his good friend and now sharing the son's distress, was not enjoying his job. He was wondering why he ever wanted to become a judge. He put his hand on Dan's shoulder to comfort him.

"I'll tell you what Dan," he said. "I'll hold off any decision for another week. Perhaps someone will come along. There are a couple of families that I'm going to talk to."

Dan rode home carrying a heavy load for a twelve-year-old boy. Dave's wife, Nor, was there, cleaning house and cooking. She was quiet and efficient. Within three hours of her arrival, she had cleaned the house so it was spotless and prepared a big meal. Earlier, when she'd arrived, Betty Sue had been crying, but Nor's kind words had quickly helped the young girl. Talking without pause, the lonely girl followed Nor as she worked. After saying good-bye to each child with a generous hug, Nor picked up the large pile of laundry she had wrapped in a sheet, placed it on top of her head and walked home.

Three days later, Judge McCool rode up in his buggy. Dan had seen him coming so he was on the front porch to meet him. To his surprise, the judge asked him to climb in and take a ride. They went down the dirt road far enough to park under a good shade tree. The judge wanted to discuss his plan with Dan without Joey and Betty Sue hearing.

He laid out a plan that gave Dan more hope than he'd had in over a week. The judge's plan was to appoint himself the guardian of the three children, as well as the executor of the estate. His house was full to overflowing, and he would not be able to take the Collins kids in. They'd remain in their own home. Dan would be head of the house. With Dave and his wife to help, and Dan's sense of responsibility, the judge was confident that the farming would be taken care of. He would meet with Dan each week to go over any financial or business transactions that needed to be taken care of.

Immediately on hearing the plan, Dan stuck his hand out for the judge to shake. For the first time since the storm, he took a deep breath and smiled. They rode back to the house, and the judge explained the arrangement to Betty Sue and Joey. "Dan is your brother," he said in conclusion, "but now he is head of this house. I expect you two to give him the respect you would give your father."

This confused Joey, because he already felt more respect for his brother than for his father. He was still mad and hurt because he felt his father had abandoned him, along with his mother, brother and sister. He was determined to block out the memory of Josh Collins.

Two days later, someone came to their house who added to this confusion. It was the first time any of the Collins children had ever seen their Aunt Teresa DeVeau, from New Orleans. She was riding in a buggy with a top on it to keep out the rain and sun. Her husband, Lance, was driving. She was seated in the middle of the rear seat holding an umbrella. Lance pulled the buggy up to the hitching post in front of the Collin's house. After tying the horses he went around and helped his wife out of the buggy. She was careful to keep the umbrella between herself and the sun.

The Collins children had never seen anyone dressed in such fine clothes, and they'd never seen an adult with such smooth skin. They were lost for words and could not keep their eyes off their aunt. They knew who she was, because her husband had been to their house several times in the last few years. Also, they knew Judge McCool had been speaking of her lately.

It was polite custom to wait until invited to dismount from one's horse, buggy or wagon. But it was obvious that Teresa had her own rules and did not intend to follow custom. Only after climbing the steps and moving into the shade of the porch roof, did she speak.

"I am your Aunt Teresa," she said. "I have come to look after your welfare."

After a minute of silence, Dan said, "Welcome, Aunt Teresa and Uncle Lance. Judge McCool has been helping us. And we sure have some good neighbors!"

She shifted her eyes from Betty Sue to Dan. "You must be Dan. You look much like my brother did at your age. Thank goodness this precious young girl does not look like her father.

"One thing you must learn in life is never trust a judge. And seldom should you trust a neighbor. My husband and I must speak with Judge McCool. Have one of your darkies go tell him we are here."

"There's no one here to go with your message except me," Dan said. "I'll be glad to go. Or maybe *you* would rather go to his office in West?"

She let out a long sigh, thinking about her situation. Finally she spoke.

"We obviously don't wish to spend the night in this house," she said. "As much as I detest the idea of getting back in that buggy, I think we should go to town. After we have told the judge how to handle the mess that my brother left, we will spend the night in town. I hope they have decent accommodations."

As she boarded the buggy with the help of her husband, she held her umbrella carefully. Not a ray of sunlight was to touch her skin.

As he watched them pull onto the dirt road headed toward West, Dan was thinking about the strange fact that they did not say a howdy or hello, and the even stranger fact that her husband did not speak a single word. He remembered Uncle Lance was quite talkative when visiting *without* Aunt Teresa. He was startled out of his thoughts, when his sister shouted, "Isn't she wonderful?"

Dan was puzzled and disturbed by such a statement, because he was thinking the opposite. And then, his head already spinning, he heard Joey say, "That sure was a fine pair of horses pulling their buggy!"

Dan made himself realize that his younger brother and sister would be of little help — if any — with the troubles ahead.

CHAPTER 13

On the old home place,
When you lose two,
Hold tight to each other.
What else can you do?

Dan did not sleep well that night. He didn't know what to expect, but he figured whatever it was to be bad. While eating breakfast, he heard a buggy drive up in the front yard. All of a sudden the part of breakfast he had eaten felt like rocks in his stomach.

He was somewhat relieved when he went out and found Judge McCool, sitting in his buggy in the front yard. He walked down the steps to tie the judge's horse to the hitching post, saying, "Howdy, Judge. Come in and have some breakfast."

"Morning, Dan. I've had breakfast, but I could use some coffee." The judge was thinking he had never seen a twelve-year-old so close to being an adult.

"Let's sit here on the porch. It's cooler than inside. I'll fetch the coffee," Dan said. He was thinking it might be best if Betty Sue and Joey didn't hear what the judge had to say.

By the time he'd returned with the coffee, both his brother and sister had joined the judge. The green-eyed girl was excited. "Judge, did you see my aunt?" she asked.

"I sure did, Betty Sue. We had a long visit yesterday afternoon." He had decided to tell them all the news. Secrets don't last long anyway.

"Your aunt wants to do something I don't think any of you want to see come to pass. She thinks it would be best for her to adopt Betty Sue, and for you two boys to go live with some of the folks that want to take you in. She wants me to sell this farm and livestock and divide the money between the three of you, with her appointed executor until you come of age.

Dan spoke up quickly to ask, "She can't make us do that, can she?"

The judge was slow to answer. The pause gave Dan time to add another question, "What about the plan we had before she came?"

Finally the judge answered. "It partially depends on how determined she is to have her way. If I decide against her plan, she may go back to New Orleans and we may never hear from her again, or she can take it to a higher court. Considering the circumstances of the case, there's a good chance they'd agree with her and not me."

It was normal for Dan to be quiet, but even Betty Sue was quiet after Judge McCool spoke. It was obvious that even Joey was paying close attention. After a long silence, the judge said, "Tomorrow morning I have a meeting with her, scheduled for ten o'clock. Why don't the three of you think on this and come to my office between nine and nine-thirty? We can talk some before she shows up."

Joey ran to untie the judge's horse, as if he thought the problems would vanish when the judge drove away. That afternoon the three of them had the longest conversations they had ever had with each other.

The next morning, when the three of them entered Judge McCool's office with its large chairs, desk, bookshelves, books and table, they smelled leather and old books. Joey and Betty Sue expected it to be somewhat like his home. They were quite impressed with the difference. After the three were seated in the chairs that were too large for them, Dan spoke.

"Judge McCool," he said. "Betty Sue has something she wishes to tell you."

The nine-year-old girl sat up as high as she could in the large chair. "Judge McCool," she said, "I would like to go live with my aunt."

The judge was not surprised by what he just heard. He knew it would make his job easier. At he same time, he wanted to make sure his job being easier, or not, did not influence the decisions made here today. He had a strong feeling that Teresa DeVeau came to her old home planning to carry two things back to New Orleans — her niece and the promise of money from the sale of the farm her brother had left. He knew the best he could hope to accomplish would be a compromise resulting in her getting only one of these.

His thoughts were interrupted by Dan. "Judge, please don't let her split us up. We just lost our maw and paw. We need each other."

"Dan, I know how much you need and want to stay together. That's why I came up with the plan we had before your aunt showed up. But your aunt and your sister have changed the situation. The one thing I am sure would be reversed, if this ended up in a higher court, is a twelve-year-old boy raising a nine-year-old girl, against her will. With your sister not agreeing, I believe it is something we cannot possibly justify. Your sister's wishes must be considered. We can possibly reach some compromise on the farm and livestock.

Their meeting was interrupted when Teresa entered the room without knocking. She was followed by her husband. She was startled to see her brother's children there.

"I thought I had a meeting with you, Judge McCool," she said to the judge. "I didn't expect my niece and these brats to be here."

"By 'these brats' do you refer to your nephews?" he asked, obviously offended.

"They are boys now. Trouble is, some day they'll be men," she said. "Collins men. They're destined to live and die like all Collins men. That is to say, they will die before they can become old men, and they'll die drunk. As far back as anyone can remember, all Collins men die drunk. I'm here to insure my niece doesn't see them follow their family fate."

"Dan, Betty Sue, Joey — go outside and wait for me over near your wagon," the judge said as he rose from his chair. He knew he had made a mistake, having the children in the meeting, and he was determined to stop the damage now.

When Dan started to speak, Judge McCool interrupted him as he walked to the door and opened it. "Please, Dan, do as I ask without another word." The three minors left the room.

When he turned to Teresa his face was red with anger, but his words were firm and composed. "You obviously care nothing for those boys," he began. "But that doesn't give you the right to abuse them. Whether you intended it to be or not, what you said here today was extremely hurtful to them. Any judge in any other court would agree with me. I'm going to tell you how this will be handled, and if you choose to oppose me, you will spend many days in this county and will not win a single court case."

He knew that being in this town and county was something that she found to be quite miserable. He also knew that the case he could not win in a higher court was letting a twelve-year-old boy raise a nine-year-old girl. "You may take Betty Sue to New Orleans and adopt her. I will have the authorities there check on a regular schedule to make sure the two of you are proper parents. When and if the two males decide to sell their farm and livestock, the entire amount of the sale will be divided equally between the two of them."

Teresa started to speak. He cut her off immediately.

"You do not have permission to speak," he said, "and if you do, Betty Sue will remain here. I do not want the girl or those boys to hear any more of your cruel words. You go out the back door. In two hours I will have papers ready for you to sign. The children will go home and pick up Betty Sue's things. She and whatever she wishes to carry with her will be here for you to pick up after you and your husband have signed the proper documents. That is, if she still wishes to go with you."

He opened the back door, and they left without a word. With a heavy heart, he walked out the front door and across the yard to the wagon where the children were waiting.

"Betty Sue, are you sure this is what you wish to do?" he asked.

She nodded and said, "Yes."

The judge got down on one knee, looked the pretty little girl in the eyes and said, "You have two hours to change your mind. Your brothers will drive you home, so you can get the clothes and other things you wish to carry to your new home. If you are sure this is what you want to do, you are to be back here in two hours with your things."

The Collins boys were quiet. Between losing their parents and their sister, and the things they had heard from their aunt, they were in a state of shock.

***

Dan succeeded in holding back his tears when he hugged his sister to say, "Good-bye."

As they watched the buggy carrying their aunt, uncle and sister away, they saw their aunt pick up the bag containing Betty Sue's clothes and drop it in the ditch alongside the road. When Dan went to pick it up and place it in the wagon, he was unable to hold back the tears. He would never open the plain cloth bag, but he would value it and keep it for many years.

Joey, in his troubled young mind, found a way to blame his father, not only for his mother's death, but for the loss of his sister as well. Like most children his age, he'd been told, by his mother and others, "The father is the head of the house. He's in charge."

His experiences told him that whoever was in charge of his world had done a terrible job.

CHAPTER 14

Only one can learn
What I must know.
Others can help
Lead me to the show.

As time passed, with the help of Judge McCool, Dave and his wife Nor, Dan was doing well as a farmer-rancher. With the help of their neighbor, Lyle Slaughter, they'd driven a carload of horses from Memphis each year.

Joey was the topic of most of Dan's worrying. One day, he confided to Dave about it.

"Dave, I know you like to let us figure things out for ourselves. And I know you know that Joey just doesn't pay any attention to anything we say. What are we going to do? He just lives in his own imaginary world."

"It's true he doesn't pay attention to us most of the time," Dave agreed. "However, there *are* times he listens very carefully." Then he fell silent.

"Dave, I know you want me to figure out where you're going. This subject has me so frustrated. Please don't make me wait and figure out what you are thinking."

"Notice how he listens and learns when we are talking to him about hunting or horses?"

"Sure, Dave, those are the only two things he shows any interest in!"

Dan waited. He knew getting answers from Dave took some patience, so he just waited. After he'd given up hope of Dave continuing, he prompted him. "Horses and hunting — they're the problem, not the answer."

"I reckon you should think on it," Dave answered, as he put his ax on his shoulder and walked away.

The next morning Dan felt a little lighter. "Dave, why don't you take Joey and go get some firewood? You all can talk about hunting and horses."

"Sounds like a good plan," Dave said. "It won't take us but about half a day to get a wagon load of wood. We may just do some hunting before we come home. Tell him to bring a shotgun, one load of buckshot and one load of birdshot."

The next morning Joey came out with the twelve-gauge shotgun and the two shells as instructed. Dave drove to a creek bottom full of trees where they had their pick of just the right size trees to split into firewood. On the way, Dave talked of stalking technique. Joey paid close attention.

With a crosscut saw, Dave on one side of the tree and Joey on the other, they soon had the ground covered with wood cut just the right length for firewood.

"I can load the wagon," Dave said, while they were eating lunch. "You go up the creek and bring back some meat. Put the birdshot in one barrel and the buckshot in the other. Use the birdshot on quail, rabbit or a squirrel. Only use the buckshot on a deer, hog or a bear."

"Ain't never seen a bear," Joey said as he carefully loaded the double barrel gun, according to instructions.

"There's not as many as they used to be. You need to learn how to be still and quiet to get close enough to shoot one. The main thing is make sure each shot brings down whatever you're shooting at. Make sure when you shoot, you make a clean kill. Remember, move slow and quiet, and stay in the shadows. The more time you spend waiting, looking and listening, the more game you'll bring home."

After about an hour, Dan heard the twelve gauge explode. As he was finishing up loading the wagon, he heard it explode again.

In a few minutes Joey showed up, displaying a cottontail rabbit. "Look Dave," he said proudly, "I got this one!"

"Good work! Fried rabbit tomorrow. Did you get a hog or a deer?" Dave asked.

"I almost got a deer. I was trying to get close enough, and he heard me and took off. I took a shot at him, but he was running too fast. Dave, we'll need more wood before winter's over. Can we come back and do this again tomorrow?"

"Can't go hunting tomorrow. That would be in violation of the code of good hunting," Dave said, with a serious look on his face.

"What do you mean?" Joey asked as he put the shotgun in the wagon. "You never told me about any code." He climbed up on the seat beside Dave.

"The code is: if you pull the trigger and the gun goes off, something must drop dead. If whatever you were shooting at didn't drop dead, you can't go hunting the next day. You did good with the rabbit, and if you hadn't wasted that other shell, you could allow yourself to go hunting tomorrow."

"Dave, I think I can allow myself to go hunting anyway."

"I thought you wanted to be a good hunter, not just somebody who goes hunting. Anybody can be somebody who goes hunting," Dave told the boy, slapping the horses with the driving lines to start the wagon in motion.

"You know I want to be a good hunter!" Joey said.

"Then you don't have a choice. You must follow the code."

The horses started up the hill out of the creek bottom, and as the hill became steeper they went to pulling hard. They spread their back legs and staggered from side to side. But the wagon didn't go up the hill.

"Dave, they can't pull this wagon full of wood up the hill!" Joey shouted. He'd never seen horses in such a strain.

"Get up, there!" Dave said, laughing, as he cracked his whip over the horses.

"What happened, Dave?" Joey asked, because he was having trouble understanding what he was seeing. The horses were pulling the wagon up the hill with ease.

"What happened, Dave?" he repeated. "After you cracked your whip, they didn't have any trouble pulling up the hill."

Dave waited a few minutes for Joey to think about what he had seen before he answered, "Always remember: hosses and mules, like folks, will sometimes lie to you."

All the way home and for days after, Joey thought about what he had seen and heard that day.

Nor had cooked pork roast, sweet potatoes, greens and corn bread for their supper. Dan knew the weather was cold enough for the pork roast to keep until tomorrow. He fried the rabbit, and they both enjoyed it.

The next morning, during breakfast, Dan asked Joey his opinion of the horses they were breaking that had not been sold. He was surprised at the detailed evaluation Joey gave him of each one. The older brother vowed to talk with his younger brother about horses and hunting as much as possible. He soon learned how to give him work that didn't involve horses or hunting. When he had such work for Joey, he scheduled the work so he could tell Joey that after the work was complete, they would go hunting or go work with horses. Joey listened carefully to instructions and performed the work quickly.

***

Joey continued to become the kind of horseman and hunter he daydreamed about. He continued the practice of taking only two shotgun shells, or if he carried the rifle, he only carried one bullet. During the second year of his hunting, by the code, he evolved to carrying the rifle on a sling over his shoulder with one bullet for the rifle and two shells, both birdshot, in the shotgun. This would allow him to bring down two birds, squirrels or rabbits. Later, Dave put a sling on the shotgun so when Joey was stalking with the rifle ready, he could sling the shotgun over his shoulder. Dan also bought him a smaller rifle for shooting rabbits and squirrels. With the small rifle he always shot small game in the head. They both had grown tired of biting down on meat that was full of birdshot.

The third year, Dan only fattened up one hog for sausage and bacon. Joey was bringing home more meat than they could eat. If a neighbor was sick or just needed meat, Joey would show up at their house with plenty. He liked excuses to take meat to neighbors, because it spread his reputation as a hunter.

When someone asked him why he only carried one shell or bullet for each barrel, he liked to try to look modest and say, "Ammunition is heavy. If you don't need it, why carry it?" This from a hunter who carried two guns.

CHAPTER 15

Riding through life,
It's always best
To have a horse
Better than the rest.

By choice, Joey was not a great student. He did manage to graduate eighth grade from the school in West when he was thirteen years old. This was also the year he caught up with his brother in height.

Also in his thirteenth year, while he was helping Dave and Dan unload a carload of horses in Memphis, he saw a tall sorrel mare come off the train car that took his breath away. He couldn't take his eyes off her. He studied her, looking for flaws, and he couldn't find any. After this careful study, he shouted, "Dave, Dan, look at that mare! Did you ever see a horse so pretty?"

Dave could usually find a reason not to answer such a question. In this case he just said, "I reckon not."

Joey asked the question the other two were puzzling over. "Why would those dummies in Texas put a mare like her in a load of horses they're selling by the head?"

"Mr. Ragsdale's no dummy," was Dan's response.

Joey said, "Well then, someone who works for him must be. What do you think, Dave?"

"About the question you raise, 'Why is she here?' I reckon you ought to think on it."

Later Dave led out the gray mare by the name of Maggie, with her loud cowbell clanging. Over the years Maggie had led every horse home they'd received from Texas. She'd been a good saddle horse, a good plow horse, a good wagon horse, and she'd produced ten mule colts. Right now there was another one in her belly.

The sorrel mare didn't challenge her. She positioned herself off to one side, behind Maggie — but a little in front of the others.

Later that night, Joey said to Dave, "I've heard that horses can't buck in water. What do you think?"

"I think a horse can buck, if it wants to. They have more trouble bucking you off on deep plowed ground, and even more trouble bucking you off if they're in water up to their belly. What are you thinking?"

"There must be something wrong with that mare. I can only think of one reason why that mare is here. If those boys in Texas could ride her, she would never have been put in the stock car. The question is, can *we* ride her? If they got on her in a horse lot with hard ground, even if they can ride as good as us, the mare could be too much."

Dave was pleased with Joey's thinking. This was the first time anyone had heard him express the thought that someone else on earth might be able to ride as well as he could.

Dan quietly enjoyed the excitement his brother expressed when dealing with horses. Dan was not usually spontaneous, but this was an opportunity he couldn't resist. "Joey, you like that mare," he said. "You handle her the way you think best."

The young Joey could not have been more pleased.

Three days later, when he roped her in the horse lot, she came directly to him. This confirmed his suspicion that she'd been handled. This was not the first time she'd had a rope thrown around her neck. Joey put a halter on her and tied her to the snubbing post. He backed off, waited for her to set back and fight the snubbing post. When she didn't, he untied her and just held the rope in his left hand. She just kept all four legs straight under her, both eyes on Joey. He picked up the saddle pad and walked to her head so she could smell it. She showed some curiosity but not much fear. When he placed it on her back, she flinched but didn't bolt. He took it off and repeated the process several times without much reaction. He then went through the same procedure with the saddle. Joey was beginning to think he was wrong about her being hard to ride. He then pulled the cinch up tight and turned her loose.

She took a step and then decided she had worn the saddle long enough. After bucking for several minutes, it was obvious she could buck harder, with more athletic ability than any horse these men had ever seen. When she reached the point of deciding she was not going to buck the saddle off, she ran down the side of the fence, testing the posts by slamming the saddle into the oak boards attached to them.

Joey, afraid she would hurt herself — and sure she would soon demolish the saddle —threw his rope around her neck. Just as she had done when he roped her earlier, she quietly walked to him.

He knew that if he had been in the saddle and somehow stayed there while she bucked, he would probably have a broken leg from being slammed into the fence. She stood quiet while he took the saddle and blanket off. His thoughts were confirmed about why she had come with a load of horses being sold by the head.

The next morning, when Dave arrived at the horse lot, Joey was busy. With a roll of twine he was tying small limber switches from the fruit trees to the boards inside the horse lot. The switches extended about two to three feet inside the lot. Dave was pleased with what he saw. He offered to help. It took them more than an hour to complete the task.

"Joey, we might not have very many peach pies this year, but I think you came up with a plan that may work," Dave said with a smile.

Just as planned, when the mare stopped bucking and decided to punish the saddle with the oak boards, the switches slapped her in the face. It only took two tries to convince her that wearing the saddle wasn't the worst thing that could happen. Joey was relieved.

"You still thinking about taking her to the pond?" Dave asked.

"Yeah, I'm worried about how I'm going to keep her in the pond after I get on."

"Well, remember, a horse follows its head," Dave said. He hitched a horse to the turning plow to plow the field.

The next morning Joey was in the lot early leading the mare around in circles. It was obvious he had figured out what Dave was trying not to tell him. If you try to lead an unbroken horse straight away, they can hold their ground and refuse to follow. When you pull from the side, they need to step to you to keep their balance. It's fairly easy to lead in a circle and then slowly transition into leading straight away.

His next step was to do what they did with horses they were training to drive. With a long rope on the bridle, Joey stepped behind the horse and pulled. The mare turned as if looking at him over her shoulder, then followed her head until she was facing him. He did this many times until she was giving her head easily, on either side, and turning to him when asked.

Dave, finished with the plowing, was watching over the fence. Joey smiled and said, "Don't need to plow that field for me tomorrow. We're going to the pond."

It was obvious the youngster had been patient as long as he could. He'd been willing to take several days in preparation instead of just climbing on, as they did with other horses.

All this preparation paid off. When Joey got on in the pond, the soft mud on the bottom and the water offered enough resistance to soon discourage the sorrel from bucking. When she tried to leave the pond, Joey just pulled on one rein, and she found herself going back into the deeper part of the pond. After the third day in the pond, he led her to the plowed field and stepped on. By this time, she had decided that having him on her back wasn't so bad.

For a week Joey rode her every day — in the pond, on the plowed ground and in the lot with switches tied to the fence. Then he went to the pasture to gather cattle and found out she was an even better horse than he had imagined. After a few days of riding through the pasture and letting the mare become accustomed to his weight on her back, he realized that she had a longer, stronger stride than any horse anyone in this neighborhood had ever seen.

Everyone who saw her offered to buy her, with the exception of Judge McCool. He remarked, "She needs someone Joey's age on her, not someone my age. However, if anyone challenges you to a race, let me know. I want to put some money on her and Joey."

She offered to buck now and then, as she would for the rest of her life. Joey didn't get excited. He just pulled on one rein, then asked her to move ahead, and she cooperated.

CHAPTER 16

The young
Learn from the old,
But sometimes, they
Are just too bold.

The deafening noise of unshod hoofs pounding on wood rolled on like thunder as the horses came out of the railroad livestock car, over the ramp, into the railroad holding pens. The horses, starving for water, went directly to the watering troughs along one side of the pen. The troughs had been filled for their expected arrival. These thirsty horses had just made the trip from Fort Worth, Texas, to Memphis, Tennessee, with no food or water along the way.

Left for nature to decide, the dominant horses in this extremely thirsty herd would drink too much water and possibly founder, leaving no water for those lower on the pecking order. But when the dominant horses had drunk their share, a black man with gray hair stepped into the pen and swung open the gate that was near one end of the troughs. The frightened horses would have bolted from this movement, but before they had time to, a tall, young white man jumped into the pen. With perfect timing he cracked his whip near the other end of the water troughs. It sounded like a lightning strike. The horses that had been drinking bolted through the open gate into the next pen, and the black man with white hair closed the gate between them and the water. After this was repeated four times, the troughs were empty, and all the horses had some water in their stomachs.

Anyone watching would have deduced that this was not the first time this older man and the tall boy had worked as a team. With excitement in his voice, the young man said, "Dave, these look even better than the last bunch."

"I reckon I'll think on it," Dave replied. He had seen a lot of these horses come in from Texas and knew not to try and judge them too quickly. He knew his young companion was looking for one that could outrun the wind, while he was looking for one with a quiet disposition.

He said, "Joey, we better saddle our broke horses and be ready when Dan gets back."

About that time a man only four years older than Joey, not quite as tall, but heavier built, came at a fast walk across the railroad tracks. "Well, what do you men think of this bunch?" he asked.

"You know Dave, he's not gonna tell us what he's thinking. I think they may be a little better than the last bunch," Joey said, with a grin on his face.

Dan liked seeing the excitement that new horses brought to Joey. You could see it a mile away. He looked at Dave, who was looking at him, and they both knew they were enjoying the same thoughts about the lanky, optimistic young man.

Dan climbed up on the fence and studied the herd. When he finished counting them several times he said, "Looks like the count's okay. While you men saddle up, I'll take the draft over to the railroad office, and we can head for the river. Looks like it's gonna be a cold night." He knew Joey was at the age where he liked being called a man.

When Dan returned, Dave was sitting on a short stocky bay gelding near the gate that led out of the alley, into open country. At the other end of his lead rope was Maggie. Now her gray coat had turned white, and her back was swayed. But it was easy to see that she thought highly of herself, in spite of her advanced age. Long before this bunch of young horses arrived at their new home, they would know not to cross her.

Joey was sitting quietly at the other end of the alley on his tall sorrel mare, holding the roan gelding that was carrying Dan's saddle. Dan was always amazed at Joey's ability with a horse. The high-strung sorrel mare would not stand quiet for anyone else. With Joey on her, she was relaxed, looking like she was asleep.

Without a word, Dan opened the gate that allowed the new bunch of horses to enter the alley. He stood back as they moved into the alley between him and Dave. Dave and Maggie started out of the alley at the south end, and the herd followed. Joey came up and brought Dan his roan. They were on their way. The horses' new home was over a hundred and fifty miles due south. As those that came before had, they would soon stop and eat their fill of good river-bottom grass and drink all the water they could hold.

Memphis had grown north of the railroad tracks. There were not many houses on the south side, and most of those were not much more than shacks. An empty strip of land ran between the shacks down to the river. That strip of land and the grazing land down by the river belonged to the railroad. It was

113

there for people to move cattle, or in this case horses, to and from the railroad loading pens. Livestock needed some grass in them before starting a trip on a rail car. And they needed it even more when they arrived at their destination. The railroad had their own police to make sure no cattle or horses stayed on the grass more than a few hours and that local folks didn't turn their milk cows onto the precious river-bottom grass.

Dave and the gray mare, with her bell clanging, were in the lead. Truth was the mare could lead this herd home without any help. Dave's job was mostly making sure the herd didn't run over anyone. A little closer to home, Dave would take her halter off, and she would take them on home without any help. She knew the way as well as the men did. When one of the horses fresh from Texas, thought about moving out in front of her or up even with her, she would slowly turn her head and look at the upstart. What this horse language communicated, humans may never know. But the three men knew that the horse that had threatened to take over this operation, a few minutes before, would go hide in the middle of the herd. The young horses didn't want Maggie to look at them. But they sure wanted to follow her.

Dan and Joey were mostly off to each side, their whips ready, keeping the herd from taking off between the shanties. Without Maggie, it would take several more good riders to handle these fresh horses.

With the river and the shade trees on the west side, the sun went down early and the earth gave up its warmth. The three cowboys shivered, even though they had coats and gloves.

The horses grazed for about three hours. Not until they finally began to lay down to rest did the men get off their horses, so they could graze a while. The saddles were left on, in case the Texas horses got restless. Dan and Joey stayed close to their saddled horses and tried to take turns getting a nap on the cold ground. They didn't have much success. But a few minutes sleep tonight would help tomorrow. By this time tomorrow the horses would be settled into a routine. Most of them had been trailed in this fashion before, and by tomorrow they would be trail broke.

There was no need in talking to Dave about closing his eyes. He would simply say, "Reckon I don't need to." He sat on the cold ground and never took his eyes off the herd of horses. He had worked for the young men's father, Josh Collins, most of his adult life. He still had a small place of his own. Many days, after he

115

had worked for twelve hours or more on the Collins place, he'd then go home and work on his own.

His small house was built just a few feet off the dirt road, with a path back to the outhouse, a pen for chickens and one for a few pigs all crammed together. The land was valued by its owner and for good reason. Not many black families owned property. The small farm could produce a few bales of cotton each year and enough corn to feed the pigs and chickens. Not one square foot of land was unused. There were neither trees nor any lawn on this place.

The Collins always had horses that needed educating in the art of pulling a plow. Dave could use their horses, so he got his plowing and hauling done, and the Collins got their horses trained. The arrangement resulted in the best horseman for miles around never owning a horse.

CHAPTER 17

Railroads come.
Railroads stay.
Battle the railroads,
Or move away.

When the tired crew of three arrived at the Wesfall home outside of Batesville they all wore a smile. This was always the best part of the trip. A robust young man by the name of Coat came out to meet them with a big smile. "Mrs. Wesfall said she'll have your supper ready in about thirty minutes. I don't know why she needs another thirty minutes! She's been cooking all day." Coat was a few years older than Dan, over six feet tall and over two hundred pounds. His blue eyes sparkled, and he always wore a big smile.

Dave liked to joke, "That man's smile weighs about fifty pounds."

The Wesfalls had surrounded the large field that included most of the land between their house and town with a barbed wire fence. The wire gap at the north end was open so the Collins horses could be driven in to rest for the night. The tired crew of three could get some sleep tonight. But first, they would enjoy a big supper on the Wesfall's back porch.

As they approached the house, a flock of gray guinea hens squawked and flew to the shelter of a blackjack oak thicket. Closer to the house, actually in the back yard, gray Dominica chickens ran for the hen house.

Harvey didn't get up from his rocker. He had aged and enjoyed too much of his wife's good cooking. With the help of a walking stick he could still get around. He had learned to use the walking stick like another hand, or at least an extension of the one he still had. When he wanted to get on a horse he would get on a stump, or if he was home, on the wood block that Coat cut and placed in the back yard. He would lead the horse up beside the block. After he labored to climb up on the block, if the horse was not close enough, he put the walking stick, with the handle down, across the horse's rump. When he pulled on what would normally be the part of the walking stick that touches the ground, the turned down handle motivated the horse to sidle up to the one armed man on the block. Then he could step on with ease. Coat liked to joke, "Mr. Wesfall's horse is walking stick broke." It was well known that once he was up there he could ride for many miles.

Mrs. Wesfall was aging better than most women in this part of the world. According to Coat, "She stays young and slim fattening the rest of us up."

Everyone had eaten too much before she brought the pie out. However, after looking at it and smelling it, they all knew they could handle at least one piece. As they were enjoying washing the pie down with good coffee, Dan ask Coat to tell him how he got that name. They had all heard the story more than once, but all of them knew they would enjoy hearing it again. Old Harvey Wesfall lit up his pipe and made ready to enjoy hearing it again himself. The aroma of a good pipe spread over the porch as the Dominica chickens searched for scratch in the back yard.

"I was just ten years old when your Papa came to my house and said he had to go to Fort Worth, Texas, and wanted me to take good care of his horse. He told me to walk and trot him each day. I confess I did enjoy making a few runs on him, both bareback and with the saddle. One time I was riding bareback, and that brown gelding wanted to run. I was pulling on the reins to slow him down, and pulling on his mane to hold on, and pulled myself up until I found myself sitting on his head, right behind his ears, with him running full out. Still scares me to think about it. Thank goodness he was such a good gentle horse. When he stopped, he dropped his head down, and I stepped off on the ground. But I fed him good, and he was in good shape when your paw came back from Fort Worth."

Coat, one of those people who could laugh and talk at the same time, laughed now as he went on, "I had a total of four dollars in my pocket when he left our house, after his trip to Fort Worth. That was more money than I had ever seen.

"A little more than a month later, he showed up and wanted me to help him drive horses from Memphis to West, Mississippi. Mind you, I was only ten years old. Dave was there. Ain't I telling it true, Dave?"

"You was ten years old and weighed about ten pounds," Dave put in. His smile was almost as big as Coat's.

Coat continued laughing and talking, saying, "By the time we got to West, I was thinking I *might* be a cowboy. I was so tired, I didn't know if I *really* wanted to be one. Your folks fed me up, gave me some grub and told me to report back here to the Wesfall's place.

When I left, I had six dollars in my shoe, and Dave gave me this pair of spurs he'd made. They were too big, but I grew into them. Thought I was rich.

"I met up with a fellow soon after I left West — not much older than I was. We had a good time riding together. When we got back here, Mrs. Wesfall fed us up like nobody else can. Mr. Wesfall offered to hire me on. I wasn't sure I needed a job, rich as I was. So the next day, me and my new friend lit out for Memphis.

"Your paw had warned me I'd need a blanket on the trip. We didn't have any blankets. At home, on a cold night, we slept between the feather mattress and the one filled with shucks. My maw pulled a huge wool coat out from a chest and said that would have to do for a blanket. Back then, I could have fit in one sleeve of that coat."

Mrs. Wesfall spoke up and declared, "That boy wasn't nothing but bones and hide! Not very big bones and a thin layer of hide."

Everyone laughed, because Mr. Wesfall working him and Mrs. Wesfall feeding him had changed his appearance considerably.

She wanted him to get on with his story so she told him, "Go on, Coat. Tell about your name."

"Well, this fellow traveling with me said, when I crawled into the coat, he couldn't see me. All he could see was coat. Then he started calling me 'Coat.' I had met several other people named Thomas. Somehow, I didn't like it they were using my name. I was the only person I ever heard of with the name of Coat, and I liked the sound, 'Coat Calcoat.' But I never did tell my maw. She went to her grave not knowing I'd changed from the name she gave me. She said it was from the Bible." For a brief time his smile faded.

"Well, I'd made the mistake of telling the fellow traveling with me about the money in my shoe. That last night on the road, we stopped at the spring where you always water your horses. While we were getting a drink, he made like he accidentally fell into me and knocked me into the water. Had to take those wet shoes and socks off to let them dry. You all probably already guessed the rest. When I crawled out of my coat the next morning that no good scoundrel was gone, along with my six dollars. When I got home and showed Maw the spurs Dave made for me, she didn't pay any attention. She didn't ask about the money. She just cried and hugged on me. She said she was just glad to see me alive. To this day I don't understand why she didn't ask about the money."

Everyone had a good laugh, but Joey always felt a mixture of sadness and anger when someone mentioned his father.

When Dave stood up it looked like it hurt a little, he was so full. "I reckon I had better go see to the horses," he said. "Mrs. Wesfall, thank you for such a fine meal. Mr. Wesfall, it sure is good to see you again."

Coat walked him to his horse. Before he mounted he looked at Coat and said, "Coat, you said you didn't understand why your mother didn't mention the money and cried because she was happy just to see you. When you have young ones of your own, you'll understand." He tipped his hat as he mounted and headed down to the herd.

Joey said to the others, before following Dave, "Thank you, folks. Nobody in Mississippi can cook better than Mrs. Wesfall. Matter of fact, nobody any where can cook as good as Mrs. Wesfall."

Dan wanted to talk a little more, so he rolled a smoke as the others rode away. "Guess you know about the railroad, Mr. Wesfall. They say it's going all the way from Chicago to New Orleans. Is it coming close to Batesville?"

"Too damn close. You look out there and see the town. It's coming between here and town. They came through here and said they're going to buy some of our land. I told them, 'What you offer to pay for my land will determine if you're going to buy.' They said they didn't know, but it would be a fair price. I don't like the idea of them taking my land, if I don't agree to the price. I don't much like how they do business."

Dan could understand. "They're coming right through West," he said. "I'm glad we are out far enough they don't want any of our place. If they can hold to the schedule, I hear they plan to have it complete, at least this part of it, by next year. If they get it done, I guess we can stop driving horses and start hauling horses. The folks in the railroad yard in Memphis say they will unload them in Memphis to let them eat and drink. Put them on the south bound and drop them off in West. It'll cost a little more, but when you divide by the number of horses, it's not so bad. To tell the truth, it's just in time. It's getting harder and harder to get through the countryside. The town folks don't want us driving through town, and more folks have fenced their fields off. We're finding we have to get on the road more than we like. More than the other folks on the road like, too."

About that time Mrs. Westfall showed up with the usual flour sack full of food. She shoved it into Dan's hands.

"You folks are the best part of these drives," Dan said. "If we'd not been able to make a little money on the horses, it would have been worthwhile just to have met the Wesfalls."

"Lord," said Mrs. Wesfall, with both hands gesturing in the air, "what would we ever have done if your paw hadn't brought Coat into our lives? We never would have been able to get by. I still have a good man, but let's face it, a plow has two handles. You sure need two hands. You folks brought two good ones into our lives. Besides that, we love him to death."

To show that the love was returned, Coat just showed his big smile, walked over to her, planted a kiss on her cheek and gave her a hug.

CHAPTER 18

Time to grow,
Time to share.
Where is
My sorrel mare?

With a new herd of horses there is always plenty of work. Dave's young son, Little Dave, was working hard to show that he could work alongside the men. Joey's sorrel mare had always been nervous with anyone except him on her back. One day he told Little Dave to get on her and lead a horse to the plowed field. He jumped up there, and the mare was as calm as she would be with Joey in the saddle. Everyone was pleased and complimented him on his horsemanship.

When Joey got an opportunity he talked to Dan about it. "You said I had grown too big to be a jockey. I guess we found a new jockey."

"What good is a having a jockey going to do when no one within five counties will run against your mare?" Dan asked, laughing.

Joey shrugged his shoulders and went back to work. With Joey as a jockey, they had run the mare in four match races and won all four easily. They'd made more money racing her than they'd made selling any ten other horses. They decided it would've been better not to outrun their opponents so badly, though. Their opponents weren't coming back for any more of the sorrel mare.

One day their aunt's husband, Uncle Lance, came by. They always enjoyed his visit. He laughed a lot and talked a lot, unlike when he was with his wife. This time he brought a friend along by the name of Wayne Trudeau.

Both Uncle Lance and Wayne Trudeau were a little uneasy. They said they'd just dropped by, but there was a heavy cloud of business in the air.

When Wayne Trudeau asked what he would take for the good sorrel mare, Joey intended to get rid of him like he had all the others who had asked the same question, since he definitely did not want to sell her. He just gave them a ridiculous price.

"Mr. Trudeau, I'll take five hundred dollars," he said, sure that the price would get rid of the Louisiana man. Instead of walking away, Trudeau reached in his pocket, counted out five hundred and handed it to Joey.

Joey would never forgive himself and never forget the lesson. If he ever had another horse or anything that was not for sale and someone asked him the price, he would say, "Not for sale."

It was painful to watch them leave with the mare tied behind his uncle's buggy. To make things worse, it brought back memories, for Dan and Joey, of seeing their sister carried away in the same buggy.

This fine horse went on to bring Wayne Trudeau fame and fortune on the racetracks in and around New Orleans.

Dan tried to console his brother by talking about how much money five hundred was. With her winnings in the match races and her selling price, she had brought them more money than they normally made from two carloads of horses, teaching Joey and Dan that one good horse is worth more than a carload of average ones.

***

Lately Dan had noticed a faraway look in Joey's eyes. Dan knew his brother was dreaming, but he couldn't figure out what the dreams were about. He was pretty sure it was not horses or hunting. Two days after the sorrel mare was led away, Joey came in with the words that told Dan what his brother had been dreaming about.

"I'm thinking about heading west," said Joey.

Dan couldn't keep from being depressed. This farm had been home to a family of five. Now it was to be a family of one.

Joey had been thinking about problems his leaving would create for Dan. Mostly the problems related to operating the farm.

"You won't have to drive horses anymore with the train coming through town," Joey said. "Well, you'll have to drive them from town to here, but Maggie can handle that without you. As for breaking them, Dave's getting a little long in the tooth, but you and Little Dave can handle it."

"Where are you going?" Dan asked. His mind was not on horses. He dreaded seeing his brother ride away.

"I want to go to Fort Worth and try to find out where that mare came from," Joey answered. "I know I'm too late to homestead some land. Wish I'd been born fifty years ago. I keep thinking about those folks that ended up with big ranches."

That brought a smile to Dan. He knew he and Dave had not cleaned all the daydreaming out of

Joey's head. This also brought a question to Dan's mind. "You going to take the ten-gauge shotgun or the twelve?"

"If it's all the same with you, I think I'd like to take the twelve. You know, I've shot game with both. If you're close enough, the result is the same. The twelve is a little lighter and easier to carry. You know I like to carry a rifle and a shotgun.

"One reason I want to leave, there's not much game left around here. Hell, by the time I get to Texas, there may not be much left out there."

"Joey, after you leave, there'll be a lot more game around here. And I'll bet, after you've been in Texas a while, there'll be a heck of a lot less out there. How will you travel?"

"If I had my choice, I'd be on the sorrel mare. That's not an option, so, if you are okay with it, I'd like to take the bay gelding we just broke. I thought about taking the train but finally decided to go horseback, so I could get a good look at the country between here and there. I've never seen a mountain! Been thinking about swinging north through the mountainous part of Arkansas, so I can see what the world looks like from a mountaintop. Then I'll go to Fort Worth. I don't know where I'll be going when I leave Fort Worth."

Dan had learned from his father and Judge McCool not to leave loose ends. "Two things we need to talk about. First, this farm is yours and mine, equal."

"Brother, you go ahead and operate like it's all yours," Joey told him. "Whatever you can make off of it, it's all yours. I won't be here to help. But when and if you decide to sell, let me have my part. What's the second thing?" Obviously, Joey had thought through his answers to questions he expected his brother to ask.

"The second thing is the five hundred," Dan said. "It's yours. Take it with you. You may find something in Texas to spend it on."

"Mighty good of you," Joey responded. "I been thinking about when Coat was ten years old and his trip back to Memphis. I'll just take a hundred. You put the four hundred in the bank, and if I find a girl or a horse pretty enough to spend it on, I'll write a draft."

Then he did something Dan never expected. Joey walked over to Dan, put his hand on his shoulder and with a tear in his eye said, "All the time I was growing up, without a maw and paw, I thought I had a bad deal. I know now, you and Dave gave me a better raising than most people that have a maw and paw. I didn't make it easy for you, and I am truly sorry."

Dan stood up and embraced his brother — something he hadn't done in all these years. With a tear in *his* eye he said, "You have nothing to apologize for. I'm sorry there were times I just didn't know what to do. We made it together. But we would never have made it without Dave and Judge McCool. They were more than just friends.

"The judge said, 'Just do your best. That's all a mule can do. You can't get it right every time, maybe not even most of the time. If you do your best, every day, things will work out."

"And Dave, besides all the work he did while teaching us how to work — Dave made us think."

CHAPTER 19

Time to travel.
Who will I meet
In the hills
And on city street?

Joey rode the bay gelding to the Wesfall's, where he visited with them and Coat. Mr. Wesfall was in an uproar about the railroad taking some of his land. Mrs. Wesfall made riding a horse to Fort Worth sound like a trip around the world, twice. Coat said he'd be glad when things settled down. He asked a lot of questions about Joey's travel plans.

With the requisite flour sack of food that Mrs. Wesfall fixed, the young man on the bay horse headed for Memphis.

There was a bridge across the Mississippi River at Memphis, and Joey was surprised to see how much traffic there was on the bridge. He and the bay were both frightened by the sounds of travelers and the sight from the bridge. The churning muddy water below the bridge was not a sight either of them liked. After he crossed the river, the traffic soon thinned out, and he realized the traffic on the bridge was a result of people like him, coming from many miles up and down the river to cross. Likewise, after crossing, they scattered out, up and down the river, and the roads were almost empty.

He allowed that the hills and mountains of Arkansas were pretty.

Roads were made for wagons. A team of horses or mules had to work hard to pull a loaded wagon up a hill. Then going down the downhill side, the loaded wagon tried to run over the team. Therefore, to the extent possible, roads were built around hills and mountains instead of going over them. When the road turned north or south to avoid a steep grade, Joey just kept riding west. He enjoyed getting off the road.

The amount of game he encountered was astonishing. For the life of him he couldn't figure out why he'd heard so much about hungry people. He was passing up far more game than he and twenty more men could eat. He usually just killed a rabbit, squirrel or a couple of quail each day. Each evening he enjoyed stopping near the top of a hill or mountain, looking out over the country and cooking his supper. He let deer, bear and wild hogs go about their business.

About half way up one mountain he came across a family in a one-room cabin. They were nice but apologized for not having food to share. Joey rode on a little further and made camp. The next morning he killed a doe, field dressed her, carried her back and hung her up in the yard for the family that was hungry in the mist of plenty.

This delay resulted in his being on top of the mountain in mid-day. He decided to go down the mountain even though it would result in his camping this night in lower country. He figured he could get along without the view from a mountaintop for one night.

The bay gelding had turned out to be a good choice. It was as if he had learned his rider's way of moving quietly and then standing very still to look and listen. He was a good horse for a hunter. Often when Joey could not hear the sounds made by game, the gelding's ears would rotate and tell the hunter where the game was. Later that afternoon when they stopped to look and listen, Joey thought he heard a strange sound. The sound, riding on the breeze, would come and go.

Joey finally decided it was the wind itself blowing through the forest. As he rode on and stopped on top of the next ridge, the sound was clear and it was the most beautiful sound Joey had ever heard. He and the horse both cocked their heads to the side, so their ears could pick up as much of the music as possible. Joey could not understand the words, if there were words. Amazed and entertained, he waited and listened.

After listening a while and deciding which direction to travel to find the source of the beautiful music, he moved on. He soon came to a stream, and as he moved upstream, he found a quite common sight to be the source of the music. Two women were washing clothes, one beating the clothes with rocks in the stream as the other was hanging clothes on tree limbs. A wagon and a good team of draft horses were close by. The ladies' voices, accompanied by the sounds of the stream, were unlike anything he had ever heard.

About the time he decided they were not singing actual words he heard a familiar sound that sent fear through him to the extent he stopped breathing. He knew what a gun being cocked sounded like. He believed the two hammers he had just heard being cocked were on a double barrel shotgun that must be pointing at his head or his spine. The beautiful music had made him careless, and the running water had blocked his hearing. He slowly released his fingers from the reins and slowly raised both hands over his head. "I mean no harm," he said.

The voice behind him was not beautiful like the voices in front of him. "What are you doing snooping around here?" that voice asked.

"I'm just passing through on my way to Fort Worth." Joey answered, thankful that the gun pointed at him was quiet.

"Don't try to lie to me," the voice behind him said. "I know when a man's passing and when he's stopped."

"I was attracted to this spot by the beautiful voices of the two ladies," he said. "I only stopped a few minutes to enjoy the music the ladies were making." The realization came to Joey that in all his years of handling guns, this was the first time he knew of one being pointed at him.

"Why you going to Fort Worth?"

"I'm going to look for a job. My brother and I have a farm in Mississippi. Can't make enough on one little farm for both, so I'm going looking for work."

Joey was thankful that he'd been careful not to wear new clothes for the trip. He didn't have a new saddle or a new pack behind it. Nothing about his clothing or gear suggested any level of prosperity.

The man pointing the cocked shotgun at him walked around and stood near the horse's head. "Let me see your hands," he ordered.

Joey held his hands out for the other to examine. "My name is Joe Collins," he said. "I'm from West, Mississippi."

The stocky man, about forty years old, in bib overalls, said, "Those *could* be the hands of a farmer." He pointed the shotgun toward the sky and eased the hammers down before introducing himself. "I'm Carson Finley. I had a farm in Ohio, but I'm on my way to South Texas, where I plan to have me a much bigger place.

"You being a young man, if you don't know you'll soon find out that this country is set up for the rich to get richer and the poor to get poorer. Only thing is, I plan to trick the setup. Come on up to the wagon, Joe, and meet my wife and daughter. I'd invite you to supper except there ain't no game around here. All we have is some greens the women gathered."

Joe didn't argue about the game even though he knew better. He'd planned to try to change his name from Joey to Joe, but he'd surprised himself when he'd introduced himself as Joe while a man had a gun pointed at him. He was in for an even bigger surprise when he was introduced to the Finley women.

"This is Joe Collins from Mississippi," Carson said, "and this is my wife Onzo and my daughter, Vergie Mae."

Joe was speechless. Onzo was a handsome woman, probably in her early forties. But Vergie Mae was a young woman, about Joe's age, with red hair, freckles and green eyes. He had known girls with red hair and freckles back home, but none as pretty as Vergie Mae. It took him a minute to get over his reaction to seeing such an attractive young lady. He stumbled a bit but managed to say, "I was attracted to the beautiful music you two ladies were making. I sure did enjoy listening, and I'm sorry if I startled you."

Onzo smiled and said, "When we looked up and saw you for the first time, my husband had his gun pointed at you. So we weren't startled, Mr. Collins. What about you?"

"I was scared to death. I stopped breathing, but my heart started beating faster," Joe said. He hoped they didn't know that the sight of their daughter had his heart beating fast again now. "As far as I know, that's the first time anyone pointed a gun at me. I hope it's the last."

After a minute of awkward silence he continued, "There's a little light left. I think I might get lucky, if I spend that time looking for some game. If I find any, I'll bring it back for you folks to have for supper."

"Take more than luck for you to find any game around here," Carson said.

Joe just rode back to where he'd remembered crossing some hog signs. After deciding which way they were going, he started after them, leading the bay. He moved slow and stopped often to listen and watch the gelding's ears. When they heard the hogs up ahead, he moved back and tied the bay to the branch of an elm tree. He checked the wind to make sure the hogs couldn't smell him, then he moved toward them slowly. After moving to where he could see them, he waited until a half-grown hog came into view. A full-grown wild hog often has a strong flavor. One about half-grown is tender and has a delicious flavor. One shot from Joe's rifle, and the pig dropped dead.

By the time he had cleaned it and carried it back to the Finley wagon, Vergie Mae had a large fire going. She had heard the shot and somehow knew this young man would bring something that needed cooking. While she melted some bacon fat in a pan, Joey stripped the loins and back straps from the pig and sliced some into pieces about one inch thick.

Carson commented on how lucky Joe was to find the hogs on this hill. He said they must be the only game within a hundred miles.

Vergie Mae cooked the pork while her mother cooked corn cakes and greens. Joe realized he had not heard Vergie Mae speak. He wanted to ask her a question, any question. But when he looked at her, he was speechless. Carson had been talking, and Joe realized that he had not listened to one word the older man said. He hoped he wasn't expected to respond.

The young lady with red hair and green eyes was humming under her breath the entire time she was cooking.

With a knowing smile, Onzo interrupted his thoughts by placing a plate in his hands, along with a fork and knife. "As our guest, please help yourself," she said.

"Thank you, Ma'am. Sure looks like a fine meal," Joe said. Something about Onzo caused Joe to relax and regain his composure. Soon everyone was eating, and all talking stopped.

After the meal was finished and coffee poured, Onzo placed a pan near the fire and asked Vergie Mae to go to the creek and bring back a bucket of water to wash the dishes. As Vergie Mae started to the creek, Joe said, "Let me get that bucket of water for you."

The lovely young lady kept walking to the creek. Just as she scooped up the bucket of water, Joe caught the bucket by the handle and relieved her of the load. When she said, "Why, thank you, Sir," the sound of her voice caused him to feel much like he did when he heard the hammers cocked behind him earlier that afternoon — but for a different reason.

She kept walking toward the fire, and he didn't mind, because he liked to watch her walk, hoping no one would notice. Viewing her from behind, in her dress that touched the ground, his imagination began to run wild.

Carson broke the spell by saying, "Don't you be spoiling my daughter. She don't need help with a bucket of water."

Onzo had another knowing smile on her face.

Carson slept under the wagon, while his wife and daughter slept inside the wagon. Joe slept near the fire, using his rolled up saddle blanket for a pillow. He woke up at daylight to find Carson putting the harness on his team while his wife arranged things in the wagon and their daughter cooked breakfast. Both women were singing softly as they worked.

When Carson saw Joe was awake he came toward him with something in his hand. Joe rubbed the sleep from his eyes and found himself looking at a printed brochure. The brochure told about a place called Fowlertown, Texas. There were pictures of peas, melons and ears of corn, bigger than any Joe had ever seen. The brochure described a rich land with abundant water just under the surface. New windmills had been invented to pump the water to the surface to irrigate the land so an abundant crop could be guaranteed each year. No longer did the farmer have to depend on the weather.

With the bustling city of San Antonio just to the north and the port of Corpus Christi to the south, a market for any crop you chose to grow was insured. This rich land with abundant water was selling for just two dollars an acre. If you bought at least eighty acres, you got an option to buy another eighty acres for the same price the next year. There were stories of farmers who paid for their new farms with just one crop, with money left over to expand.

"This is the best opportunity to get ahead of the game that has ever been available in the settlement of this country," Carson declared. "We sold our farm in Ohio for five dollars an acre and will have a much bigger operation in South Texas. Within a few years, all of this land will be sold. You better come down and get your share while there is an opportunity like this."

Joe looked at the brochure without answering.

Carson went back to the business of getting ready to travel.

By the time Joe finished his breakfast, Vergie Mae was standing there waiting for the plate and coffee cup. She put them in the wagon to be washed later. Within minutes the Finley's were pulling out onto the nearby southbound road, waving goodbye.

He realized he had not commented on what a fine team of horses they had. He also wondered if he would ever again see anyone who made him feel like Vergie Mae Finley did.

Unlike the Finleys, he took his time putting the saddle on his horse and moving out. He knew he had to go to Fort Worth.

CHAPTER 20

West of West,
The trees are green.
The hills are high.
Some men are mean.

Joe rode in a westerly direction up the Arkansas
Mountain. After about an hour, he found his path
blocked by a rock outcrop. Joe could have climbed
over the rock and continued west, but the bay gelding
certainly could not. Joe turned south, looking for a
break in the rock outcrop that would allow him and
his horse to continue in a westerly direction.

The trees and brush were thick. He found a game
trail that made traveling a little better, but the animals
that made this trail were obviously not as tall as a man
on horseback. Occasionally, he dismounted and led
the gelding, to avoid tree branches that blocked his

way when he was horseback. Even then, the saddle horn sometimes crashed into a tree limb and slowed or stopped progress. Walking was difficult, as the ground was rough and covered with rocks.

The top of a rock about two feet above the ground invited him to sit and rest. He sat down and commented to the gelding, "Damn brush and trees are so thick, it's like being in a cave."

Just before getting up to continue, he heard what sounded like a woman screaming in the distance. He waited, quietly listening for a repeat, hoping to determine the direction. He knew patience was better than going in the wrong direction. While waiting, and listening intently, he opened the shotgun in his lap, removed the shells loaded with birdshot and replaced them with shells loaded with buckshot. After a minute — that seemed like an hour — he distinctly heard a man shout, "Nooo." He quickly left the game trail and tried to run in the direction of the shouts, southeast.

The limbs of the undergrowth were hitting him and his horse in the face. Joe didn't pay any attention to this, but the gelding did and held back, trying to avoid them. After trying to drag his horse and making little progress, Joe removed the rifle from the saddle.

With the rifle in one hand and the twelve-gauge in the other, he continued without his horse.

It was still slow and tedious. Finally, he came to a place where the brush was not so thick, and he could run faster. He jumped a ditch and found himself on the side of a dirt road. After looking in both directions, he saw the tracks on the road. A wagon had passed, going south, and horses had traveled in the same direction, following the path of the wagon. Without thinking, he ran as fast as he could.

He didn't have far to go. Just around the first bend in the road he saw the Finleys' wagon in a small clearing on the left side of the road.

Carson Finley was tied to a tree beyond the wagon. He was obviously in a painful position, with his hands tied high and his legs tied low. Between Carson and his wagon, Joe could see a man leaning over what looked like a pile of clothes. Joe stopped.

His presence was revealed to the other man when Carson shouted, "Kill him! Kill him, Joe!"

A huge black-bearded man rose up. He started walking toward Joe, a Bowie knife in his hand.

Joe froze.

"This pup ain't gonna kill nobody," the huge man said. "Just put the guns down, boy."

Joe swung the rifle on to his shoulder, using the sling. He pointed the shotgun at the huge man.

"Don't come no closer, or I'll use this shotgun on you," Joe said. He noticed the Bowie knife and that the man's hands were already covered with blood.

Carson was shouting for him to shoot, but Joe didn't want to kill. He was calculating his chances of stopping the giant of a man by using the shotgun as a club.

Just as the man reached for the barrels of Joe's shotgun, Carson shouted, "**HE MURDERED MY WIFE!**"

Joe pulled both triggers. His attacker was dead before he hit the ground.

Joe ran toward Carson. Before he got to the tree where Carson was tied, he looked between Carson and the wagon at the most gruesome site he had ever seen. All of Onzo Finley's clothes were in a pile beside her. Her body was covered with blood. Her head was no longer in proper position in relation to her body. It was attached to her body only by a small amount of flesh.

Before he could even comprehend the sight in front of him, Carson said, "There's another one, and he's got Vergie Mae."

Joe looked up to see the other man coming out of the brush about fifty feet away. He had a Bowie knife like the other man's and was holding it to the throat of Vergie Mae. Vergie Mae had no clothes on. The man held her in front of him as a shield.

Joe raised his rifle and took aim. The man shouted, "Drop that gun or I'll slit her from ear to ear!"

Vergie Mae's white skin was a contrast to the big man. He was dark, his hat and clothes were dark, and the forest behind him was dark. Only one eye and about an inch of his head was visible from behind the girl's head.

Joe squeezed the trigger. As his target fell back, the knife sliced across the girl's throat. She fell on top of her attacker.

Joe laid the rifle down, because he knew the man was dead. He told the sobbing girl to be still while he examined her throat. He was relieved to find the cut was not very deep, and no arteries or veins were severed. Being careful not to let her see the dead man's head, he lifted the crying girl's naked, bloody body and laid her in the grass a few feet away. He took off his jacket and covered her.

He didn't want her to see the man with a portion of his brains blown away. He didn't want to look at it himself.

"You're safe now," he told her. "The cut's not deep. It'll be okay."

He turned and told Carson she was not injured badly and would be fine, but she needed to be taken to a doctor. As he took his knife out and cut the rawhide holding the farmer against the tree, he could see that his friend was in a state of shock. Hell, he was too. He and Carson were both crying.

The older man stumbled to the wagon, pulled out a blanket and covered the horrible sight that had been his wife. Joe followed him to the wagon. He handed Carson another blanket and motioned toward Vergie Mae.

Both men were wrapped in sorrow and anger.

After a few minutes, Joe was able to collect his thoughts. "Carson, how far are we from a town?" he asked.

"About four or five miles, I think. The folks in the last town said it would be about fifty-five miles to the next one. I figure we traveled about fifty miles since then."

"Carson, I know you are suffering, but we need to put your daughter in the wagon. You take her to town to a doctor. After that, go to the sheriff or whatever they have for law and send them out here. Tell them to bring a wagon. I'll see to it that Onzo's body gets to town. You don't need to come back. Stay with Vergie Mae."

When the wagon pulled away, Joe sat down and tried to understand what had happened here today. "Why did it happen?" he asked himself. "How could anyone be so mean? Why? What should I have done differently?" No answers came.

After a few minutes, his gelding came walking down the road, holding his head to one side so he wouldn't step on the bridle reins that were dragging on the ground.

Joe lost track of time, but finally heard horses coming up the dirt road. A tall red headed man with a large red mustache rode up to him, stepped down from his horse, and extended his hand. "My name is Godwin," he said. "I'm the sheriff in this county."

"Howdy, Sheriff. My name is Joe, Joe Collins."

"Where you from, Joe Collins, and what business you got in Arkansas?"

"I'm from a town called West in Mississippi, and I'm on my way to Fort Worth, Texas."

Sheriff Godwin didn't answer for a minute as he looked at Joe, his horse and his guns, several times. Then he walked around and looked at the three bodies. When he came back to Joe he said, "Lots of people

151

will be glad to learn we can finally count these two men dead."

"You knew about these men? Why in hell didn't you do something about them before now?" Joe asked. He was angry.

Sheriff Godwin hesitated a few minutes, because he understood the young man's anger. "Mr. Collins, you be at my office tomorrow morning between eight and nine o'clock, and I'll tell you more about the Harp brothers. I only have one more question for today. Why did you shoot with the young lady in the line of fire?"

"She was *not* in the line of fire. I could see his eye, so I had a clean shot. I figured if I laid my rifle down when he told me to, Vergie Mae would end up like her mother did."

Without comment Sheriff Godwin went to help his men load the bodies. Joe was pleased with the respect they showed when handling Onzo's body. He thought it fitting when they threw the bodies of the two men in the back of the wagon like sacks of dirt. The wagon pulled away slowly with the mounted men following behind, leading the dead men's horses. It reminded Joe of a funeral procession.

CHAPTER 21

West of West,
Death brings tears.
They will flow
For many years.

The young hunter had never minded before when he found himself alone. After thinking on it for a few minutes, he realized he didn't want to be with anyone else *or* alone. He just didn't want to be, period. Not wishing to stay at the scene of the horrible crime, he climbed on his horse and started toward town.

Not very far down the road, he came to a clear stream. He realized that in his entire life he had never wanted to bathe more than he did now. He went up stream, out of sight of the road, bathed in the cold mountain water, then ate two cold biscuits that had been in his saddlebag for several days.

After cleaning and reloading his guns he wrapped himself in his blanket, hoping sleep would replace the thoughts in his mind. Determined to forget what he had seen and heard today, he closed his eyes, but when he tried to close his mind, it didn't work. He was to learn, like countless others who have tried to forget a terrible sight, that the more you try to forget something, the more clearly it's stamped in your mind. The sight of his drunk father riding away, the sight and sound of his aunt saying that all Collins men die drunk, the sight of his sister leaving with his aunt, the sights and sounds he had seen today — all fought each other for dominance in his mind. The sights he had seen today won the battle.

He didn't know how long he had been rolled in his blanket, but he knew he'd not had any sleep. He also knew it was useless to try to forget, and useless to continue trying to go to sleep.

Enough time had passed for his hobbled horse to finish grazing, because Joe found him lying down resting. After coaxing him to his feet, removing the hobbles, putting on the saddle and gear, Joe and the bay headed toward town.

As he rode into a town, about the size of West, there was a little light beginning to show over the mountain to the east. Since he'd been spending most nights on mountaintops, this was the first time he thought about the fact that these valleys got light later each morning and dark sooner each evening. It was later than he thought, and he was glad to see a café opening for business.

He was reminded of the nights when they drove horses from Memphis and sometimes got no sleep.

The ham, eggs, biscuits and coffee gave him a little energy. As he paid for his meal he asked the waitress, who was also the cook and dishwasher, for directions to the sheriff's office. After she gave him directions she said, "You must be the bounty hunter."

The statement didn't register with Joe. He just said, "No, Ma'am," and headed for the sheriff's office.

He met Sheriff Godwin coming out of his office. "Good morning, Joe Collins. I'm glad you got here early, because I need to leave the office for a bit. We don't have a full time preacher. We share him with four other towns. He had plans to leave early this morning, but he's staying long enough to bury Mrs. Finley. I'm on my way to the funeral. You're welcome to come along, or you can wait in my office if you like."

On a little rise just south of town they came to a small church, and just south of the church was a small cemetery.

The Finleys' wagon was parked near an open grave. As Joe and the sheriff walked to the open grave, the preacher, dressed in black, came out of the church. Four men followed him who carried a coffin. The men were the same who had been with the sheriff yesterday afternoon. They were followed by Carson and several other people.

Joe looked around for Vergie Mae and found her sitting in the wagon seat just a few feet from where he was standing. Her neck was bandaged, and her head was hanging down, as if she didn't want to see what was happening.

Two ladies came forward to place flowers on top of the coffin.

Joe listened carefully to the preacher's words as he gave thanks for Onzo Finley's life and expressed sorrow for her passing. He was surprised that in the last sentence of the preacher's prayer, he thanked God for sending the young man who had taken the lives of the two Harp brothers. In all his thoughts since the killings, Joe had not considered that he might have been sent by God to do the Lord's work when he aimed the guns and pulled the triggers.

Without speaking to anyone, Carson climbed into the wagon seat and drove away. Joe never did see

Vergie Mae raise her eyes. His sadness was reinforced by the thought that he would never see her again.

Just before they reached his office, the sheriff said, "I need to step in the telegraph office for a minute." As he was in there quite a while, Joe moved to the bench near where his gelding was tied. When the sheriff came from the telegraph office, he was walking slow, reading over and over the two telegrams in his hands.

Then he stopped and studied Joe's horse and saddle like they puzzled him. He motioned for Joe to follow him and went inside. After they were seated he said, "I sent a telegram to the sheriff in West, Mississippi. He verified everything you told me, except he said your name is spelled with a 'Y.' He said you're a hunter but not a bounty hunter."

"I think I like the name Joe, instead of Joey, and because I'm moving to another location, I thought this trip would be a good time to make the change," Joe explained. "I been thinking on it for quite a while."

"Well, the spelling of your name relates to what I'm about to tell you. With your rifle on one side of your horse and your shotgun on the other, you look more like a bounty hunter than most bounty hunters I know. You make good decisions under pressure and can shoot as good as anybody I ever knew. You never heard of the Harp brothers, have you?"

"No, Sir, not until you called their name yesterday."

"Joe, I've met some *mean* men in my business, but the Harps are — or were — the meanest men I ever heard of. The oldest was the biggest one, called Big Harp. The other one was much bigger than most men were and he was called Little Harp. They roamed up and down the Mississippi River for several years — murdering, raping and stealing. No telling how many folks they killed. There are dozens of lawmen and bounty hunters looking for them. They've committed crimes in every county and parish from New Orleans to Ohio.

"Yesterday was the first time they've been seen this far from the big river. That should answer your question about why I haven't done something about them before now. They always kept moving and haven't been seen in these parts. I guess the number of men after them along the Mississippi resulted in them changing to the Arkansas River.

"I regret to report that what you saw yesterday is, or was, typical. They preyed on families traveling, like the Finleys, or families on farms or in cabins that are remote. Big Harp liked to rape and murder women in front of their men, like you saw yesterday. Little Harp liked to take them off to a private location.

"One reason we have this information about them is they often liked to keep older children for a while as slaves. The young ones, that cried, they killed. They liked to kill children by swinging them around by the heels and bashing their heads into a tree or large rock. Several children that they used for slaves have escaped to tell what they witnessed.

"The thing that allowed the children to escape and slowed the Harps down was their love for whiskey. I wager that if they hadn't found some whiskey in the Finleys' wagon yesterday, all three Finleys would've been dead when you got there.

"There is a larger reward out for each of these men than anyone else I know of. I've contacted the United States marshal's office in Fort Smith. A deputy marshal will be here this afternoon to verify the identity of the Harp brothers. He's bringing a draft for the reward. After he identifies the bodies and signs the draft, you can take it to any bank in the country and deposit or cash it."

"Sheriff, are you sure these men are the Harp brothers?" Joe asked.

Without answering, Sheriff Godwin handed Joe two wanted posters, each with a picture of a Harp.

There was no doubt about the identity of the dead men. The amount of the reward, ten thousand dollars for each man, startled Joe. "Are you sure that even though I didn't kill those men for the reward, I'm going to get this money?"

"Read the poster carefully. Notice it reads: 'Paid to anyone who turns them over to a law enforcement agency.' I'm a law enforcement agency, and you turned these terrible outlaws over to me.

"If we didn't know the owner of the horses they were riding, you'd be entitled to them, too. The family that owned them was killed except for one son, who was not at home when they struck. This results in the horses being part of his inheritance.

"Not only do you get the money, I speak for many people when I say you have my admiration and appreciation for taking care of these two. You done good."

"You say that, and I appreciate it," Joe said. "The preacher said the Lord sent me, and I have a huge sum of money coming. Why do I feel so terrible?"

"Son, if you didn't feel terrible after what you were part of yesterday, you wouldn't be human. Time will help."

As it turned out, the U. S. deputy marshal didn't bring the draft. Joe had to travel several days out of his way to Fort Smith to pick it up. It was obvious that the federal judge had arranged to have Joe come to Fort Smith, so he could have his photograph taken with Joe. He insisted Joe hold his shotgun that killed Big Harp in one hand, and his rifle that took care of Little Harp in the other, as they stood for the picture.

Then the judge talked long and hard, trying to get Joe to become a deputy United States marshal. All he got was his photograph.

CHAPTER 22

West of West,
Are we what others see?
Or are we
What we would like to be?

Joe was travel-weary. He wanted to get to Fort Worth as soon as he could. After buying a new jacket and supplies, he pulled out of Fort Smith and traveled through Oklahoma across the Arbuckle Mountains.

When he finally crossed the Red River and entered Texas, he promised himself he would think on it long and hard before taking the long route to anywhere ever again.

However, the country between the Red River and Fort Worth was to his liking. It had rolling hills covered with grass and fields waiting to be plowed in preparation for spring planting. As he came near

North Fort Worth, or what most people called the stockyard area, he was amazed at the activity — like his father twenty years earlier.

Miles away from the stockyards, the steam rising from the packing plants dominated the sky. The bottom of a huge cloud of steam pointed the way to its source.

The roads kept joining up with other roads, funneling Joe and others to this cloud's source. The closer he came to it, the more crowded the road was. There were buggies, wagons, people riding horses or mules, people leading cattle, mules, horses and dust. Lots of dust. He was amazed to see wagons carrying cages that held cattle, goats, sheep, chickens, ducks and hogs.

As he was getting over the surprise of all the activity, a man rode up beside him riding a camel. Joe's normally nice, quiet gelding was snorting and jumping like he wanted to bolt back to Oklahoma. Joe had seen pictures of camels but never dreamed he would share the road with one.

Occasionally, a car or horseless carriage came by, startling animals and causing great disturbance. Joe was thinking his gelding's idea of getting away from this excitement was possibly the best thing to do. When he entered the cobblestone street, Exchange

Avenue, where the business of the stockyard was conducted, the explanation for all the excitement came in the form of a huge banner that had been stretched across the road. The banner read, "WELCOME TO THE FORT WORTH FAT STOCK SHOW."

Joe laughed while looking at his gelding. He was in reasonably good shape, but after the long trip certainly had no fat on him. "Don't get any ideas about the Fat Stock Show, old buddy," he told him, "because if they're looking for fat, you'd probably come in last."

He rode to the end of the street near the packing plants, which had large signs painted on the buildings. One read, "Armour Packing Company," the other, "Swift and Company." After sitting on his horse a few minutes — marveling at the size of the buildings and the acres of pens filled with cattle and hogs — he rode back up the street and tied his horse in front of The Stockyard National Bank.

He was concerned about leaving his horse and gear out of his sight, on a street crowded with so many strangers. But he saw there were police on every corner and two standing in front of the bank. They looked at his horse and guns and watched him carefully as he entered the building.

The bank was huge compared to any he had ever been in. A man wearing a black suit with a vest came up to him to say, "Good day, Sir, how may we serve you?"

Joe was suddenly aware of how much he needed to shave and take a bath. "Howdy, I'm looking for a man by the name of Walter Ragsdale," he said. "I was told he has an office in this bank."

"He does not have an office in the bank," the well-dressed man replied. "However, he has an office in this building. Just go up those stairs. His office is the third door to the left from the top of the stairs. His name is on the door."

"Thank you, Sir."

The door to Walter Ragsdale's office was open, so Joe took his hat off, stopped in the doorway and said, "Howdy."

To Joe's surprise the man with white hair and a well-trimmed white mustache looked up, stood up, smiled, reached out his hand and as he gave Joe a firm handshake said, "Joe Collins! Or is it Joey Collins? Either way, welcome, come in and have a seat. It sure is good to see you."

"Mr. Ragsdale, I'm pleased to see you as well. But how do you know who I am?" Joe asked.

"How do I know who you are? Because you're famous, and your brother is worried about you. About a week ago I got a telegram from your brother, Dan,

165

asking if you, Joey, had showed up here. I wired him back that I hadn't had the honor of seeing you. Then a few days ago, I looked at the front page of the newspaper, and there you are, Joe Collins, the bounty hunter, with a gun in each hand, standing beside the federal judge. As soon as my wife saw that picture, she said, 'That's Josh Collins' son.' Evidently, Dan saw the same picture in the newspaper in Mississippi, because I got another telegram from him asking about you. If you haven't contacted him, I suggest you send him a telegram without delay, so he won't continue to worry."

"Dan has been a parent as well as a brother, because I was just a snot-nose kid when our parents passed," Joe explained. "With the troubles I caused growing up, he just naturally got in the habit of worrying about me. But I don't want to keep causing worry, so I better ask you to excuse me, so I can take your advice and send him a telegram. Did I see the sign right, there's a telegraph office in this bank building?

"By the way, I'm not a bounty hunter," he added.

After the telegram had been sent to Dan, Walter insisted they should go see his wife. Joe didn't have any idea why. When they entered the restaurant, an attractive lady with white hair had a warm smile and greeting for Walter. When she looked at Joe she smiled again. Her eyes sparkled as she said, "Joey Collins, you look so much like your father, I recognized you as soon as I saw your picture in the newspaper."

While the three of them sat down to have supper, Walter and Judy Ragsdale explained the crowded conditions during the stock show. Most hotel rooms had several people in them. Most of the people from out of town were living in tents, some in green areas around the stockyard, but most in parks and open space along the river. Every tree had animals tied to it, and makeshift pens were everywhere.

"There's only one place in this part of Texas available for you to stay, and that's at our house," Walter seemed pleased to explain. "I have a pen in back of the house where I keep my buggy horses. We can put your bay in with my team."

Joe's objections were ignored. With such distractions, Joe didn't have the opportunity to ask the questions he wanted to ask. The Ragsdales' house was in walking distance, so the three of them walked, Joe leading his gelding.

The house was small but quite comfortable. It was the only house Joe had ever been in that had running water and electricity. He felt uncomfortable. But the Ragsdales acted like he was an old friend they'd known for years. They explained that they'd been married only five years — so they were not man and wife when Josh came to visit, years ago.

Walter explained that it had taken him most of his life to get her to say yes. Judy admitted that not saying yes many years ago was a mistake on her part, but she sure was glad Walter waited.

Walter teased her with a smile and said, *"Perhaps she was worth the wait."*

The house had running water, but not hot water. Judy heated two large kettles of water on the wood stove for Joe to carry to the bathroom and dump into the tub with some cold water. When he had bathed in the warm water he found a kettle of hot water on the floor, by the door, for his shaving. It was obvious he would have to wait until morning to ask questions, because as he was shaving Walter came by and said, "Goodnight."

Joe allowed that electric lights were a big improvement over kerosene lamps. And these were the friendliest people he'd ever met.

Early the next morning he woke to the sound and smell of bacon frying. By the time he dressed and came out of his room, a breakfast of bacon, eggs, biscuits and molasses was waiting. Judy walked over to Joe, gave him a hug, then walked over to Walter and gave him a kiss. Then she hurried out the door.

As Joe covered his last buttered biscuit with molasses, he explained that for years people — who knew it was none of their business — had been asking how their father came up with the money to buy the first train carload of horses from Walter. It was common knowledge that you just did *not* make enough money on a small Mississippi farm to buy a train car full of horses. Perhaps it wasn't any of his and Dan's business either, but they never could figure it out themselves.

Walter sipped his coffee and explained, "Josh and I agreed not to discuss our business arrangement with others. Someone not so trustworthy could have come along to complain about not getting the same treatment. I guess that's no problem now, with Josh dead all these years, and me going out of business. We agreed that for the first two years, when Josh sold a horse he would send me the money for that horse. Up front he only had to pay the railroad and take care of the horses. True to his word, after two years he had enough money to pay me and the railroad when the third carload arrived in Memphis."

"Mr. Ragsdale, as I understand the story, my father was only here a few days. How could you know you would get your money?"

"Your father and I built up a trust. I knew him to be a man of his word." With a smile he added, "For insurance, I checked with the bank in West, and they said his word was good. You see, a good name is worth more than money. With a good name you can make money. However, no amount of money can buy a good name."

"Thanks for telling me that," Joe said. "Dan will be pleased to learn the answer to that question, too.

"Now, the next question is the main reason I came to see you. About five years ago, when we unloaded a carload of horses in Memphis, a sorrel mare came off that train that took my breath away. She was the best horse I'd ever seen, and I still haven't seen another horse as good as her. I was wondering why you shipped her with the others, and I was hoping you could tell me where I could find another horse like her. Do you remember the mare I'm talking about?"

"I remember her," Walter said, taking another sip of coffee and smiling. "I remember her. The men I sent to my ranch to bring the horses here for shipping wanted to buy her. I couldn't sell her to them, or keep her, because the deal I made with your father was that I'd not cull the good horses or the sorry ones. If you think about the horses you received, you'll agree, you got some that were poor specimens. We shipped them, and we shipped her, and other good ones, because that was the deal we made.

"The answer to your question about you finding horses like her will take a while," Walter continued. "Let's put that off for a bit and take in the activities at the livestock show."

During the walk to the stockyard, Joe asked about the comment Walter had made about going out of business.

"Judy and I are retiring," Walter explained. "She sold her restaurant where she worked all her adult life, and where she'd worked a few years before she ever was an adult. Years ago she bought that restaurant and devoted herself to making a successful business. She damn near worked herself to death, but she made a go of it. Now the lady who has not been out of this county, except to visit my ranch in the adjoining county, wants to travel. She's working at the restaurant now to help the new owner through the livestock show. Not many women or men have accomplished as much as my Judy.

"My business is a little different. I don't have any good food to sell. It's built on personal relationships. I'm trying to make sure my regular customers have someone they can depend on. I have a ranch with good water and grass a few miles northwest of here.

Effective next month, I have it leased to my neighbor, who'll run cattle on it. I hope you have time to take a trip up to my ranch and see the good band of mares I've acquired over the years.

"The large building you see there across the street from the bank is the Livestock Show Barn. Most of the livestock will be judged inside that building. The people most responsible for this great show plan to build a building big enough to have the rodeo inside the building."

"A rodeo inside a building?" Joe was obviously amazed.

"That's what I said, Joe. Mark my word, in a few years you'll see that happen right here in Fort Worth.

"I need to go to my office and meet with a man who is taking over some of my accounts. You're welcome to come along, if you want to, or you can look around and meet us at the restaurant for lunch.

"I do hope I can talk you into taking in the rodeo this afternoon. And we still need to talk about horses like the mare you mentioned. I'm anxious to hear your opinion of the horses that we'll see in the calf roping this afternoon."

"Sounds good to me. I'll see you at lunch," Joe said.

CHAPTER 23

Where are the good ones
Out west of West?
…The fast ones, that can
Better the best?

Joe was still amazed at the variety of activity. He watched the cattle show for a while, impressed with the better ones, glad he didn't have to judge between the few that were clearly of higher quality. After watching several classes, he was doing good to pick the few that would place high. Choosing between the number one and the last place was easy, but choosing between the first and second place was another matter. His imagination kicked in. Instead of playing the spectator or judge, he played at thinking like a rancher who was trying to decide which cow he would buy to take to his ranch — that he didn't own. In his mind, the stakes were high, because the survival of his ranch depended on his choice. The longer he studied, with this mind set, the closer his picks were in line with the judges. He became so engrossed in his mind game, he didn't realize how late in the morning it was, until the cattle judging was over. He hurried to meet the Ragsdales for lunch.

As it turned out, there was a line waiting to get in, and he was not late, because Mr. Ragsdale was near the end of the line. After inquiring about Joe's morning, the older man asked, "Joe, what are your plans? Where are you going from here?"

"I don't know. I came looking for horses like the mare we talked about this morning. I told my brother I was born about fifty years too late. I'd like to have a big ranch — but with the homestead days over, I don't know if that's possible."

"Judy is inside helping, but she won't play favorites. We'll wait our turn to get a table. You realize those people that ended up with large ranches not only homesteaded — they had to fight to hold onto the land and cattle. They fought other people who wanted to take what they had, including Indians and rustlers, and they fought to survive against Mother Nature."

"If anyone came to take my land or livestock, they'd have a fight on their hands," Joe said.

Walter smiled and was about to comment when someone behind them shouted, "Move on up or get out of line!"

Walter looked at the man hassling them and said, "Buford Wilson, all you're doing is making noise. Come here and meet my friend. Joe, this is Buford. Mostly he just makes noise. He's taking over some of my accounts, and I sure hope he doesn't screw things up too badly. Buford, this is Joe Collins."

Buford laughed in surprise as he shook hands with Joe. "Hell, Walter," he said, "this man is a bounty hunter. Aren't you afraid he'll turn you in to the law?"

"Hell yes, I been worried about that. I have some information he wants, so I may be able to stay out of jail until he learns what he wants from me. He wants to retire from bounty hunting at a young age."

"I bet he will too, if he doesn't hang around you too long," Buford said as he laughed. "Joe, your friend here is going to be playing in the sand in Florida or California, or the snow in New York, pretty soon, so when you need to buy or sell some livestock, let me know. It's good to meet you, even if you are hanging out with Walter."

As they were seated in a corner table for two, Walter said, "Buford makes a lot of racket, but he's a good man."

The fried steak was slow in coming, because the restaurant was packed. So Walter got back to talking with his young friend. "Joe, there is one place that I know of where good land is cheap, because, in this region, the will to fight is as important as it was years ago. The Big Bend area of Texas is called that because it's where the Rio Grande River makes a big swing south into Mexico and then a wide swing back up before continuing to the Gulf of Mexico. It creates a large area that shares the border with Mexico on three sides.

"When people live on or near a border with another country, I think they most always benefit in some ways and suffer in others. That probably applies to both sides. I've never been there, but I understand there are vast grasslands that offer some of the best grazing in Texas. The country is covered with lots of game — deer, antelope, bear and mountain lions. Whether its true or not, I don't know. The story is, the grass is so good, that in the old days during the winter months, buffalo would come all the way from Canada to graze in the Big Bend."

Their steaks were placed in front of them, but Walter kept on talking.

"Along with this good grass, there are mountains that are rugged with canyons that have straight walls, and traveling through these mountains is almost impossible. As rugged as the mountains are on *this* side of the border, they're even more rugged on the Mexico side. I understand there are still bands of Apache Indians living there. The Mexican army can't send troops into these mountain areas after the Indians and have the solders come out alive.

"The lawlessness is contagious. The renegade Indians and Mexican bandits are not the only problems. We Americans contribute bandits and outlaws to both sides of the border. Rustlers steal livestock in New Mexico, drive them to the Big Bend area to sell on this side or the other side of the river. Then they steal livestock in the Big Bend area and drive them to New Mexico to sell.

"In years past, some renegade Texas Rangers were paid by state governments in Mexico to bring in Indian scalps. Well, it's almost impossible to tell an Indian's scalp from another person's with dark hair. So, they killed and scalped hundreds of people, on both sides of the river, without paying attention to whether they were Indians or not, and sold their hair to state governments in Mexico.

"You add troubles like these to those furnished by Mother Nature, and you can see why only those willing to fight can survive. However, the land we're on right now — and all land east, west, north and south of here — was once just as lawless. Someday the Big Bend will be a good place to bring up a family. We just don't know when the drought will end, or when law and order will prevail."

Joe was astonished at what he had heard. He and his older friend ate without talking.

On the way to the rodeo arena, Joe said, "Mr. Ragsdale, the more you talk the more questions I come up with. I have more questions now than when I met you. For instance, you said the land in the Big Bend is cheap. How cheap is cheap?"

"I understand there is quite a bit of land that homesteaders abandoned and is now back in the hands of the state of Texas. In most cases the published price of this is fifty cents an acre, from the state. A person who owns land there can buy adjacent land from the state, for less than an outsider can. There has been and still is a drought in that area. Most people are trying to ranch like they did years ago, and it doesn't work.

"A man came through here a few months back with some well-bred cattle that were in bad shape. He was determined to get as far from his Big Bend ranch as possible. He wanted a herd of cattle he could drive to Montana. The shorthorns he was driving were nearly dead from living in the drought and the drive up here. They would never make it to Oklahoma, not to mention Montana. Buford Wilson had a set of longhorn cross cattle, and the man wanted to make a trade. They finally made a deal. The man got Buford's cross cattle in exchange for the shorthorn cattle and the deed to the ranch in the Bend.

"The folks around here have been having a great deal of fun at Buford's expense, teasing him about the ranch he's stuck with. Most folks consider the deed to be a worthless piece of paper. Some of our friends ask him if he's paid the taxes on his ranch, every time they see him. When you give folks around here something to pick on you about, they do a real good job of razzing you. Of course, Buford being one of the best at razzing people, we sure like to unload on him when we can. Judy is going to join us in our box seats later."

Joe's head was spinning with more questions than ever. Every time Walter answered one question, several more came to mind.

He watched the best roping he had ever seen. The speed with which the roping horses came out of the box and the hard stops they made caused great excitement deep inside the young man. After it was over he looked at the seat beside Walter and said, "Mrs. Ragsdale, good to see you. I didn't see you come up here."

"Perhaps that's because I've only been here an hour. I see I can't compete for your attention with a roping horse. However, I'm going to make a prediction that your fascination with these roping horses will be short-lived. Tomorrow, when you see the cutting horses, you'll forget about the roping horses — just as surely as you failed to notice me today."

Joe's face was red with embarrassment. He looked to Walter for help.

Walter laughed and said, "Joe, I might be of some help dealing with the men around here. When it comes to dealing with Judy, you're on your own."

Their laughter helped Joe relax. These very friendly folks were a joy to be around.

The next day after lunch, Judy and Walter had some things to do, so Joe went ahead to take in the rodeo. Later, when Judy arrived at the box seats, neither Walter nor Joe was there. Finally, she saw Joe sitting on the fence, watching the start of the cutting competition. Walter walked up to Joe for a few minutes, then came to sit with his wife. "Didn't Joe want to come sit with us?" she asked.

"I don't know," Walter said with a laugh. "I spoke to him twice, but he's so into studying those horses he didn't respond. He's in a trance. I was afraid I might startle him, and he may have a right fist that could do what his father's did. I thought it best to come sit with my lovely wife and leave him alone."

After the first herd of cattle were used up, and a cattle change was in progress, Joe joined the older couple. They looked at each other knowingly when he said, "I didn't know you folks had showed up.

"These cutting horses are great. When the rider stops reining and turns them loose, they work the cow with so much strength and speed, it's amazing. Some of them are the same horses that competed in the roping yesterday. I'm having trouble figuring out what the judge is looking for."

"Some of the contestants will declare they share that problem with you," Walter said. "The cutting horse and rider are supposed to drive the cow out of the herd and keep it from returning. When a rancher needs to cut a cow from the herd, for whatever reason, he wants it done without causing a stampede. So the judge gives points to the horse that drives the cow out quietly, without disturbing the other cattle. Then he wants to see the cow held as near the middle of the arena as possible and out away from the herd — without reining the horse.

"A few years back, the horse and rider had to drive the cow through a gate into a small pen in the middle of the arena. Now they need to hold the cow while the cow's instinct makes it want to return to the herd. To make things more exciting, there are turn-back men, on horses, encouraging the cow to return to the herd. If the horse gets out of position or loses working advantage, even though he may keep the cow from returning to the herd, the judge takes off a few points. If the rider reins his horse after the cow is cut out, he gets penalized. I must tell you, there is considerable disagreement about how the competition should be judged."

It was obvious Joe was not only listening but also studying every word.

"The horses that are winning are built like each other and like the mare I was talking to you about," Joe remarked. "She had a little more height than most of them, but otherwise she looked much like these."

"That mare and the better horses in this competition are mostly from the Steel Dust line. Steel Dust was a great stallion that raced in short races, usually a quarter-mile or less. That's why his type are called quarter horses," Walter explained.

"Short racing was big in the seventeen hundreds, in colonial times, in places like Virginia and the Carolinas," Walter, a student of horse history, explained. "Those folks didn't have a long racetrack. They just cleared traffic out of the road and raced, usually less than a quarter-mile. Then in the early eighteen hundreds, it became big in Illinois, Kentucky and Tennessee. Steel Dust or his ancestors came from these horses. The story goes that, at the end of the War Between the States, he was stolen from someone in Tennessee and brought to Texas. He defeated all horses that ran against him. Legend has it that he never was defeated.

"However, his victories on the track are not his most important accomplishment. He passed along his strength and speed, in generous proportions, to his sons and daughters. People crossed his offspring with the better mustangs, because they're tough and have natural instinct for working a cow. The better horses you see on ranches and in roping, cutting and other rodeo competition are the results.

"The problem is, there's no registry or studbooks to identify Steel Dust horses. So now most everyone that has a horse for sale claims it's from the Steel Dust line. Therefore, buying or trading for one can be a bit tricky. You have to be careful who you deal with and examine the horse thoroughly."

The cutting continued. Just when Joe thought he'd seen the most exciting horse activity the world had to offer, the rider — who was next to last in the competition — while he was driving a cow out from the herd, reached up, slipped the bridle over his horse's ears and let it drop to the ground. The horse, without a bridle, worked the cow better than any others had during the entire competition. The crowd went wild, and the young man from Mississippi added to his list of dreams that he wanted to ride cutting horses.

CHAPTER 24

West of West,
We live, we decide —
Sometimes for right,
Sometimes for pride.

On the way to the Ragsdales' house that evening, Joe asked, "Mr. Ragsdale, do you think I would be wise to buy ranch land in the Big Bend?"

"Wise? I'm not going to go that far," Walter answered. "You said you'd like to have a large ranch. I told you about that area because if I were a young man your age, unmarried, I'd probably go there. The idea that I think it a good place to get a start doesn't mean it's the right thing for you to do. Only you can decide that."

After they fed the horses, Joe asked, "Do you have a map at your office of that area of Texas?"

"Better than that, I have several here in the house."

Long after Judy had gone to bed, the two men were looking at maps and discussing the Big Bend country.

***

"You two were up most of the night," Judy said as she placed a big breakfast in front of them. "Did you make any money or decisions?"

"Not only did we stay up late, I couldn't sleep after I *did* go to bed," Joe confessed. "I had a powerful urge to wake Walter — your husband said I should call him Walter — so I could ask him more questions. Let me get to the main one. How should I approach Buford Wilson about buying the ranch he owns? Can I pay you to help me get it for the best price? What do you think I'll have to pay per acre? How big's the ranch?"

"So you made a decision," Walter answered, with a smile. "First, let me confess — I had trouble going to sleep also. I think I came up with an idea that will be good for you, as well as for Judy and me. But for my idea to work you need a ranch.

"Therefore, I'll do everything I can to help you buy Buford's land for a good price — and I'll accept no pay or commission. He knows you can go to the state and buy land down there for fifty cents an acre. I suspect he would be pleased to receive thirty cents an acre. I would recommend offering him twenty cents, knowing he'll raise all manner of hell and insist that I'm insulting his intelligence. Then, he'll ask a higher price. If you don't mind, I'll tell him I know someone dumb enough to buy his worthless land for twenty cents an acre. He'll quickly figure out that you are 'the someone' and insist on dealing direct with you. When he approaches you, tell him you're having second thoughts about the offer. You think you perhaps made a mistake offering so much. Don't let him know you'll pay a penny more."

"I'll never understand such dealings," Judy said. "I'm not sure you're teaching this young man a proper lesson. I think he should ask Buford what he wants for the land and take it or leave it. That's a more honest approach."

"I don't remember you complaining when I sold your restaurant for far more money than you thought it was worth," her husband said. "Do you think you should give the new owner some of his money back, even though he's quite pleased with the deal?"

Not wanting to continue the conversation, she shook her head as she went out the front door.

The negotiations with Buford went as Walter had predicted. After two days of dealing, they agreed on the price of twenty-five cents per acre. Walter kept insisting that it was too much. Buford kept reminding them that the previous owner told him there were branded cattle and horses that he'd been unable to round up. These were included in the agreement Buford made when he bought the ranch. Walter and Joe kept reminding Buford he had no proof that there was livestock on the land. Walter repeated stories about problems with bandits and the problems caused by the drought. After all the details were agreed on, Buford left Walter's office with a smile on his face, complaining about how they had taken advantage of his good nature.

Walter said, "Joe, that's what I call a good deal. He would probably have been pleased to sell for twenty cents, and you were willing to pay thirty cents. When the buyer would've paid more and the seller would've sold for less, they both feel good about the deal. I hope you're pleased."

Joe was indeed pleased, even though he was uneasy knowing he had bought a ranch sight unseen.

"Walter, when you first mentioned this ranch, you said something about the old way of ranching. What were you talking about when you said it won't work?"

"If you talk to as many ranchers as I have, you learn that open range never did work well. Ranching's not so much the horse and cow business as it is the grass business. How can you manage your grass if your neighbors' cattle and horses are grazing on your land — and all the while only God knows where your livestock is?

"As most ranchers know, there are two ways to expand a ranching operation. You can gain more land, which is to say you have more grass, or you can upgrade the quality of your livestock.

"Years ago, my friend Charlie Goodnight told me that when he first bought better bulls and turned them loose on open range, he upgraded his neighbors' cattle at his expense. He was the first one of the big ranchers to tell me that fenced-in pastures are much more efficient than open range. One reason he moved into Palo Duro Canyon was because the steep walls of the canyon acted as a fence, to keep his neighbors' cattle out and his cattle on his ranch.

"Those who are not willing to change get left behind. For example, I remember the man who sold your ranch to Buford saying he was going to Montana or Canada to find open range. He complained bitterly because some of the people in the Bend were fencing in their land. We'll probably never know, but I predict he'll have no more success in Montana or Canada than he did in the Bend."

This was the first time Joe had heard the words, *your ranch*, directed at him. Hearing these words distracted him for a minute, made him want to saddle up and head to the Big Bend.

"Now that you have a ranch, I have a proposition that I believe may be good for both of us," Walter said, interrupting Joe's thoughts. "Judy and I have been fortunate and are comfortable financially. However, we never know what the future holds. One thing people our age worry about is outliving our money. We aren't in need of cash now, but we may need income in future years. Getting a check each year for the lease of my ranch is part of that plan. Tomorrow, I'd like for you and me to ride out to my ranch and look over the herd of brood mares I've collected.

"I'm reminded of a conversation I had with your father. He said when most people use the word 'farm' in Mississippi, they think of cotton. There were other ways to make money but most people thought the only way *was* to grow cotton. It's somewhat like that in East Texas too. In a like manner, west of here, when you say 'ranch' most folks think cattle. Ranchers are quick to point out that they need to keep the number of horses down because a horse eats more than a cow. There's some truth to that, but I also know an average horse will bring three times as much money as a steer.

A good horse may bring even more. I've been up-grading my mares for years and know they're high quality. I'd like to see you take them to your ranch. When you sell a colt or filly out of one of them, send me one-fourth the sell price. This should provide me some income for years to come.

"We need to work out a plan for the division of the proceeds when you sell a mare based on how old she is and how many colts she's produced. Also, we need a plan to use when you decide to keep an offspring or when one dies, or is stolen. It may be somewhat complex, but we can come up with a plan that's fair to both.

"Before you answer, you need to see the mares and know that you'll be expected to keep careful records. And that reminds me! I've been dealing with ranchers and farmers all my life, and I want to tell you one difference I've noticed between successful and unsuccessful ranchers and farmers. A rancher or farmer must recognize that his endeavor is a business. The more accurately and carefully he records all phases of his business, the more successful he's likely to be. There's a saying that the difference between a cowboy and a cattleman is, 'The cattleman makes notes.'"

The next day Joe was impressed with the quality and number of mares. They looked at just under two hundred good mares, and quite a few of them were going to foal later in the spring. He promised himself that he would make sure this worked out to be a good deal for him and his older friend. Walter revealed that he'd made a similar deal regarding his cattle with the neighbor who had leased the land. Joe realized he had a new friend who not only was a businessman, but one who was constantly thinking. He was reminded of Dave, who could be counted on to remind him and Dan to think on whatever the subject happened to be.

"I'm excited about visiting your ranch, Joe," Walter said, after Joe closed the gate for the trip back to Fort Worth.

"Now I need to answer the question that brought you to my office in the first place," Walter said. "There are several ranches you could visit to find the kind of horses you saw in the cutting and roping at the rodeo. None of them are better than the two I'm going to tell you about. An Englishman by the name of William Anson lives south of San Angelo on his Head-of-the-River Ranch, near a town called Cristoval. The ranch is at the headwaters of the Concho River. He is the youngest son of a highly bred English family. Still wears English clothes and boots and speaks like he came from England yesterday, even though he's been here for years and is a well established West Texas rancher. A few years back he was raising horses to sell as polo ponies. He learned that the quarter type horses had better speed and stamina for polo.

"Then the English got into a war in South Africa called the Boer War. With his contacts in England, he began filling contracts and shipping horses and mules to South Africa. I bought some of the horses and mules for him and handled the shipping of many of them. The last time I spoke with him, he had shipped over thirty thousand head from Texas, Oklahoma, New Mexico and Colorado.

"All the time he's been doing this, he's kept the best ones for breeding stock on his ranch. He didn't have the same agreement to ship the good ones and bad ones like I made with your father. If you can imagine the best horses out of over thirty thousand, you know the horses on his ranch will be good. He had good Steel Dust horses even before this Boer War, so he's been breeding good horses in addition to the good ones he kept out of the shipments to South Africa. It's safe to say that the worst horse on his ranch is probably a very good horse.

"Not only does he have good horses, he's a man of his word, someone you can depend on to do what he says he's going to do. If I wanted to buy stallions to breed to these mares, my first stop would be William Anson's Head-of-the-River Ranch.

"Judy and I will be leaving for California next month, and I'm looking forward to going. Don't tell her I said this, but I wish we were going with you. I hope we can visit the Big Bend area soon."

"I hope you can visit soon too. I don't have any way of knowing what the living conditions will be like, but whatever they are, I'd love to have you folks visit. You said you'd recommend two horse breeders," Joe said, trying to make notes in the bouncing buggy.

"Yes," Walter said. "The other one I would recommend is another good man by the name of William, or Bill, Fleming, in Gonzales County, east of San Antonio. On his ranch between Seguin and Gonzales, on the Guadalupe River, he raises horses that have come to be called Billy horses. There are other good breeders and many of them got some of their bloodstock from these two.

"Keep in mind the market is constantly changing. A horse is only worth what the next man's willing to pay. There are times like during that Boer War when common horses bring good money, and there are other times when you need really good horses to get a good price. Only ranchers with very good livestock survive hard times.

"Write down everything you know about the breeding of each horse. Keep up with which mares have been exposed to which stallions and the mare that each colt is out of. Then, you can look back and get guidance about how to breed horses that the next man's willing to pay top money for. Finally, keep in mind that one really good horse is worth more than a herd of common horses."

CHAPTER 25

An idle mind
Is the devil's workshop.
Out west of West,
The devil never stops.

With the Fat Stock Show over and Joe beginning to think about leaving town, he realized he had not taken time to do something he'd intended to enjoy soon after arriving. When he reviewed his activities in his mind, he was amazed that he'd been so busy that he'd almost forgotten about his plan to enjoy this activity. He fully intended to visit a house of prostitution and lay in bed with a naked woman. When he spotted women on the street looking like they might be employed at such a place, they were usually going or coming from a smaller street that turned off Main Street. Finding himself alone in town one evening, he nervously followed two such females down this street. As they passed the place where they could see between the two buildings on their right, they stopped talking and walked much faster.

When Joe walked to a position where he could see between the buildings, he knew why they had changed their gait. He could see a fight in progress in the alley. As his eyes adjusted to the dim light, he saw three men having a hard time against one. It was obvious the one was better than two, but not three.

After a minute or so, the one finally hit the ground face down. Two of the others reached for the unconscious man's pockets. Joe's first instinct was to go into the dark area between the two buildings and try to rescue the man who was being robbed. Realizing the downed man was unconscious, he knew it would be three against one — him — in a dark alley. He also knew it was unlikely anyone would come to help him against the three. Holding his position on the lighted street, in a firm but calm voice he said, "Move away from that man."

The three looked at him. The biggest one said, "Move on, mister, this ain't none of your business."

Hoping to talk until someone else came along, Joe asked, "You think there's something in his pockets worth dying for?"

As the three stood still thinking about what they had heard, the smaller one pulled out a knife. It soon became obvious that Joe was not going to leave, so they advanced toward him.

He made his plan to hit the one with the knife, hoping that he could dodge the knife and then ward off the blows expected from the others. He remained still while they moved closer.

When they were within three feet they stopped, and the smaller one with the knife said, "I seen you around town. They say you the man who killed the Harp Brothers."

"They had it right. You three want to join The Harp Brothers?" Joe's voice showed no fear.

The man put his knife in the scabbard and said, "Not me, I'm gonna get the hell outa here." As he ran toward Main Street the other two followed.

Joe breathed a sigh of relief and said under his breath, "Joe, you are one really dumb son of a bitch."

Realizing the downed man was beginning to regain consciousness, Joe didn't get close, because he was afraid the man might mistake him for one of the attackers and take a swing. When the man did manage to rise up on all fours and look at him, Joe could not have been more surprised. He was looking at the battered face of Coat Calcoat. "Coat, you look like hell."

"Joey, you look like an angel." Blood and dirt couldn't hide Coat's big smile. "I was expecting the next one I saw to be the devil telling me which fire was mine. "What happened? Three men were beating the hell out of me. I wake up and here you are."

"What I saw, you were doing pretty good," Joe said. "In the dark I didn't recognize you, but I was thinking, with a little luck, that man could handle any two of them, but the third one tipped the scales against you. When they saw it might be two against three, instead of one against three, they decided not to hang around and high-tailed it toward Main Street.

"Let me help you up and see if you can walk around the corner to the watering trough. You need to wash some of Texas off your face." He chose not to mention the reference to his so-called bounty hunting, although his reputation had come in handy.

After Coat dipped his entire head in the watering trough several times, the dirt and blood were gone but cuts along with redness and swelling were not pleasant to look at. Both of them rolled a smoke.

Then Coat felt in his pocket making sure he still had money before saying, "I sure would like to buy you a drink, Joey. I been lookin' for you for several days."

"I took a page out of your book and changed my name too," Joe said as they walked to the bar. "I'd be pleased if you'd buy Joe Collins a drink.

"What the hell are you doing in North Fort Worth, and why the hell did you end up in a dark alley with those three yahoos?"

Coat laughed even though it obviously hurt to do so. "We was shooting craps, and me being raised in the streets of Memphis, I knew more about the game than they did. After I took most of their money, they decided to take it back with a different game. I sure am glad you came along. To think, after I been lookin' for you for two days, you find me in a dark alley and save my ass." The drinks were poured, and Joe waited patiently for the answer to his first question.

After downing the first and ordering another, Coat continued, "You remember how upset Mr. Wesfall was about the railroad taking his land? Well, they took part of it anyway.

"Then two men, who called themselves 'developers,' came to the house and offered to buy the part of his land along the railroad right of way. He quoted them what he considered to be a ridiculous price to get shed of them. They told him he had a deal. He ended up selling them the whole place for God knows how much money. Then he had a big auction and sold everything on the place except me and Mrs. Wesfall.

"He and Mrs. Wesfall hightailed it to New York. They plan to get on a ship and go to Europe. I asked him where in Europe? He said all of it. Do you suppose they'll let Mrs. Wesfall use the kitchen on that ship? I can't imagine her not cooking. They plan to come back to America after their trip to Europe is over. Said that'll be several years from now.

"You know, I'm fond of them and they've been good to me. They gave me some money and offered to give me a horse. I told them to sell the horse in the sale. I was planning to travel out here on the train. They sold the horse for a good price and gave me that money along with what they had already given me."

Laughing while he talked, he leaned close and said, "You can bet your ass I didn't tell anyone on the train about the money like I did when I traveled from your house to Memphis, years ago.

"By the way, I played some cards on the train and made a little more money."

Joe had made a rule not to have more than two drinks on any one night, but as he talked to his old friend he allowed he should forget that rule. After ordering another round he asked, "Coat, what do you plan to do now?"

"I figured there should be plenty of good jobs around here. When I got here, I headed for the packing plant.

"On the way over there I got to talking with a guy who came here from Europe five years ago. He lives with his older sister and her husband. He went to work at the plant soon after arriving here. Joe, he's been working there five years, twelve hours a day, seven days a week. They let him off one day to play on the company baseball team against the other packinghouse. He had never even seen a baseball before in his life and naturally contributed to his team losing. Said he doesn't think he'll get off to play baseball again, but he sure is glad he got that day off.

"Now I don't mind working. Long hours and hard work don't scare me. Mr. Wesfall was a hard-working man, and he taught me how to work. However, being closed up in the same place where I can't even see the sky half of my life is a frightening thought — sounds a lot like prison to me. You told me you planned to come here, so I was hoping I could find you and you might know about a better job.

"By the way, I read about you killing the Harp Brothers. I want you to tell me about how you got that done. I told some folks on the train I was a friend of yours, and after that, they were sure enough scared of me. They even moved to a different car."

"Coat, I think I may have a job that'll fit you pretty good. Right now, I need to go find a pillow for my head. This whisky has got my head feeling about as bad as yours looks. Tomorrow, can you meet me for lunch at the restaurant two blocks down toward the packing plants on the right?"

Without waiting for an answer, he left the bar and headed for the Ragsdales' house. When his head felt like this he heard his aunt's shrill words clanging around inside his brain like a loud bell — "All Collins men die drunk."

The next morning he didn't feel good, but the voice inside his head was not dominating his mind. He told Walter and Judy about Coat and his plan to hire him. Judy thought it was a great idea, and Walter reminded him to repeat his instructions to his employee several times. "I worry about your friend's gambling and think you should make sure he doesn't get out of hand."

Joe arrived at the restaurant about eleven o'clock, long before noon, to find Coat waiting for him, and waiting to ask, "Hey Buddy, you cut out of the bar mighty fast last night. Are you all right?"

"Yeah, thanks. I just had a little more liquor than I needed. Thanks for asking, and I can offer you a job. Do you know where the Big Bend is?"

"I pay a nickel a day extra to have one in my hotel room. So far, I have no reason to get up early. I haven't even bothered to set the time and wind it up."

"Not a Big Ben alarm clock," Joe said, laughing. "Look at this map. See this area along the Rio Grande River? I own a ranch right about here somewhere."

Coat frowned and said, "Bullshit, are you sure those guys didn't hit *you* in the head last night while I was out?"

"You think that's hard to believe? Listen to the rest of the story. I have six train carloads of fine mares, and I want you to see that they get to my ranch in good condition. If you want the job, you will take them south to San Antonio, unload, feed, water, and rest them for one or two days — the railroad could not be sure about that. Then you put them back on train cars going west to this town right here, Sanderson. I'll meet you there, and we'll drive them southwest to the ranch. Then we go to work building fences."

"And I guess while I'm doing this, you'll be running for President of these United States. So when I get to Sanderson, I'll be met by the president," Coat replied, thinking he was the butt of some kind of joke.

"Listen, Coat, I know it may sound a bit strange, but I'm as serious as tuberculosis. I got a big chunk of reward money for what happened in Arkansas. Guess you could say I've made some business deals since I arrived here. I'm a fellow with a big job ahead. I may not be able to pay as much as you could make in one of those packing plants, but you said you didn't want to work in the same building every day. Working for me, the scenery will change each day, at least for a while. The job starts in one week, and I'll pay fifty dollars a month, furnish food and a place to sleep. I can promise the food won't be nearly as good as Mrs. Wesfall's.

"I had planned to take the mares down there and ride back up to a ranch south of San Angelo. Right about here on this map. The man who has an outfit called Head-of-the-River Ranch has some good stallions. I hope to buy some to cover these mares and raise some of the best horses the world has ever seen. If you agree to take the mares on the train, I can ride from here to the Head-of-the-River Ranch, pick up the studs and meet you in Sanderson. How's the job sound?"

"Wild!" Coat answered. "I thought I'd never be as surprised and excited about a job as I was when your papa came to Memphis and hired me when I was ten years old. By God, this comes pretty damn close. I'll take the job if you're sure you didn't make all that stuff up."

"It's all real, and I'll buy lunch today. Since you need to give me ten days or two weeks head start, one week from today you're on the pay roll. If we don't order lunch soon, they'll probably run us out of here.

"This part of Texas we are going to is pretty wild," Joe added. "If you don't have a gun, you better buy one and practice using it."

CHAPTER 26

West of West,
Men are strong —
When they are right,
When they are wrong.

After going over the plan one more time with Walter and Coat, and getting a warm hug and smile from Judy, Joe rode the bay gelding west from Fort Worth. Each mile they covered allowed Joe to relax a little more. Although he hoped he would never be put in a position to collect any more bounty money, he knew he had no choice except to finally stop arguing with people who recognized him as a bounty hunter. His relief came from the realization he would not have to hear people mentioning his father each day. He had hoped this would be the case when he left Mississippi. Now, he again told himself he would leave those memories behind and live in a place where his father's name would not keep coming into conversations.

Several times Joe thought about going south to look over the town of West, Texas, and see how it compared to West, Mississippi. Between his desire to see his ranch in The Bend and the memory of his promise he had made to himself, never to take the long route to anywhere ever again, he headed for the Head-of-the-River Ranch.

The first day he rode west to Weatherford and south to Stephenville. Several times he tried to get off the road and go across country as he had in Arkansas. Each time he came to a wire fence and had to spend valuable time going back to the road. Several times he passed one or more men building fences.

The last couple of weeks he and Coat had made several trips to Walter's ranch. Not only did it give his bay gelding the exercise needed to prepare for this trip, it gave Joe another opportunity to go over the plans for moving the mares with Coat. Coat was tired of hearing these plans, insisting he had them memorized and would remember them as long as he lived. But each evening, Walter would remind Joe to go over the plan with Coat at least one more time.

Both younger men had purchased good forty-five caliber Colt handguns and practiced shooting on each of these trips. As they moved the mares into the pasture near the road, Joe and Coat had carefully written down the markings and brands on each mare. Joe carefully copied all this information and gave the copy to Walter. He wanted to insure Walter he would keep good records; and in case something happened to him, Walter would be able to claim the mares.

Most of the land he traveled over was covered with blue bonnets and Indian paintbrush flowers. It was early spring, the weather was mild, and he could see the possibility of doing something he had been dreaming about for a long time. He had never seen so many beautiful wild flowers in his life. The only thought that repeatedly caused sorrow was the thought of never seeing Vergie Mae Finley again.

***

After three days of travel across a country covered in flowers, he arrived in San Angelo. There he had a good meal, bathed, shaved and enjoyed a good night's sleep in the hotel, while his horse was bedded down in a good stall in the livery stable. Dawn found him on the road to William Anson's Head-of-the-River Ranch near Christoval.

Before noon he was on a road that ended at the most beautiful ranch headquarters he had ever seen. Several hundred yards past a large three-story house, a large barn dominated the flat landscape. The land around the barn was divided into pens made of strong wood poles. Wire fences extended out from the barn and pens, like spokes on a wagon wheel. Some of the wire fences disappeared over low rises in the land, while others simply extended farther than the eye could see. Activity at the barn caught his attention, so he rode on past the huge house.

This open country is not a place where one can arrive unnoticed. As Joe rode up to the barn, William Anson was standing in the middle of the road with feet wide apart. The tops of his shining boots came up to his knees. His pants were tight at the knees and waist but flared out on each side of his upper legs. Joe couldn't figure out the purpose of this but was not about to ask. William Anson's hat was plaid with a narrow brim, not what one would expect to see on a ranch in West Texas.

He was expecting Joe, because Walter had sent him a letter letting him know when Joe would arrive. Joe didn't know about the excellent personal references Walter had included in this correspondence.

"Greetings, Joe Collins, and welcome," said William Anson.

"Greetings to you, Mr. Anson. Our friend, Walter Ragsdale, told me a good deal about your operation.

Even though he told me to expect to see a beautiful ranch, I was not prepared for anything so grand. I passed quite a few impressive ranch headquarters on the way down here, but none to compare with yours."

"Thank you. Your compliments are appreciated. We lost so much the first few years, it's hard for me to believe we learned how to profit from this operation. It will soon be time for lunch. Let's put your horse in a stall and go to the house so you can rest a few minutes and meet the lady who worked alongside me to help build this place. Better yet, ride to the hitching post at the house, and we won't have far to carry your gear."

Joe dismounted and walked with the Englishman, who walked briskly to the large house.

William Anson and his wife, Shirley, were pleasant and friendly but more formal than anyone Joe had ever been around. He felt welcome but not as much at home as he had felt in the house with Judy and Walter.

William had Joe put his shotgun and rifle in the rack near the front entrance along with several others. As soon as they were seated in the large parlor, the subject turned to horses. Joe told William about the deal he had made with Walter, including his need for stallions.

William Anson enjoyed telling him about his ranching business from start to finish. "When I came here I thought I knew what a good horse was and planned to show Texas what good horses looked like. I brought some thoroughbred and standard bred stallions with me. After crossing them on good mustang mares, I had a herd of horses that were close to useless. I sold mature geldings for ten dollars each and was glad to get them off my grass at that price.

"Only the demand for well bred cattle, which I brought from England and Scotland, kept me from losing everything. Thank goodness, ranchers, for the most part, have decided to change from longhorns to shorthorns and Herefords.

"One day Shirley and I went to a horse race in San Angelo and watched a Steel Dust stallion outrun horses that I thought looked quite superior to him. I began to change my opinion about what a good horse was. About a month later, we went to a rodeo in San Angelo and saw horses like this Steel Dust stallion used as roping and pickup horses. After talking to the people who owned these good cow horses, I knew what I wanted to do. My main market back then was for polo ponies, and I was right in thinking this type of horse would be a good polo pony. I am pleased to report that the people who play polo agree with me.

"Now, I have good men like you coming to buy the quarter horses we've been raising for the last ten years. These horses are a cross between the quarter-mile racing horses, called quarter horses, and good mustang mares. These mares are descendants of horses the Spaniards brought here several hundred years ago. The Spanish horses were mostly Arabians. Arabians have great stamina, and I think living in the wild has increased this to a high level.

"Most of these mares were never wild horses but are from the ranches where their ancestors, who were once wild, have been working cattle for over a hundred years. They not only have tremendous stamina, but they have a strong instinct to work cattle.

"I have found that working in a minor percentage of thoroughbred blood can be quite beneficial or quite disastrous. It had to be a thoroughbred I describe as 'tight twisted.' That is to say, his muscles are shorter and heavier than most thoroughbreds. Not exactly what one thinks of as a typical tall, elegant thoroughbred. It's reported that the sire of Steel Dust had a thoroughbred dam.

"Perhaps you noticed the fenced pastures extending out from the barn area? Each pasture allows the horses or cattle to range out quite a few miles and still come to the barn for grain. With the exception of breeding season, we run the stallions in a pasture with other stallions of the same age. By alternating cattle and horses, we avoid having horses across the fence from other horses and cattle across from other cattle. I had several horses injured badly from wire cuts when horses were across a wire fence from each other.

"In the conduct of our ranch work, we always ride stallions. Geldings are for selling and mares are for selling or raising babies. Three things contribute to their good disposition — breeding, lessons learned running with other stallions, and work under saddle. This time of year I feed grain to get the stock in shape for breeding season. This afternoon most of the stallions will come up looking for grain, and you can pick out the ones you wish to purchase."

"Mr. Anson, I need more stallions than I can purchase. Is there a possibility of purchasing some and leasing some from you?"

"I think we can work something out. Let's get the purchases out of the way, then we can talk about the leases. Right now, Mrs. Anson has some pie ready that is made with antelope meat, and I hope you enjoy it as much I."

Joe did indeed enjoy the delicious meal, and he liked the straightforward way his host presented business deals designed to satisfy both their needs. By the time dessert was served, it was agreed that Joe would buy three stallions and lease four others. He was surprised when William stated that Joe could pick out any young stallions he wanted. This was defined as any stallion four years old or younger on the ranch. "None will be held back," William told him. "The choice is yours."

After lunch they saddled two older horses and drove the four-year-olds into the pens near the barn. This gave Joe time to look at the stallions moving as well as standing. After they drove them into a large pen, he sat on the rail for several hours studying the fine stallions, particularly their movement. His plan was to get three four-year-olds, three three-year-olds and one two-year-old. It was close to dark when William walked up to the pen and asked which horses Joe had selected. Joe asked him, "William, would you do something for me?"

William in his fine British accent answered, "I would be most pleased to do what I can to help. It is getting dark. Should we wait until morning for you to continue the selection?"

After a fine dinner with the main dish being the best steak Joe had ever tasted, they moved to the large parlor where William carefully prepared and lit his pipe while Joe rolled and lit a cigarette. The British gentleman said, "I was about to say, I don't like to brag, but you can't get a steak like that from a longhorn. That was from a shorthorn steer. What did you have in mind that I might do to help you with your selection?"

"Mr. Anson, I was just thinking about the fact, that was the best steak I ever tasted. I was also thinking how I would be most pleased if you would select the stallions for me."

With a frown on his face, William paused for some time. It looked as though he was carefully studying his pipe. Finally the frown turned to a smile. "Did my friend Walter Ragsdale tell you to ask me to select horses for you?"

"No. He did tell me you're a man of your word, and I would be wise to consider carefully any advice you gave."

William Anson thought for a full minute, then responded, "I have made a habit of letting buyers pick out the horse they wish to purchase. Seldom do they select the one I consider the best. Now you have turned the wheel. When I select the horses, you will surely leave here with the best young stallions I own."

Joe pulled the small tablet from his shirt pocket, made a quick note on it and placed it face down on the table. "Which horse would you select from the herd I was looking at this afternoon?" he asked.

"The bay with white high on his tail," William replied, without hesitation.

Joe turned the tablet over to reveal the printed words, *coon tail bay.*

"We chose the same horse!" William shouted. "Joe Collins, it is my prediction that you will be successful as a breeder of great horses! Is there a main characteristic you based your choice on?"

"I liked the looks of most all the stallions, but I thought the coon tail bay moved with more quickness. As they played with each other, I liked the way all of them moved, but when he made a quick move, it was easier for him. It required less effort."

"Lad, you put him in a pasture with the best of the mares you got from Walter, and you will have colts that are as good as any in this land."

Then he added, "If you can keep the raiders from Mexico from stealing them. The area of the Big Bend where your land is located is close to the border. I will rest easier if you tell me that you are going to put the stallions you are leasing in pastures on the north side of your ranch — away from the border."

"I'm anxious to look the country over, and I assure you I plan to put your horses and the best of my

217

livestock in the pastures where they're less likely to be stolen," Joe answered.

"Good, and I need to tell you about a most interesting man." William settled down in his chair, enjoying his pipe, as he spoke. "One day about six years ago while riding on the western part of my ranch, I came upon a man crawling across my pasture on all fours. Naturally, I thought he must be injured or terribly ill. As I closed the distance between us, I could see that he looked as healthy as you and I do now. He rose and introduced himself as 'Korus Korus.' I asked him what the bloody hell he was doing. He claimed to be a dentist in route to the city of Alpine, where he planned to open a dental office. I asked if he intended to crawl all the way, or if he might consider walking. He answered that he had a love of plants and found the plants on this part of my ranch most interesting.

"To make a long story short, as they say, Korus Korus knows far more about plants than anyone I ever encountered. I persuaded him to spend the next three days with us, and I learned more about my own grass than I had in all the years before he showed up. He told me which grass was best during the winter, spring, summer, and fall. The most valuable lesson was how to know when to move livestock off the grass, because it needed to produce seeds for next year.

You will notice as we ride across the ranch tomorrow that some pastures have no horses or cattle grazing on them. I had known the value of rotating livestock on different pastures, but he taught me how to do it in a timely fashion in order for the grass to recover quickly. If you can find this man and get him to talk about your grass, I am sure you will find it beneficial.

"Oh, I almost forgot, he casually mentioned two places where he thought there was water below the land. The best two wells on this place are on those two spots. The water produced by each of these two windmills has created small creeks that run across several pastures.

"I found his information so valuable and his company so interesting, I offered to give him a horse for his journey to Alpine. Alpine is a little north and west of your ranch. He thanked me and turned down my offer. He never rides horse or buggy. He walks everywhere he goes. And he did not eat my wife's cooking, much to her disappointment. As we walked across the land he would eat seeds from one plant, leaves from another and root from others. I told you he was on all fours when I found him; he claimed he was examining plants. I am sure he was, but I also suspect he was grazing. The last time I talked to someone from Alpine, I was told that Korus Korus still has a dental office there. If you do see him, please give him my warmest regards."

***

The next day, as they rode back toward the headquarters of Head-of-the-River Ranch, William stopped to gaze at a herd of antelope in the distance. "I wish I had one of my long range rifles with me," he said to Joe. "We eat so much beef, most of the ranch hands and I, for that matter, enjoy deer or antelope. Those are some distance out of range for our saddle guns, and if we ride closer they will surely run."

Without comment, Joe removed his rifle from beneath his right leg, stepped out of his saddle, and handed the bridle reins to William. He scooped up some dust, dropped it to check out the wind, then sat on the ground, took careful aim and fired. As he removed his rifle from his shoulder, nothing happened, and William was sure his young friend had missed. The distance was about two times as great as most would consider in range for a thirty-thirty. Then, as Joe was putting his rifle back in the boot, attached to his saddle, the legs of a young buck folded as he crashed to the ground.

"Bloody hell!" William shouted. "I hope you never have reason to take a shot at me."

CHAPTER 27

We make friends.
We learn from danger —
Far from the hands
Of a Texas Ranger.

Roberto Arredondo had worked for the Head-of-the-River Ranch for nearly one year and had not spent one dollar he had earned. He told William when he went to work that he was going to work for one year, then he was going back to Mexico to marry the girl he loved, Itza. William had been the one to point out that Roberto only lacked a few weeks finishing a year's work, and the other hands were giving him a hard time about his marriage plans. William suggested that Roberto work for Joe the next few weeks and help Joe take the horses to the J bar C Ranch on the Rio Bravo.

Roberto liked the idea, as it would result in him being several days closer to Itza when the year was over.

Now he found himself riding Joe's bay gelding with the reins in one hand and a rope dallied around his saddle horn in the other. Joe was riding the coon tail bay stallion with the other end of the rope around his saddle horn. Between them, six young stallions were tied to the rope. When William first suggested this, Joe had serious doubts, because young stallions are generally hard to handle, especially around other young stallions. William told him it would work, if they kept them moving. The stallions were accustomed to running in the pasture with other stallions and had been turned in a pen together as soon as the decision was made regarding which ones Joe would be taking to his ranch.

"When you stop to rest," William advised, "Put them on a picket line or hobble them, and don't rest any longer than necessary. You have experience driving horses, so you know the most important thing is to keep them moving. Keep them tired. The first two hours will be the most difficult, so I will ride behind for a few miles to help keep them moving south."

As it turned out, William Anson knew what he was talking about, and after about two hours the horses were trotting with their heads down, making Joe's and

Roberto's jobs reasonably simple. The two men made the two hundred mile trip in four days. When they arrived at the ranch — that Joe had decided would be known as the J bar C — the horses were tired, but the men were exhausted. They were quite relieved to find a reasonably well-built corral for the horses and a three-room ranch house with beds in all the rooms.

As Joe was about to fall onto one of the beds, Roberto said, "Wait," and made a sound with his tongue that sounded exactly like a rattlesnake. Joe could see that he'd brought a stick from outside. Roberto examined the rooms carefully and found one rattlesnake, which he killed and threw out the front door. When he came back in, Roberto told him he knew there was a snake in the house because he had smelled it. "It is good. With a snake in the house there will be no rats and mice," Roberto explained. Without removing their boots they each collapsed on a dusty bed and immediately fell asleep.

When Joe's eyes opened several hours later, his first thought was regret that it was still dark. He'd have to wait for daylight to look around his ranch. He found his way to the door without waking Roberto and was pleased that even though there was no moonlight, there was enough light from the stars for him to see his horses and barn. As his eyes adjusted to the dim light, he saw a snake in front of him and froze. After waiting a few minutes, he realized this was a stick, not a snake. He picked it up and used it to feel the ground in front of him for real snakes.

He circled around the buildings and corrals and then made a wider circle. He continued making wider circles until he realized light was beginning to come from the eastern sky. The land was reasonably flat to the east, with rolling hills to the south and north. When he turned to look west, beyond the buildings, mountains reflected the morning sun. Having noticed them yesterday and again now, he couldn't decide if he needed to be pleased or worried about fresh signs of cattle on his land. The excitement he felt as he walked back to the ranch house was unlike anything he had ever experienced. Then a pang of sorrow came over him, because he had a vision of the wagon carrying Vergie Mae Fleming as it traveled south into the Arkansas hills and disappeared.

They had lived on sausage and biscuits for the last two days, and Joe was surprised to smell food cooking as he walked between the house and barn. He knew Roberto hadn't opened his pack during the trip and was pleased to see Roberto carrying a skillet containing meat with a generous proportion of chili pepper on top. After placing it on the table, he reached back to the stove and handed Joe a metal plate containing tortillas. Joe threw a thank you at Roberto, filled a tortilla with meat and took two big bites. The taste was excellent, but the peppers were so hot he couldn't speak for several minutes. With watery eyes and a silent promise to his mouth that he would take smaller bites, he finally said, "This is great, Roberto. Did you have the makings for all this in your pack all this time?"

"Si, Señor, except for the snake."

As far as they could see, there were no fences on the ranch save those pens and corrals around the house. The horses needed to graze, so they hobbled them before turning them out to graze and drink from the spring-fed creek just south of the house. Roberto suggested taking a ride over to the mountains. Joe could see his Mexican employee studying the mountains carefully and held back his urge to ask why.

After about two hours of riding at a walk, south along the base of the mountains, Roberto saw something that caused him to turn and ride west to the mountains. There was an opening about twenty yards wide with a small stream of water trickling out through the middle of the opening. They rode through the opening into a small canyon where they found a meadow and startled several mule deer, sending them scurrying up the rocky mountainside. Then Roberto, looking pleased, explained, "The trail the deer used was difficult for them, and it's the only trail out of this small canyon — except the way we rode in. It would be almost impossible for a horse to use their trail. If we put some poles across the deer trail and the entrance, the stallions will have enough water and grass until we return with the mares."

The first day of their trip Joe had explained the need to go to Sanderson and get the mares, but Roberto hadn't responded. Joe had decided the Mexican didn't understand. Now he realized that Roberto not only understood, but he had come up with an excellent solution to the problem of feed and water for the stallions while they were gone. "That's a good idea, Roberto."

Finding poles and brush to close off the canyon helped Joe understand how badly they needed basic tools such as an ax, saw, posthole digger, and a hammer — not to mention a wagon and team. The grass growing around an old abandoned wagon was evidence that it had been years since it last hauled anything. Roberto insisted he could make a buckboard using some of the wagon parts and a few additional parts they could bring back from town. The trouble was, a wagon would be needed to haul the parts and tools necessary to perform work on the abandoned ranch.

During the two days before departing for Sanderson, Joe was impressed with the work Roberto completed. He never had to tell him or suggest what should be done or how to do it. Roberto went from task to task without waiting for orders or suggestions. When a gate needed the hinge repaired or a horse needed feet trimmed, Roberto did the job without anyone telling him to. This reminded Joe of Dave, who had taught him how to work on a farm in Mississippi, years ago and miles away.

In the middle of the morning, the day before the trip to Sanderson, two men rode up to the ranch house. Without getting off his horse, the older one introduced himself as Buck Yoakum and the other man as his son, Lloyd. "My son and I operate the ranch just north of here. Do you know who owns this place?"

"I suppose that would be me. My name is Joe Collins, this here is Roberto Arridondo. You are welcome to the J bar C."

"And you folks are welcome to our place, the Double Y, which joins the north end of your ranch. Let me ask an important question on a subject that caused problems between the previous owner of your ranch and me. How do you feel about fences, Mr. Collins?"

Joe could feel the tension in the question. "Mr. Yoakum," he said, "if you and Lloyd would call me Joe I'd appreciate it. I've talked to some ranchers that have a good deal more experience than I have on the subject of fences. The more successful ones tell me if I'm going to take care of my grass and improve the quality of my livestock, I need perimeter fences and cross fences. Won't you lighten up the weight on your horses and visit a while?"

For the first time, smiles came on the faces of the Yoakum men as they climbed from their horses and shook hands.

"The last man who owned this place would become quite hostile if someone mentioned a fence," Buck explained. "We'd been friends and neighbors for several years, helped each other at roundup time, when someone was sick or any other time we could. He was a good friend and neighbor, but when we started talking about fencing our place in, he went into a rage. Said this is open range country and he plans to see it stays that way. You hate to lose an old friend, but we lost him as a friend long before he pulled up and drove north."

"I plan to start building fences as soon as I can get some wire and posts," Joe explained. "First thing we need to do is go to Sanderson and drive right at two hundred mares back here, from the railroad yard."

"I don't see enough men to drive that many mares," Buck responded, "and I don't see a wagon to bring supplies and tools back. Would it make you mad if Lloyd helped you drive the mares, and I drove my wagon for you to fill with supplies?"

"That's mighty neighborly of you. I grew up on a farm, and I know how important it is to have good neighbors. I would sure appreciate the help. You must make sure you let me know when we can help you."

"That's the way around here. Ranches in other parts have more hands than most of us. By helping each other, we can get by with fewer men in the bunkhouse."

As the men rolled a smoke, Buck continued, "With this ranch just being abandoned, I've let some of my cattle graze here. I'll get them gathered and moved as soon as I can. You have some cattle grazing here too. Since the ranch was abandoned, we've had one roundup. Just like we always did in an open range situation, when we gathered a cow and calf we put the brand that was on the cow on the calf. Not a great crop, but the ones with a circle J brand are yours and the ones with a double Y are ours. There are a few with other brands on your place, but not many."

"When I was in Fort Worth, the man who sold me this place told me the brand was circle J. I decided to use my initials J bar C. I can just add bar C to the circle J and with time those with a circle will be gone. How many cattle do you think I'll find with the circle J brand?"

"Cows, calves and all, I guess around three hundred head, mostly longhorns but some shorthorn cross.

"I better tell you about the biggest problem we all share. Just on the other side of those mountains, west of here, is a canyon called Panther Canyon. It's called that because quite a few panther travel through it and sometimes hang around to eat our livestock. Panthers are a big problem, but not the biggest problem the canyon presents. You see, south of you there are some high bluffs along the Rio Grande River, and most of the year the river is swift. Bandits from Mexico have a hard time driving our livestock directly south and getting across the river. It's possible, but not easy. Because of that damn canyon they don't need to. It runs quite a few miles north of here, and when bandits drive our livestock into the canyon, they are as good as in Mexico. It's like a funnel keeping the livestock heading south. They can stampede horses or cattle south down Panther Canyon using the walls of the canyon like a fence. At the mouth of the damn thing the river is shallow, and the water moves slow because it's wide, perfect for crossing. The biggest problem we share is not fences, and it's not panthers. It's that damn canyon and the way the bandits use it."

Joe was quiet for a minute, letting what he'd heard soak in. "I have six stallions penned in a blind canyon a couple of miles south of here. We figured they have grass and water for the next few days while we're gone. Based on what you just said, I'm thinking maybe I should move them."

"That's a decision you'll have to make," Buck announced. "If they were mine, I wouldn't be worried, because of the short time they'll be there. We've noticed the banditos usually raid a pasture where stock has been for some time, leading us to speculate that they send a scout to spot the livestock they plan to steal. There looks to be considerable planning to their raids. I seriously doubt that they will find your studs, have time to make plans, then come get them before we get back. Plus, we've shot a few of the buzzards. They probably won't risk getting a bullet for six horses. When they make a run, they like to fill Panther Canyon up with horses or cattle."

CHAPTER 28

Out west of West,
The border is trouble.
The ignorance of Man
Causes it to double.

"Joe, I don't like to do many business deals with a good neighbor or friend, because things sometimes go wrong," Buck continued. "When that happens I stand to lose, not only on the matter of the deal, but more important, I may lose a friend. If you don't want to make the deal I'm about to propose, there won't be any hard feelings. What if I leave my cattle on your grass for a couple more months, until you get some fences built? During this time I have a fenced pasture, with decent grass, you can put your mares in. When you get your fences built, we move my cattle and your mares."

Joe paused. In his mind he could hear his old friend Dave saying, "I reckon you ought to think on it."

His new friend could see Joe struggling with the decision. "Any time between now and when you get fences built," he told Joe, "either of us wants to move the horses and cows, we should do so without any hard feelings."

"Mr. Yoakum, Buck, I accept that offer. I won't have to worry about herding horses and can concentrate on building fences."

Late the next afternoon the four men arrived in Sanderson, Joe riding the coon tail bay. Roberto rode a four-year-old roan stallion and led the bay gelding for Coat to ride back to the ranch.

Joe had worried whether or not the wagon team Buck was driving could keep up. The horse was a gangly sorrel gelding. He and the bay mule didn't make a handsome pair, but as it turned out they didn't know that and just did their job.

After putting the saddle horses in the livery and making arrangements for the wagon team to join them later, Joe hurried to the store with the wagon. He made arrangements for Buck and Roberto to buy the things on his list as well as anything else they thought might be needed.

He went to the railroad office and confirmed that the train carrying Coat and the mares was scheduled to arrive before dawn the next day. The man in the railroad office told him, "The only freight to be unloaded in Sanderson is your horses, and I don't want any time wasted unloading your broomtails." Then he added, "I'll be the one getting my ass chewed out if the train's delayed."

"Don't worry, we have a long drive ahead of us, so we'll do the job of unloading as fast as possible," Joe assured him.

Joe had made arrangements to keep the loaded wagon inside the barn at the livery, and Roberto insisted that he was going to sleep in the barn to guard the wagon. When Joe objected, Roberto smiled and insisted, "I am welcome in the barn, and that is where I'll sleep."

When Joe, Buck, and Lloyd entered the hotel, Joe realized why Roberto chose to sleep in the barn. A sign on the wall behind the counter, with large letters, read, "NO NIGGERS OR MEXICANS ALLOWED."

The next morning as Coat walked toward him, Joe thought that Coat's smile got bigger every time he saw him. "Coat," he said, "how did the trip go?"

"Joe, things just went great. Two mares limped a little when we unloaded in San Antonio, but by the next day they were walking sound. Must have been just bruised a little. I know you're in a hurry to get these girls headed to your ranch, but just as soon as possible we need to have a talk."

"Okay, Coat, let me introduce you to our neighbors, Buck and Lloyd, and to a good hand who will be gone in two weeks, by the name of Roberto."

After each of them had had an opportunity to shake hands, Roberto said, "Señor Joe, I thought you may want to know, there was a man in the livery last night looking for a job."

"I better not leave until we get unloaded. Will you go tell him to come talk to me?" Joe asked.

"No need. I told him last night you might hire him. That's him, walking this way."

Buck spoke up to say, "I think I better get started. With this wagon loaded my team'll need a head start, if we're gonna keep up with your drive. If you pass us up, don't wait, just drive to our place. Lloyd knows where to put the mares."

Joe had bought two saddles at the store. He roped one of the mares that had white marks on her withers. These white marks indicated that someone had used a saddle on her that didn't fit well. But more importantly, it was a sign she might be broke to ride. Roberto offered to ride her, but the new hand, Russell

Allsup, said, "It's my horse to use, so I'll be the first one to ride her." And as it worked out, after about a half dozen crow hops, he and the bay mare got along well.

The horses were tired after the ride on the train, and that's just the way Joe wanted them. With Lloyd in front and a stout sorrel mare taking her place as lead mare right behind him, the drive to the Double Y was completed without any major problems. It was dark when they finally closed the gates on the pens and corrals at the Double Y. The mares would be moved to their pasture tomorrow. The concept of neighbors helping neighbors when there was need had dictated the construction of bunkhouses with room for guests.

Mona Yoakum, Buck's wife and mother of Lloyd, had anticipated the hungry crew and had a big meal prepared. With hair that was beginning to gray, she was a little heavy on her feet and quite attractive. She reminded Coat and Joe of a little younger version of Mrs. Wesfall.

As soon as everyone had a good meal, Coat said, "Joe, let's go check on the mares one last time." Everyone laughed when he added, "After looking after them the last few weeks, I feel sorta like their mother. You know, like a mother hen with a lot of really large biddies." Everyone laughed, and Joe noted that Coat's combination of talk and laughter was still contagious.

It was obvious Coat had more on his mind than the mares. Once outside, the two old friends paused to roll a smoke, then walked slowly toward the corrals.

"Joe, there was an incident on the train," Cote said. "Just a few miles out of Del Rio, there was a train robbery. I guess I should say there was an attempted train robbery. Earlier I'd been playing cards with the railroad security guards and one man they called a railroad detective. I'd won a little of their money but, unlike those guys I shot craps with in Fort Worth, we became friends. During this attempted robbery there was a gunfight. One of the bandits slipped up behind the detective and surely would have killed him, if I hadn't shot the bandit before he shot the detective. I didn't get any bounty money like you did for killing the Harp brothers, but the detective was so pleased he offered me a job.

"I really like the idea of riding on the train, playing cards and drawing pay. It's like a dream come true. They tell me there are more attempted train robberies and more successful train robberies on the run between San Antonio and California than in all the rest of the nation combined. I guess that confirms your statement a few weeks back, about this being a wild part of the country. I told him I wanted the job, but I'd committed to work for you. Then he said the offer was good for two months. I can work for you for two months, if you want me to, but then I want to become a railroad security guard."

"Coat, if I was running a railroad, I sure would hire you on as a security guard or detective or something. I look forward to working with you the next two months, and appreciate you working with me during that time instead of taking the job with the railroad right away. It looks like coming west may turn out to be good for you and me."

Coat's smile got even bigger as he remarked, "By the way, Joe, it didn't hurt my cause any when I told them I was a friend and employee of Joe Collins, the bounty hunter. They all said they'd like to meet the man who brought down the Harp Brothers."

CHAPTER 29

Out west of West,
Hearts can break.
Can we live with
The mistakes we make?

By the time Roberto's two weeks ended, Coat had the building of fences down to an art. With Russell Allsup and two men from Mexico, Coat could build over a mile of fence each day. Joe was working from dawn to dark trying to keep them supplied with fence posts. It soon became obvious he didn't have enough trees on the ranch for the fencing job. Before daybreak one morning, he hitched his team and headed his wagon toward the town of Marathon, where he was hoping to buy a load of posts. About halfway there, he came on a two-man crew building fences with good sturdy cedar posts. Joe stopped to ask where they got such good posts. After finding out they had several wagonloads in inventory, and who supplied them, he finally convinced them to sell him a load. It was agreed that Joe would bring them a load to replace the posts he was purchasing and get his money back. Joe promised he'd have the replacement load to them in two to three weeks. He didn't think the men believed him, but they would find out that he was a man who was determined to do what he said he was going to do.

He pushed the team hard going home, arriving in the middle of the night. He roused his sleeping hands and explained he was going to buy some fence posts and would be gone the best part of a week. After packing his gear, with his repeating rifle on one side of his saddle and his twelve-gauge shotgun on the other, he rode east on his coon tail bay. His men were left standing in the yard, wearing only their long johns, scratching their heads and trying to make sense of the actions of the man they were working for.

He rode the remainder of the night and all day the next day, stopping only to let the bay eat and drink. He had, in the last few weeks, concluded that having a good stallion to ride had spoiled him. He was still amazed at how much strength and stamina they had compared to a mare or gelding. The next afternoon found him riding into the small, hill country town of Rocksprings.

The man at the livery told him what he needed to know, which was how to get to the ranch whose owner was in the fence post business. Resisting the urge to head out immediately, he left his good horse bedded down in the livery and went to the hotel to eat, shave, bathe and get a good night's sleep. He did everything he intended to at the hotel, except get a good night's sleep. The restless young rancher was on the road, following the directions of the liveryman, before daylight the next morning.

Later that morning he stopped on a hilltop overlooking a rather small, dog-run ranch house along with a barn, two wagons and corrals. There was smoke coming from the chimney but no sign of movement outside the house and no livestock about. With his heart pounding, Joe Collins walked down the hill leading his horse. A harmless blue tick hound came out from under the house and announced Joe's arrival. After tying his horse he stood by the hitching rail and shouted, "Hello, the house."

The window curtain moved enough for someone inside to see him, but not enough for the person inside to be seen. The few minutes until the door opened seemed like an eternity to Joe. When it did open, his mouth was so dry with excitement he could not speak.

"Good morning, Mr. Collins," said Vergie Mae. These ordinary words from Vergie Mae caused his heart to beat so hard he was afraid she could hear it.

By biting his tongue, he created enough moisture in his mouth to reply. "Good morning, Miss Finley. I hope you don't mind me coming here, and I hope you'll call me Joe. I haven't had breakfast." He had longed for this meeting for months. Now that it was here he found he was not prepared and didn't know what to say.

"Joe, we had breakfast quite some time ago, but I have some cold biscuits left. You're welcome to them, or you're welcome to wait while I cook some fresh ones. There's fire in the stove. Please come in."

Without moving, Joe explained, "I ran into some men near my ranch, west of here, who told me they bought fence posts from Carson Finley. Said this Carson Finley lived near Rocksprings and described your father. I need fence posts."

"Well Joe, which do you want first, breakfast or fence posts? Won't you come in and have a seat? My father *is* in the fence post business. He'll be back soon, and I'm sure he'll want to hear about your ranch."

Watching Vergie Mae cook biscuits and bacon was the most enjoyable sight Joe could remember. By the time she was removing the bacon from the pan and placing it on a plate, he got up the nerve to tell her, "Vergie Mae, I hope you won't think what I'm about to say is too bold, but watching you cook breakfast is the most pleasing thing I ever remember doing."

"Joe Collins, you keep talking like that, and I bet I can find some honey for you to put on these biscuits."

As Joe finished the most enjoyable breakfast of his life thus far, they heard a wagon pull in and a loud "whoa." Carson came in with a big smile, gave Joe a pat on the back, and shook his hand.

"Boy, I knew it was you when I saw the rifle on one side of your saddle and the double gun on the other," he said. "What in the world brings you to these godforsaken hills? Vergie Mae, we need some coffee!"

For Joe it was as if he'd been disturbed from the most pleasant dream of his life. "Carson, I came looking for fence posts. I thought you'd be raising vegetables in that town south of San Antonio."

"It's the same old story. The rich man getting richer and the poor man getting poorer. The Fowler brothers were running a crooked game. Turns out the water they bragged about is there like they claimed, but it's sour. The first year you water with sour water you grow vegetables just like they showed in the pictures. The next year the crop will not be as good, and after two years of watering with that bad water the land looks like a desert and won't grow anything. Ten men can't raise a fuss on that damn land.

"By the time we came along, others had been there for several years and lost everything. I'd sent half the money to buy a farm, and I'll never get it back. Others who came earlier lost everything. I joined in a law suit to get my money back, but we all know who owns the judges in this world."

"I am truly sorry for your misfortune. Life hasn't been kind to the two of you in the last few months. How did you end up here — and in the fence post business?"

"I heard about this place being for sale cheap and come to look it over. There's no topsoil. About all it will grow is rocks, cedar, goats and deer. I'd seen a great deal of building going on when we came through San Antonio and thought I could haul these rocks there and sell them for a big profit. Turns out, even a good team can't pull a wagonload of rocks out of these hills, and there's rocks available just north of where all the building is going on.

"Met a man from Del Rio one day hauling posts and got to talking to him. He needed several more loads, and I made a deal to sell him a load. While I was cutting posts, two Mexicans came by and convinced me they wanted to cut posts. To make a long story short, my neighbors let me cut posts off their land just to get rid of the cedar. My Mexicans are happy in their lean-tos made from cedar branches and living off beans, flour and whatever they can gather and kill. I now have three wagons hauling posts to ranchers who've discovered the benefits of wire fences. Who would have thought a man could make a living in these hills with no topsoil?"

As important as Carson's story was, Joe found it hard to concentrate with Carson's pretty red headed, freckle-faced daughter moving about the room.

He managed to learn the price of a load like the one Carson had parked in front of his barn and made arrangements for the delivery of six loads to the J bar C. The heavy built man from Ohio was pleased to make the deal. He wanted to celebrate with a drink of whisky, which Joe managed to decline. Vergie Mae watched from the porch as Joe led his horse to the barn and removed his saddle while her father hitched up a team to an empty wagon and drove out to have it loaded with posts.

Joe felt more at ease as he walked to the porch, planning what he wanted to say next. With her seated in a chair on the porch and him standing on the ground, they were about eye to eye. "Vergie, truth is, I do need posts. But that ain't the main reason I'm here. I've been unable to get you off my mind and was afraid I'd never see you again, or that you'd be married to someone else. What I really need is to see you every day of my life." He paused when he saw, to his surprise, that tears were streaming down her face.

The expression on her face told him that these were not tears of joy.

"I didn't mean to hurt you. The last thing I ever want to do is to see you cry. Please forgive me. What can I do? What did I do?"

After several long agonizing moments she regained some composure and replied, "You have nothing to apologize for. I wish so many things were different. You know better than anyone that the man in Arkansas ruined me. I could never be the person someone like you would want for a wife. I'd bring shame to your house."

Joe knew he had to say the right thing now, so he spoke up quickly. He placed her small white hands in his large rough hands, looked straight into her eyes and said, "You did nothing wrong that day in

Arkansas. I took the life of two men and will regret that for the rest of my life. But I didn't have a choice and must keep reminding myself that I did the right thing. *You* didn't have a choice. The only people that did wrong that day were the Harp brothers, not you and not me. Will you please try to forget that day and live your life as my wife? I promise to do my best to be a good husband."

More tears came from her eyes, but this time the expression on her face told him that these *were* tears of joy. She didn't speak, but she nodded her head, looked at him and placed a soft kiss on his lips.

He felt tears of joy coming to *his* eyes as she gently said, "Please, wait here. I need to go into the house for a minute, and I'm afraid you'll be gone when I return. I have another confession to make." And she disappeared into the house.

She returned a few minutes later carrying something wrapped in a clean white pillowcase. She sat down in the chair and carefully removed the jacket he had placed over her naked body that day in Arkansas and handed it to him. "I didn't wash this jacket, because I didn't want to wash away what was left of you. I carefully removed the blood, one spot at a time. Often when I'm alone I put it on, close my eyes and dream that you're wrapped around me like the jacket."

"I don't have a gold ring to give to you today. Will you keep this old jacket as a sign of my promise to you?" Joe asked, offering to hand her back the jacket.

Then he held her in his arms and kissed her, knowing that he would never forget this day.

CHAPTER 30

West of West,
Life will change
For better or worse,
On the Texas range.

Three weeks later, Joe, along with Coat, returned to the Finley ranch driving the buckboard Roberto had made from old wagon parts found on the J bar C. The crew at the ranch wanted to do something to celebrate the wedding, so they painted the buckboard white and bought a new, bright red wagon seat with springs.

A buckboard is nothing more than a short wagon. Without the length of a wagon and without the springs found on a buggy, it jars your teeth out when you hit a bump or a hole. A spring seat relieves the jarring a little but causes the person sitting in it to be launched into the air — thus the name, buckboard.

What made this one stand out and caused everyone to stare was that, for some unknown reason, people just don't paint buckboards. While everyone was accustomed to seeing painted wagons and buggies, not one of the hands could ever remember seeing a painted buckboard. The freshly painted buckboard with a bright red seat was quite a sight. The bay gelding Joe rode from Mississippi and the bay mare, cut out to use on the drive from Sanderson, made a team that matched reasonably well.

After loading Vergie Mae's personal things, they were married in the church in Rocksprings. Coat stood beside Joe with his big smile. The lady from a neighboring ranch had visited Vergie Mae several times, and Vergie Mae had visited her. This neighbor came to stand with the bride who wore a beautiful white wedding dress her mother had made for her before they left Ohio. A white scarf, neatly folded around her neck, concealed her scar. Carson purchased a new pair of bib overalls like the ones he wore every day of his life.

They stopped for one night in Del Rio and the next night in Sanderson. Then they drove to the J bar C.

Vergie Mae had tied the blue tick hound on the porch of her father's house so he wouldn't follow. She and Blue were good friends, so they both shed a few tears over parting, and he howled as the buckboard left Carson's ranch. When they went to the buckboard late in the morning, after spending the night in Del Rio, the blue tick hound named Blue was seated on the bright red spring seat waiting for them. He had chewed through the rope and a piece of the rope was hanging from his collar. After a joyous reunion between Vergie Mae and Blue, Joe smiled and said, "Looks like we'll have a good dog on the J bar C. If your father objects we can tell him not to blame us. Blue made the decision."

As the young couple and Blue bounced along, their cares bounced away. They laughed and smiled at each jackrabbit and butterfly they saw and made a game out of which one would be the first to see the next beautiful scissors tail swallow.

Joe told her about growing up in Mississippi without a mother or father. He admitted how he'd wanted to go astray but how Dave, Dan and Judge McCool had somehow managed to raise him to understand right from wrong — and how he was still trying to figure it out. He told about spending time with Judy and Walter Ragsdale. He said he was looking forward to them coming to visit and meeting his lovely bride.

He enjoyed telling her about Korus Korus, the dentist in Alpine, who walked from Alpine to the J bar C and spent several days telling Joe about every plant on the ranch. "Each season we have different grass that comes up green, even during winter. Korus taught me how to know when I needed to move livestock off and let the grass produce seed for next year. He also told me where we would get water when we drill wells. We haven't drilled yet, but you can bet there'll be water where Korus Korus told us we can find it.

"One of the best things about this area is there aren't as many insects as in other places. They say it's because of the altitude and low humidity.

"Can I call you Vergie instead of Vergie Mae?"

"Of course you can. I always wished my name was Virginia — but when you say Vergie, it sure sounds good. I've been so lonely here in Texas. The only thing that kept me from going crazy was thoughts of you.

"I grew up on a small farm in Ohio with no brothers or sisters, but we had lots of neighbors and someone was always visiting. My mother and I were always singing, and most of the neighbors liked to sing as well. Us kids could walk to each other's house, and not a day went by without visiting. You can imagine, there was a lot of talking, playing and laughing.

"My father always said we wasted lots of time. He said it was a waste for girls to go to school and learn to read. We didn't have books in the house. Mother never learned to read, and she considered this to be normal.

"Joe, I learned to read a few words by reading labels on cans and sacks, but I want to learn to read and write. Will you teach me?"

She was hurt when he laughed out loud, but relieved after he explained. "I'm not laughing at you. I was thinking about how shocked those teachers who finally got me through the eighth grade would be if they knew I was teaching someone how to read and write. Mrs. Collins, I would be honored to be your reading and writing teacher. Let's buy some books when we stop in Sanderson." This brought tears of joy to her eyes, which he didn't understand.

For the first time in her life she saw antelope and mule deer. She saw many strange birds and plants.

He enjoyed telling her about their neighbors, about Panther Canyon, and about how he was building fences, using a modification of William Anson's fencing plan. The modification was to allow for the lay of the land and the possibility of rustlers coming from

Panther Canyon. "We're building fences so we can keep longhorns and mustangs in pastures next to the canyon and better breed horses and cows east of the ranch house. That way the longhorns and mustangs will be between the more valuable livestock and the canyon."

"Most men carry a hand gun. Why don't you carry one?" she asked, after noticing that he was careful to keep both his rifle and shotgun where he could easily reach them.

He laughed again. Then he reached behind the seat into his saddlebag and pulled out a pistol with holster and ammunition belt. "See here — I have one. Seems like the only time I take it out of the saddlebag is for target practice. I've about decided the only reason a man uses a pistol is because he forgot to bring his rifle or shotgun."

She was tired and sore from bouncing on the painted buckboard, but she didn't complain when he took a longer route to show her some of their good horses.

The sun was low in the west. It peaked over the mountains and was shining in their eyes when they finally came within sight of the ranch house and Coat riding to meet them. As planned, Coat had come back to the ranch on one of Carson's wagons loaded with posts. Before he got within hearing distance, Joe said, "You mustn't think Coat's smiling only because we're honeymooners. He wears that big smile most all the time."

"Howdy, Coat," Joe said next. "Nice of you to come meet us."

Coat removed his hat, gave it a swing, then held it over his heart. "Howdy, Mr. and Mrs. Collins. It is my great pleasure to welcome you to the J bar C."

CHAPTER 31

West of West,
In spite of the past,
Hearts will bind.
Love will last.

"Howdy again, Coat, nice of you to come out to greet me and Mrs. Collins. Why do I get the feeling there is something on your mind?"

"Yep, I wanted to warn you that you're not the only newlyweds about. Yesterday Roberto showed up with his bride and a most interesting story about what's going on across the river. They asked if they could spend the night in the barn and I, wanting to get myself fired anyway, insisted that they stay in your house. They resisted, but I insisted. I didn't want you to be surprised and find out from them. It's entirely my fault. Now, am I fired? Can I go now?"

"Thanks for warning us, but your plan to get fired didn't work. Come on to the house and give us a hand unloading this buckboard."

Itza couldn't speak English and looked as though she was afraid to speak anyway. Roberto told how the Mexican army was going from ranch to ranch taking cattle and horses and declaring it a tax. He'd arrived at her father's ranch the day after the Mexican army left. Her father's huge ranch, encompassing thousands of hectares, had been handed down from his father, who inherited it from his father. The beautiful Itza had been raised to be a wealthy man's wife.

Just over a year ago, when Roberto asked for her hand in marriage, her father told him to go work on a ranch for one year and not spend any of the money. Of course, he expected the young man to join with others his age and show the weaknesses of youth. He never expected the young man to show up back on the steps of the large ranch house, which looked more like a Spanish castle.

If Roberto had arrived one day sooner, he would have been drafted into the Mexican army. If he had resisted he would have been killed.

The army occupied the ranch for four days, while Itza hid in a secret room and her father was a prisoner in his own study. Knowing these men with large ranches liked to hide their money, the army officers found the best way to get their hands on it was to kidnap sons and daughters and hold them for ransom. They didn't find Itza, but they pillaged and raped, then left with the best cattle, all the horses, all the young ranch hands as soldiers and the young women as slaves.

Her father, who had hoped never to see Roberto again, now praised God for sending him. "You must marry my lovely Itza and take her across the Rio Bravo, where she will be safe. Someday we'll have a revolution to rid our country of these terrible scoundrels, then you can return. With our blood we delivered this land from the savage Apaches, and we endured the Comanches raiding from the north. Now we must rid the land of our own government. In God's name we will do it. You must keep Itza safe."

After Roberto swore that he would not join the army and would devote himself to keeping her safe, they were married in the church, which was part of the ranch compound. They were escorted to the river and walked to the J bar C Ranch, hoping to spend the night.

The next day Roberto agreed to stay and work on the J bar C. Without being told to do so, he joined the men building fences.

Coat's big smile turned to laughter when Joe told him he was fired and could go to his job as a railroad detective. "Not a detective, a security guard! But someday I just might be a detective. Detective Coat Calcoat! I like the sound of that!"

After several days, it was obvious that the production of the fencing crew and the crew handling livestock had improved, using ideas suggested by Roberto. Joe knew someone else needed to supervise the work on the ranch, leaving him free to keep an eye on the livestock and the countryside joining the ranch. When he announced that Roberto was the ranch foreman, he told everyone to consider Roberto's orders as coming from him.

There were no objections, though Russell Allsup was obviously disappointed that he didn't get the job. Russell worked hard and long, but someone needed to tell him after each task what he should do next. This was in contrast to Roberto, who was constantly planning what task needed doing next. Roberto may not have been the only Mexican with the position of ranch foreman in Texas, but he was the only one for miles around.

CHAPTER 32

West of West,
Times will change on
The plains and mountains
Where good horses range.

At least once each week, Joe rode into the mountains overlooking Panther Canyon. He often found stones with marks indicating they were gravestones. Because these mountains were so arid, wood decayed slowly. He found wooden crosses that could have been centuries old. These might have marked the resting place of a settler, fifty years ago, or a Spaniard, three or four hundred years ago. He even found remains of scaffolding such as those used by Indians for burial and marks on rocks and in caves made centuries before the Spaniards came.

On one of these trips he noticed no unusual activity and turned for home. But when he was almost out of the mountains, something told him to look back. When he did and saw a cloud of dust coming from the floor of the canyon, he turned to ride to an overlook. From there he only saw more dust, so he rode to the floor of the canyon. There the tracks told him that while he was riding toward home, a herd of cattle had been pushed south, through the canyon.

At least one of the ranches north of him was missing cattle. He rode to the river as fast as his good horse could carry him. When he arrived he saw a man on the Mexico side driving tired horses away. Joe took out his rifle, took careful aim, raised the front sight slightly to correct for distance, breathed in, held it for a few seconds — and then lowered the rifle. The man needed shooting but not as much as the one he worked for. Joe couldn't bring himself to shoot the horse wrangler in the back.

He waited a few minutes, hoping the man would turn around. He didn't. After he was gone, Joe had doubts about the decision not to pull the trigger.

Riding back he met eleven men including Buck and Lloyd Yoakum. He told them what he'd seen, leaving out the part about passing up an opportunity to shoot the wrangler. Obvious to all, there had been fresh horses waiting at the river, and the wrangler was driving the spent horses. The cattle had been stolen from a ranch about ten miles north of the J bar C, and none of the men in this group rode for that ranch. Perhaps the owner didn't know his cows were gone.

Joe found this frightening. And more frightening still was that while he had been in the mountains, they had driven past his place without his seeing them. He promised himself that in the future he would look to see what was going on behind him more often.

***

With two couples the little ranch house was crowded. There was sometimes tension, but each couple respected the other, and problems were usually solved without hard feelings. Each couple had a small private bedroom and they shared the dining room, kitchen and living room, only somewhat larger. They began to refer to it, with a smile, as "the great room."

The large front porch provided relief from the crowded ranch house and from the bunkhouse. Everyone on the ranch enjoyed spending time on the porch. Sometimes they would just sit. Usually they discussed horses, but on rare occasions other subjects came up.

Joe was surprised at how much enjoyment he felt each evening during the time set aside for Vergie's reading and writing lessons. He valued the time spent close to her, and it took his mind off other problems, allowing him to relax.

As Virgie and Itza worked together during the day they taught each other English and Spanish. Neither had a sister while growing up, but now they were enjoying treating each other like sisters.

Vergie had worked hard all her life, in the field and in the home. In contrast, Itza had been taught how to cook, sew and clean for the intended purpose of preparing her to supervise, not work. After a difficult job was complete and she found satisfaction, she would say, "For the first time in my life I feel useful."

The house was not large enough for all when Walter and Judy Ragsdale came to visit, so the men slept in the bunkhouse to leave the ranch house for the women.

The bunkhouses on most ranches didn't get cleaned until it was necessary to use a shovel instead of a broom. Most ranch cooks were men too old or crippled to be cowboys. The two young ladies on the J bar C cleaned the bunkhouse each day. Bedding was washed each week, along with the men's clothes.

As word spread from ranch to ranch, the men from other ranches began teasing the

J bar C hands about the conditions in the bunkhouse. The teasing was obviously out of envy.

The ladies took turns preparing meals. One week, one would prepare breakfast and lunch, and the other supper. The following week they would switch. They had fun, but the competition was sometimes intense. They each liked looking on and asking questions about how the other prepared food, often making suggestions. Sometimes these were welcome and sometimes not.

***

An old cowboy by the name of Henry had been working for Joe long enough to prove he could break a young horse and have it ready for ranch work faster than any other hand. However, he also knew how to finish one off and produce a solid roping or cutting horse. Joe saw to it that Henry spent most of his time making good, well broke horses even more valuable.

Henry had been raised on Charles Goodnight's ranch in the Palo Duro Canyon and had ridden on the big spreads from Montana to South Texas. He'd spent years on ranches in California, learning the ways of the Spanish vaqueros. He was the old-timer on the place, and everyone respected his knowledge and wisdom. While he liked to talk about the younger men being too young to wipe their ass, they would tease him about being too *old* to wipe his. With a smile he often complained that on this outfit, he was deprived even the pleasure a man could experience scratching a fleabite. He also allowed, "The way this bunkhouse is run, when I get too old to ride, you young ones'll probably take me out in the snow and leave me to die like an old Indian squaw. Won't be no cook job around here for the likes of me."

Joe enjoyed watching Henry when he was working with a horse. His techniques were different, but his movements and manner around a horse reminded Joe of Dave.

Most ranches only broke the horses they needed to work cattle. Well bred, well broke and well trained horses were the end product of the J bar C.

CHAPTER 33

West of West,
In mountain passes —
Horses, cattle
And jackasses.

There was an area near the mountains where the ground was always moist. For some unknown reason, water seeped out from under the mountains, even during dry weather. Many discussions about gardening or planting crops on the moist ground ended with the observation that deer would be the only creatures to harvest from a garden in the wet area.   Instead, a garden that sometimes needed to be watered by hand was planted near the springs, just south of the barn. Blue didn't allow deer that close to the house.

The first year, Joe hadn't planned on having any livestock to sell. But during his rides into the mountains, he'd found burros, a few longhorns, some mules and a few wild horses without any brands. He knew the army would buy mules and horses, and after finding out that there was a quicksilver mine on the west side of the mountains that would buy burros, he began planning to round them up. Joe knew there were flaws in his plan, because the rough country would make it impossible to control the animals. After listening to Joe's plan, Henry said, "The drive you need to make is to town."

The older man didn't elaborate on why he wanted Joe to go to town. After waiting in silence for several minutes, Joe asked him to explain.

"Go buy some corn," Henry said. "Spread it out in the canyon where you want the animals. Spread it out good, because mules, burros, and horses don't like each other. Put fresh corn out every other day for about two weeks, and then close the gate. You can be sure others have tried to drive them out of these mountains and failed."

"Henry, the only solution I can think of for that problem is to halter break each animal and lead each one out. You know, we plan to halter break them and give them a little training anyway. The time spent halter breaking them won't be wasted, it'll just make them more valuable."

It was a big job, but it paid off. The quicksilver mine was in need of the burros and paid seventy-five dollars each. These were animals most people considered useless, but they were small enough to pull carts through the tunnels in the mine.

After the mules were broke to pull, the military paid a hundred dollars for each head. They said they would pay a hundred-fifty dollars for larger mules. Joe wrote to Coat, at his San Antonio address, telling him that the J bar C needed a large Missouri jack.

Three weeks later, Coat rode up wearing a black suit with a string tie, riding a livery horse and leading the biggest jack Joe had ever seen. Laughing, Coat said, "He looks about as good as a jack can look."

"Where did you find him, Coat? And what did he cost?" Joe asked, as he joined Coat in laughter.

"There was a man on the train hauling six of them to California," Coat said. "We got in a card game, and now he's hauling five.

But before you get any ideas about beating me out of my fine ass, let me tell you how raw my *other* one is. Riding on the train doesn't keep a man in shape for sitting in a moving saddle."

"Well, get outa that saddle and rest a spell. The army wants bigger mules, and with this jack around, we should have some to deliver in a few years."

CHAPTER 34

In mountains west of West,
Danger will hide and
Fear will be learned
From a long, long ride.

The second spring on the J bar C was looking good. There had been snow in the winter, leaving adequate ground moisture. Now rain came, adding to the good growing conditions.

Joe continued to try to come up with a way to take advantage of several acres of land near the mountains that was sub-irrigated and stayed moist, even during dry weather. Several times he had tried riding across the wet area, into the canyon beyond — only to prove, again, that the wet area in front of the mouth of the canyon was too boggy for a horse to cross.

The rock outcrop on the cliffs above the area prevented anyone from looking down into the canyon from above.

Late one evening he returned to the ranch house, almost in a state of shock, with a story everyone found fascinating.

"I was determined to see what was in that canyon today," he began. "Left my horse tied to an acacia and was careful to walk close to the mountain to get past the boggy area. Knowing that getting past the boggy area would be a problem, I thought nothing of leaving my guns behind. I mean, this is just two miles from our house. Holding on to rocks when I could, I managed to work my way around to the mouth of the little canyon. I was naturally looking down, trying to stay out of the bog. I took a few steps into the canyon, still looking down to make sure I was clear of the bog. Finally, I looked up, and what I saw made my blood run cold."

Everyone was using their imagination to guess whether it was a mountain lion or a bear. Joe went on.

"When I looked up, I thought I was a dead man. Standing on top of a large rock, right in front of me, was a tall black Indian. He had one feather in his headband, no shirt and was wearing deerskin britches and moccasins. I'll declare, with him carrying a bow and arrow and standing on that rock, he looked like a giant. He had no expression on his face, and I never wished for a gun more in my life. I was trying to figure out which way to jump if he raised that bow when he said, in plain English, 'Greetings, Sir.'

"That surprised me just about as much as the sight of this man. I said, 'Howdy.' He walked down from the rock, and we had a long talk."

Joe's presentation was so exciting that no one noticed supper was getting cold as he continued. "Turns out he's a Seminole Indian from Florida. At least his folks come from Florida. The American Calvary force-marched them from Florida to Oklahoma along with a bunch of Creek Indians. When they got to Oklahoma, the government gave the Creeks a reservation and told the black Seminoles to live there too.

"The Creeks wanted to make slaves out of them and even attempted to sell some of them to white men and other Indian tribes. The Seminoles fought their way out of the reservation and left Oklahoma coming this way. This was before the war, and everyone they met in Texas wanted to make slaves out of these black Seminoles. They fought their way across Texas, finally entered Mexico over around Del Rio. The Mexican government gave his tribe a reservation in exchange for the black Seminoles helping fight Apache and Comanche."

Itza had learned enough English to follow the story and could not resist interrupting in Spanish. Roberto served as interpreter. "This is true. We had some of these people working on my father's ranch. My father often said there is no better vaquero than the black Indian. He also talked of these men helping fight the Apache and Comanche."

Thankful for verification of the Indian's story, Joe continued, "That fits his explanation. He said now that the Mexicans don't need them to fight the Apache and Comanche, the Mexican government wants to take their reservation. In the last few years, most of his people have been on the run. He came to this ranch the fall before we did and found that canyon. Get this — he has a wife and two sons. They live in a cave that's as nice as our ranch house. Come to think on it, it's a little nicer.

"This is embarrassing, to know that this family has lived on my ranch just two miles away from headquarters, all this time, and I didn't know.

"Noticing that we seldom get off our horses, he dug that low place out so it would be too boggy for anyone to ride a horse across. He took the soil and made little areas on rocks, on the side of the cliff, and on the floor of the canyon, where they grow plants. They grow corn, squash, peppers, melons, and plants I never heard of. Each plant is cared for as an individual plant — no rows. You can't get in a position to look down on the land from up above, but even if you could, you wouldn't realize you were looking at a garden, because the plants aren't in rows."

Henry hadn't spoken until now, when he said, "He must speak pretty good English."

"He and his wife both speak English and Spanish. He also speaks several Indian languages. He claims he can communicate with any Indian, and I believe him. I told him he was welcome to stay on the ranch until we talked again — and perhaps for a long time after.

"He said his most difficult task has been to keep the two boys from making noise. Now that they've been discovered, he'll be happy to let them play without worrying about them 'hoopin' and 'hollerin'."

"Those boys need to be in school," Vergie declared. "How old are they?"

"The older one's four and the young one's two. Looks like their maw and paw have been doing a good job of teaching them. The mother told me I was the first person the two-year-old had seen, except for his parents and brother. They don't have Indian names.

The father's name is John Thomas, his wife is Miriam, the older boy is Harry and the young one is Calvin.

"Do we have any supper around here?"

***

The Thomas family stayed on the J bar C and made impressive contributions. They liked living in the cave, which provided good shelter in the winter and functioned as a cool home during the hot summer. The large garden, John and Miriam now planted in rows, in the naturally sub-irrigated area, provided vegetables and melons for the entire ranch. Something John rubbed on each plant and spread on the ground kept the deer away.

John could use his rifle now without worrying about being discovered. Until John came along, Joe was the undisputed, best marksman on the J bar C. But John could match Joe's shooting skills and even taught Joe some techniques that improved his marksmanship.

Just as useful was John's ability to make plaster and to build with stones and mortar. Within two years he built Joe and Vergie a stone house. All the building material came from the nearby mountains. The new house was just in time, because Itza had a baby girl and the three-room ranch house was quite crowded.

CHAPTER 35

West of West,
Rustlers succeed and fail.
Good men die.
Will law prevail?

The Cattlemen's Association had become a tool in combating rustlers. Just how useful a tool was debatable. The meetings were usually in Alpine, and the wives socialized in the hotel lobby and shopped while the men conducted the business of the association. While the main purpose was to combat rustling, there was considerable business conducted, such as the buying and selling of livestock.

Coat was now the detective in charge of the railroad security from San Antonio to El Paso. He was often in attendance for these meetings, because the same people who stole cattle and horses from ranches often robbed or tried to rob the trains. On more than one occasion, rustlers had stopped the train, unloaded the horses and cattle, and made off with them. Coat said this was so frustrating, because it left his men with no horses to use in pursuit of the rustlers.

Always in attendance was Carson Finley. He would bring several loads of cedar posts and several jugs of whisky to each meeting. The quantity of the whisky resulted in some of the men expressing a need to check out the price and quality of the posts several times each day. It became routine for the meeting to be adjourned with the motion, "I move we go check on the fence posts."

As a detective, Coat was always asking about the methods used to protect livestock from rustlers.

***

Joe, Henry and Russell were unloading a wagonload of supplies, brought to the ranch on a return trip from a meeting of The Cattlemen's Association when John rode up, pointing out a cloud of dust south of the ranch headquarters. A few minutes after he sounded the alarm, Joe and the others were riding south as fast as their horses could travel. They found fences cut and a pasture of the best mares and colts missing. The fresh trail, left by the herd of mares, colts and rustlers, was not hard to follow. The J bar C crew continued south at top speed. When they got to the bluff overlooking the Rio Grande River they looked down on rustlers pushing the stolen horses across the river.

Most would have considered the distance too great for rifle fire to be effective. However, when Joe and John began shooting, the rustlers began to slump in their saddles, showing they were hit, even though they were able to ride away. At such a distance the bullets didn't have the killing power they would normally deliver. To escape the rifle fire, the rustlers abandoned the stolen horses and got lost in the rough landscape of northern Mexico.

While gathering the horses to drive back to the ranch, Roberto waited until Joe was away from the others and said, "I must ride to Mexico. I think one of the men who got hit is my brother. I must see that he does not die, then I will return to your ranch. Will you keep Itza and the little ones safe until I return?"

"You keep Roberto safe, look after your brother, and know we'll keep your wife and children safe," Joe told him. He took the food and ammunition from his saddlebags, passed them to the ranch foreman and shook his hand. He sat still and worried as he watched Roberto ride south.

***

It took hours to drive the mares and colts up to the high bank on the north side of the river. As they drove them back to the ranch, Joe made plans. They would build a cross fence and keep a herd of longhorns or mustangs between the river and the more valuable mares, as they had done on the land bordering Panther Canyon.

The worry over Roberto's safety was relieved when ten days later he rode in, tired but happy to be once again in the arms of his wife and children. After spending time with his family, he walked over to the porch of Joe's rock house, where Joe was waiting.

"Joe, I don't have any good news about conditions south of the Rio. I found my younger brother, Antonio. After doctoring his wounds, which were not life threatening, I took him to our uncle's house and found my mother there. It sure was good to see my family.

"I tried to make Antonio understand that he should come to America and work on a ranch. My uncle and mother understand and explained the same thing to him, over and over.

"Like many others in Mexico, he is convinced that this land, along with the cattle and horses here, was stolen from Mexicans years ago. I told him how you, William Anson, and others, bought ranches and horses and cattle and raised more horses and cattle. I told him that you are not a thief — and even if you were, it would not grant him the right to become one. I can only hope that someday he will understand, although he did not wish to believe my words."

Two months later, The Cattlemen's Association met again and devised a plan to keep a lookout on top of a mountain overlooking the mouth of Panther Canyon. Each lookout would spend a week on the lonely post. A replacement would come from another ranch to relieve him. Joe agreed to send John Thomas and two other hands to build a shelter for the lookout and pile brush to be burned when the lookout saw raiders coming into the canyon. The large fire on top of the mountain would send riders from the J bar C north and west, where there would be other piles of wood and brush waiting to be fired. Buck Yoakum's crew would set these fires, and others would repeat the warning, until ranches the full length of the canyon got the message and sent in well-armed men. The plan was to trap and kill anyone in the canyon who looked like he might be an outlaw.

At this meeting where these plans were finalized, Coat had a different look about him. When he and Joe were alone, he lost his smile and told Joe, "I like the job, working for the railroad, and I especially like trying to out-figure the plans of the outlaws. Trouble is, we're on duty around the clock, and now I'm on probation for gambling. We get on the train in San Antonio, ride to El Paso where we get on one heading east, work our way back to San Antonio and start all over again. When I first signed on, gambling was mostly for modest stakes. Now that we have cars to sleep in, professional gamblers are using the train like a riverboat. There's gambling for big bucks now, and I ain't allowed to join the game."

Three weeks later there was a raid on two ranches north of Joe, resulting in serious loss of horses and cattle. When Joe and Buck Yoakum rode to the lookout to find out why the warning system didn't work, they were shocked to find one of Buck's best hands, who had been known simply as 'J W,' dead from numerous gunshot wounds. His saddle, horse and guns were stolen along with his canteen and food.

Buck covered his bullet-riddled body while Joe looked for signs.

"There are no shell casings near J W's body," Joe told Buck. "I don't think he fired a shot. It looks like someone J W trusted rode up and got the drop on him."

His death was a heavy burden for Joe and Buck. Both of them had voted for the plan that placed the good man alone on this mountain.

With only two horses, they tied the body on Joe's horse, and Buck led him down the mountain. After stopping at the J bar C to let Roberto know he needed to send someone up the mountain with a horse for Joe to ride home, Buck carried J W's body to the Double Y on the buckboard. All ranches this far from town had a cemetery, and the Double Y would be J W's final resting place.

At a special meeting of the association, the members in attendance voted to abandon the warning fires. The rustlers knew about them and that they would be manned by only one person. Hopes for relief from the activities in Panther Canyon were at an all time low. Joe did convince the ranchers to leave the piles of wood and brush for possible use in the future.

CHAPTER 36

West of West,
Eagles fly high.
Panthers scream loud.
Good and bad men die.

Ten days after the death of J W, a rider from Mexico came with bad news. The rider, Roberto's cousin, reported that Antonio, Roberto's brother, was dead. Antonio and Roberto were not twins, but they looked so much alike, people often made the mistake of thinking they were. The cousin reported that Antonio was wounded in the shoot-out that claimed J W's life.

When the wounded Antonio had made it back to his home, he'd told his family he'd agreed to make the lookout think he was Roberto and that way get the drop on him. It was agreed the lookout would be tied up so he could not light the fire, warning of the attack.

When it became evident the rustlers were going to murder J W, execution style, Antonio tried to stop it. The others wounded him before he escaped.

The cousin also said both Roberto's uncle and mother insisted that Roberto not come to Mexico. It was too dangerous.

Each year, everyone in every church in the Big Bend area prayed for conditions south of the Rio Grand to improve, and each year the situation became worse. As a military fighting force, the Mexican army was no match for Pancho Villa's Revolutionary Army of northern Mexico. On one occasion the Mexican army, running from Pancho Villa, crossed the Rio Bravo west of the mountains near the town of Presidio and surrendered to the United States army. It was perhaps the only time a military force, not at war, had another army surrender to them. The United States army loaded them on the train at Marfa, transported them to El Paso, and sent them back across the river into Mexico. So great was their hunger, the Mexicans ate their horses and mules on the march to Presidio. Between Presidio and Marfa they ate their saddles and leather harness.

Pancho Villa kept his promise to relieve his fellow citizens of the oppressive federal government. The problem was, he replaced it with a government that was worse. Not only was his army superior to the Federales, he was also superior as an oppressive tyrant. When it came to raping and pillaging, his so-called "Revolutionary Forces" were second to none. He didn't take *some* of the ranchers' cattle; he took *all* of them. He didn't want *some* of their money; he wanted *all* of it. He even crossed into the United States to raid ranches and towns, declaring these to be a part of Mexico that was stolen by the gringos in years past. As Revolutionary Ruler of northern Mexico, he considered the towns and ranches on both sides of the river to be part of his kingdom.

Mostly because of the Mexican Revolutionary War and the threat of World War I, the need for quality horses increased each year, along with the price. The J bar C continued to grow as they sold horses and mules to the military and to others who wanted well broke horses or top breeding stock. The bunkhouse expanded, because Joe insisted that all horses and mules that left his ranch must be broke to ride or pull or both.

A statement heard often was, "As people buy more automobiles, more horses and mules will be needed to pull them out of ditches." This was certainly illustrated when the United States army, under the leadership of General Blackjack Pershing, made a drive into Mexico with orders to kill or capture Pancho Villa. For the first time, automobiles, trucks, and motorcycles were used by an army on the attack. If horses and mules were not pulling these motorized vehicles out of the mud, they were pulling them through sand, not to mention problems associated with keeping fuel in the tanks and dealing with mechanical breakdowns.

While this was happening, most of the United States' citizens were focused on trouble in Europe. On one trip to deliver horses to the army at Fort Davis, the sergeant who was taking delivery asked Joe to give him the name of all the men working on the J bar C. Joe didn't see any reason to supply the names. "Sergeant," Joe said, "with due respect, you have my name, and I don't see any reason why you would need the name of all the men on the ranch."

Without a reply, the sergeant disappeared into the quartermaster's office.

After a few minutes, the colonel, who served as quartermaster, came from his office and greeted Joe with a firm handshake. "Great to see you, Joe Collins. It's good to see you and even better to see the quality of livestock you delivered.

"You must know of the talk of war in Europe. We don't know if America is going to be involved or not. If we do need to go over there to kick their ass, you can be sure there will be no more war. We'll put an end to war.

"The official word from Washington is that each county must prepare to draft men into the army. We need your horses and mules more than we need you. We have been instructed to make a list of men on ranches that supply large numbers of horses and mules. All men on these ranches will be exempt from the draft."

"Colonel, what if some of my men *want* to join the Army?"

"They can join any time they wish, but they can't be drafted into service. We have a long list of occupations that will be exempt from the draft, if there is a draft. The list includes people who work in the quicksilver mine south of here, folks who keep the railroads running, sheep herders, even farmers who grow beans."

"Considering your explanation, I don't see anything wrong with giving you the names of the men on the J bar C." But Joe was puzzled. "Just out of curiosity," he asked, "why sheep herders and bean farmers?"

When the sergeant and colonel both began to laugh, Joe knew he had been suckered into asking the question.

With a chortle, the colonel replied, "They figure, no matter how cold the weather in Europe is, if a soldier has on wool clothes and farts inside of them, he'll stay warm."

CHAPTER 37

West of West,
Judge a man:
Prepare yourself
To see his hand.

When Joe rode up to the barn about dusk the next afternoon, he was pleased to see an old friend waiting for him. "Hello, Little Dave. I sure didn't expect to see you this far from Mississippi. Dan sent me a letter about your father passing. I sure am sorry. He was a good man and the earth is a better place because he walked on it. I shudder to think what would have become of me if he hadn't been there to help in my up-bringing. I hope you can stay a while."

"Joey, I hope I *can* stay a while. When my father lay dying I asked him what he thought about me coming out here to work for you. He said …"

"Excuse me for interrupting. I think I know what his answer was. I bet his words were 'I reckon you ought to think on it.'"

"How could you know that?" the young black man asked in surprise. "There was no one there except him and me."

"Truth is, your father had a great deal to do with my raising," Joe answered. "I spent many a day and night trying to figure out why in hell he wouldn't answer my questions. He would tell me enough to get me curious, then instead of an answer to my question, he'd say, 'I reckon you ought to think on it.' Thinking back on it now, he'd always given me enough information. He wanted me to figure things out. Dan said that Dave taught us how to think. I shudder to think what I might have become without the lessons learned from your father.

"On the subject of you working on this ranch, I have a ranch foreman, by the name of Roberto, who needs to make the decision. But I'll just bet that with my recommendation and your experience, he can find a job for you. Let's go to the bunkhouse and get you settled in for tonight. By the way, I go by the name of Joe now."

"I'll try to remember. I hope to be called Dave instead of Little Dave."

"Dave, I'll try to remember as well. That rider coming is Roberto. Let's stand here by the barn and wait on him.

"Howdy, Roberto. I want you to meet an old friend of mine by the name of Dave. He's looking for a job, and I want to tell you he can break a horse to saddle or to pull. If there's a horse race and he's one of the jockeys, I plan to put my money on the horse he's riding."

After discussing Dave's employment and agreeing on wages, the three of them continued to the bunkhouse. John Thomas was the only black man working on the ranch, and by choice, he lived with his family in their cave.

Joe waited on the front porch of the bunkhouse while Roberto introduced Dave to the other ranch hands, then told him, "Pick out any bunk not in use. You're too late for supper, but we put leftovers in the screen window for anyone that comes in late. Just help yourself."

While Roberto returned to the porch, where Joe was rolling a smoke, Dave threw his pack on an empty lower bunk. Willis was a ranch hand who did his share of work, but considered himself a fighter as well as a cowboy. He had never provoked a fight on the ranch, but he had been involved in several in local saloons.

When Dave's pack landed on the empty bunk, Willis said, "That's my bunk."

Dave picked up his pack and put it on the upper bunk. Willis said, "That's mine too. There *ain't* no bunks in this bunkhouse for niggers."

The front door opened with a bang. Joe and Roberto stepped in. Joe asked, "Dave, which bunk did you put your pack on the first time?" After Dave pointed to it, Joe picked up Dave's pack and placed it on the bunk. When he turned around he was obviously angry as he looked straight at Willis. "On this ranch each man will be judged by how he gets his work done and how he treats others. If any man doesn't like that, he can draw his pay or deal with me."

No one spoke as Joe and Roberto left the bunkhouse. When he and Roberto were far enough away that the men couldn't hear, Joe said, "We need to change plans for tomorrow. Have every man on the ranch ready to ride at daybreak. We won't get back until late, so make sure they each carry food. Put Dave on that dun mare in the lot west of the barn." With no further directions he left his ranch manager and retired to the rock house.

Roberto was puzzled, even disappointed. He'd never seen Joe set someone up for a fall, not until now. Almost every man in that bunkhouse had tried to ride that dun mare and had suffered because of it. She always waited until the person attempting to ride was in the saddle and relaxed, then she began to buck and do everything she could to hurt the rider, including slamming the rider into the corral fence. She had earned the title of 'Dun Bitch.'

The next morning at first light, Joe led his old coon tail bay stud out of the barn as Dave was preparing to climb into the saddle. As he walked to the corral gate, he called to Dave and, pointing south, asked, "Dave, you see where those mountains meet the prairie, south of here?"

When Dave nodded, Joe swung the corral gate open and shouted, "Lead the way. And don't slow down until you get to the cross fence, about eight miles out." As the mare lunged through the open gate and started bucking, Joe hoped Dave could hear him shout, "We'll meet you there!"

The other ranch hands were not easily surprised when it came to dealing with horses, but they looked like they were in a state of shock. They knew that without a corral to contain the mare, she would run to gain speed, then slam her feet into the ground, throwing the rider's weight forward. Then before the rider could regain balance, she would kick the sky with her back feet, pitching the rider over her head, and he would probably land on *his* head. This predictable behavior was why horses were always ridden in an enclosure before riding them outside.

But as Dun Bitch tried to get rid of the rider by repeating this maneuver over and over, the young black rider sat in the saddle as though the horse, saddle, and rider were one. After the first run like this, the other ranch hands waved their hats and began to cheer for Dave. They kept yelling as they rode out — watching the bucking dun mare and the black man from Mississippi disappear into the southern landscape.

A little over two hours later, with their horses at a fast trot, they arrived at the cross fence to find Dave circling the mare. He would pull her head right and make a few circles to the right, then pull her head left, and circle left, all the while keeping her at a trot.

Each man, including Willis, complimented him on his ride as the dun walked calmly through the gate. Dave had gained their respect.

The pasture they rode to contained about a thousand longhorns. Joe sent each man in a different direction with instructions to move the cattle to a low place near the foot of the mountains. After several hours, most of the longhorns were gathered near the mountains.

Joe divided the crew into two groups. "I want one group of men to move the cattle that are mostly brown into the little canyon to our south," he told them, "and the other men to move those that are mostly white onto the canyon just north of us. Roberto and I will stay here to hold those that don't fall into one of these color groups."

It was hot, dusty work, but the men liked working when they didn't have to get off their horse except to take a leak. They liked taking their turn cutting cattle from the main herd and trying to do it quietly and better than their friends. When it came to cutting cattle out, none could match Joe and his coon tail bay. He remarked that most of them were on green horses, so he had an unfair advantage.

At noon, some took their turn holding cattle in place while others ate cold biscuits, tortillas, and canned fish. They drank water from a nearby spring.

The men probably would not have stopped, but their horses needed to drink and graze. By mid-afternoon the longhorns were divided into three herds.

Joe told the men, "Ride from herd to herd, and decide which herd has the best quality cattle. I may get rid of the others."

When they rode back to report to Joe and Roberto, there was considerable disagreement. Some argued for one color and others for another. When Joe insisted they agree on an answer, they moved off where he couldn't hear and finally elected Henry, the oldest in the group, as a spokesman.

"Joe," Henry said, "we can't agree on which bunch is best. The conclusion is — there is about the same ratio of good ones and sorry ones in each bunch."

After several minutes, with only the sound of bawling cattle in the background, the rancher said, "Let me get this straight. You men agree that in each color there are some that are good and some that are not so good?"

After everyone nodded or spoke to indicate their agreement, Joe simply said, "Well men, I reckon we all ought to think on it." He touched his old horse with spurs and loped toward the ranch headquarters, leaving his men looking at each other, thinking about what they had just heard.

The day had been lost as far as ranch work was concerned, but Joe felt a sense of pride. He reckoned that old Dave and his brother Dan would be pleased. He was aware that he made decisions each day by asking himself what those two men would do in a similar situation. He felt that today he got it right.

As the sun was setting behind the mountains, he opened the gate at the cross fence and waited while each man passed. Roberto stayed close. He waited for Joe to close the gate and climb into his saddle.

"Joe, this was a good day for the J bar C!" he said. "I'd sure like to know how you came up with the idea to turn the dun mare out without warning Dave."

"When I told you to put him on her, I didn't take into account the way she throws herself into a fence while bucking — trying to hurt the rider or at least get him off her back. After I went to bed, I thought about it and lay awake, reviewing possibilities. The only plan I could come up with was to turn her out where there was no corral fence. I knew him to be one hell of a rider, but I didn't expect him to stay on very long, going across the open pasture. I was just hoping he would ride long enough for the others to see how good he was, and hoping he wouldn't get hurt too bad when she pitched him off. We have to get him in the next rodeo!"

But Roberto asked him, "Joe, how many black and brown riders did you see in the last rodeo?"

CHAPTER 38

West of West,
Some will doubt,
Others think they know
What friendship is about.

With the prairie on the east side of the ranch headquarters and a ranch owner who was always up before dawn, the hands liked to say, "On this ranch the sun comes up early, but with those mountains on the west side, she goes down early too." What they liked most was the sound and smell coming from the cookhouse before dawn. They knew Vergie and Itza would have plenty of strong coffee and good food waiting for them.

One morning as Joe was enjoying the smell of bacon frying and watching the sun come up, he noticed all the horses in the nearby corral were looking in the same direction. So was Blue. Following their example, he looked too and saw two riders coming from the southeast. As they came closer, he could see their horses were about to drop from exhaustion, and the men were about to fall out of their saddles. When they rode in front of the barn, they did fall off. Joe caught one, and someone else caught the other. Coat was the one Joe was holding, though under the dirt and without a smile, he was hard to recognize. After sitting on the ground to let his face get washed with a towel and drinking some water, Coat's smile came out, just as the sun came up.

"Looks like when I'm in really bad trouble you are always there to bail me out, Joe. This coyote is my prisoner. I went into Mexico to get him, and found out Villa's men didn't like him any better than they liked me. We been running and hiding from them for four days. In the last two days the only nourishment we had was a drink of water when we crossed the Rio Bravo. I don't think they followed us across, but you better get your rifles ready in case."

After food and drink the two men passed out in the bunkhouse. Just before Coat passed out he said, "If he moves, shoot him." Joe kept watch in case the prisoner woke up to try to escape or cause trouble.

It was almost dark when Coat woke up. Right away he asked Joe to loan him two horses, and they soon rode off for Sanderson. Joe thought it strange that Coat didn't bother to handcuff or tie his prisoner, who hadn't spoken one word.

Joe told Vergie that night, "Being a railroad detective all these years has sure changed Coat. I'm not sure if the other man is a prisoner or something else."

***

Not only did Vergie learn to read better than Joe, she and Itza learned to read and write in two languages. The reading lessons were no longer necessary.

Vergie took over the job of bookkeeper for the J bar C. Each night she and Joe talked about notes she needed to record.

The one thing missing in their life was a child. They both wanted one. He wanted a girl who looked like Vergie, and she wanted a boy who looked like him.

***

After the next meeting of the Cattlemen's Association, Buck Yoakun asked Joe to stay for a minute. When the room was clear he said, "I know you probably suspect what I'm about to tell you. I want you to know up front, I don't put any stock in the rumors."

"Buck, no need to beat around the bush, what's on your mind?"

"There's a fair amount of puzzlement among some of the association members as to why your ranch has only been raided once, and on that occasion, you got all your livestock back. Some of them have been raided three or four times. A number of the men don't like your friend Coat Calcoat. They say he spends time with some folks who are known to have bad reputations. I think they don't like the idea that when they play cards with him, he leaves the table with a good deal of their money. You have to admit, he's mighty nosy about the business of the association. They still talk about your ranch foreman having a brother known to be one of the rustlers."

"I think my ranch foreman is a man of good character, who has absolutely nothing to do with the business of the rustlers. I assure you he'll help stop them any way he can. His brother was a rustler but was fatally wounded trying to keep the others from murdering J W. You know that story, and you know I've built fences that make it difficult for the rustlers to get to my best horses and cattle. Many of the members of this outfit let their best livestock graze next to Panther Canyon. If you were one of the raiders, which ranch would you pick to raid?

"And as for Coat, I have no influence on his life. If they don't like the people he hangs out with or the way he plays cards, they are welcome to tell him. Personally, I learned a long time back that he's a better card player than I am. My solution to that is, I don't put much money down when he's at the table."

Buck nodded his agreement. "Not only do I appreciate everything you just said, I've told them the same thing; and I'll repeat it as many times as necessary. Plus, I'll remind them that you and your men have the reputation of being deadly with rifles, along with your reputation as a bounty hunter. If I were a rustler, I wouldn't come close to your ranch. Don't worry, I just need to remind them. They are good men too."

CHAPTER 39

West of West,
Love abounds.
Music is lovely,
But gunshots sound.

On the way home from Alpine, Joe noticed that Vergie, who was usually a happy person, wore a smile that showed a little more self-satisfaction than usual. He always gained great pleasure from looking at her. He knew that if they lived to be a hundred years old he would never grow tired of putting his eyes on her.

"Vergie, you look quite pleased with yourself. Did you buy something or do something in town you haven't told me about?"

"Yes, I bought some material and buttons, so Itza, Miriam and I can make each man on the ranch a new shirt. I bought two new books, one written in English and the other in Spanish. Also I talked to the other wives about the way I've been feeling, and we decided I must be carrying a child."

When no reply came from her husband, she looked at him to see tears in his eyes. On several occasions, he had told her he couldn't understand why she cried when she was happy. Looking at him now, she resisted the urge to ask him why there were tears in *his* eyes.

After a long silence, he let out a yell. It frightened the horses so badly, it took him several minutes to get them back down to a trot.

As soon as Vergie determined that Joe had control of the team — and himself — she said, "We must be thinking about a school for our children. And for other children on our ranch and neighboring ranches."

"Yes," he responded.

She promised herself she would not fail to push the idea later, because she knew how important it was.

When he insisted she do nothing but eat and breathe she said, "Yes, dear." Then when he was not around, which was almost all the daylight hours, she spent her time doing all her customary tasks.

Vergie, Miriam and Itza had developed a unique style of singing together as they were working. Everyone who heard them agreed, their singing was remarkably beautiful. One would sing a song in

English, and then one would sing it in Spanish. Then they would sing together in different languages or perhaps the same language. The singing brought joy to them and entertained anyone fortunate enough to hear.

One day with all the men gone, the three ladies were in Itza's house, the old ranch house, sewing and trying to see who could sing with the most volume. They were startled out of their world of stitches and song when a man none of them had ever seen before stepped onto the porch. They'd been singing so loud, they hadn't heard his automobile when he drove in.

Vergie walked cautiously to the door to answer his knock. "Hello," she said, opening it.

"Howdy. That sure was beautiful music. I enjoyed it so much I sat in my car for several minutes just listening. Is Joe Collins here?"

"No, Sir, he's not. However, I think perhaps his brother is. You don't look much like Joe, but you sure sound like him."

Dan said with a smile, "I thought Joe must have exaggerated some in his letters about how beautiful and smart his wife was. Now after being here just a few minutes, I think he told it true."

As men came in from work, Dan enjoyed meeting each one. He and Dave were especially happy to see each other. Everyone came in by the time it was dark, except Joe. Often he was late, but as time passed even the hands that had told everyone not to worry, began to worry. Roberto sent Willis to get John Thomas. When John arrived he said they should go ahead and saddle up but wait another hour, until the moon came up, before leaving to look for him.

They were relieved when Joe's voice called out of the darkness, "Hello, the house. Don't shoot, it's me."

Everyone let out a sigh of relief and began loosening the cinch on their saddles. When Joe rode in, he said, "Don't put those horses away. We got trouble."

He saw his brother and jumped from his horse to shake his hand and hug his neck. "It sure is great to see you, but we got serious trouble. I can't visit now."

Dan couldn't take his eyes off his brother. A boy left home years ago, now here stood a man. In the light of oil lamps, he didn't look young any more. Dan asked, "What kind of trouble, Joe?"

Joe stepped up on the porch to make sure everyone could hear him, then said, "About noon, I was in the mountains when I looked south and saw a cloud of dust in the distance. Staying on the high ridges, it took me a couple of hours to ride to the cliff overlooking the mouth of Panther Canyon. I lay there on my belly and counted over sixty men and a few women preparing a camp. Beyond the area they were camping in, there was a rise, and some brush, so I couldn't see how many people were out of my sight. Judging from the smoke and dust over the rise, there must be at least sixty more, maybe a hundred. I just don't know. All the way back, I've been thinking about what to do. Roberto, we need someone to ride to the Double J and tell them to bring guns and ammunition. Tell them to keep sending the message to the next ranch until it gets to Canada, or at least Oklahoma. We'll have more time to get in position, so we'll cross the canyon and take up positions on high country on the other side. Tell Buck Yoakum to have his men take up positions on the high country on this side of the canyon. We don't have time to ride to the mouth of the canyon before daylight, so tell Buck we'll be due west of our ranch headquarters, on the other side of the canyon. He needs to have his men on this side of the canyon, between us and the J bar C headquarters. Now everyone fill your saddlebags with ammunition, get some food, and your rifles. We need to ride in ten minutes. Dan, that must be your automobile. Put the women and children in it and drive north till you run out of gas."

"Joe, the automobile is not a dependable means of transportation. I proved that on my three-week trip out here. I think it would be better for them to leave here in a wagon or buggy. I hope they can handle the wagon or buggy, because I plan to go to the mountains with you."

Vergie Mae spoke up. "Don't worry about us," she said. "We'll go to the cave that John and Miriam live in. We'll be safe there. All three of us know how to handle a gun, and with the bog out front of the little canyon, only one person at a time can enter. If anyone comes in that canyon, they'll soon wish they had stayed in Mexico. We can take care of the children and ourselves."

Joe had spent hours making the plans as he rode home. Now people who hadn't known about the problem ten minutes ago were making changes, but he didn't have time to argue. He was pleased to see that Roberto had Dave riding north to the Double J. He shouted over the loud talk as he ran to his house, "If you have two rifles, bring both — and all the ammunition you can carry! Henry, have someone get Dan and me fresh horses."

The ride to the mountains at a fast trot didn't take long, and although the climb up the mountain with only moonlight was slow, it was not a problem for these men and horses. The descent into Panther Canyon was another matter. Riding a sure-footed horse was no guarantee that a rolling rock or loose gravel was not going to cause the horse and his rider to fall. One loose rock under a horse's hoof could send him and the rider to the bottom of the canyon faster than either wanted to travel.

After holding his breath most of the way down, Joe celebrated with a deep breath as he heard the sound of each horse stepping onto the table rock in the floor of the canyon. He knew sunlight would be shining on their backs before they reached the upper ridge on the west side of the canyon.

Just after sunup, they took positions on the higher peaks of the ridge. If someone came north, in the floor of the canyon, they could shoot him even though it would be a long shot. If someone came north on the west ridge of the canyon, the men from the J bar C would be waiting directly in front with large rocks for cover and the advantage of the high ground. Each man was on the north side of a large rock that provided protection from bullets and provided a rest to keep his rifle steady.

For Joe the waiting was charged with doubt. Were the Mexicans going to cross the river? If they crossed, were they coming up the canyon? Why were they here? Were his men and his brother going to live through this? Were the women and children safe? Was he too tired to think straight?

About two hours after sunup, at least one question was answered when a group of thirty Mexican soldiers came into view, riding north on the canyon floor. Now Joe had to make a decision to turn them back with a warning shot or a kill shot. His men had been told to wait until he fired the first shot. He studied the men coming up the canyon and realized he had made a mistake in not having Roberto with him to help make a life and death decision.

Each of the approaching Mexicans wore a military uniform with three ammunition belts. He couldn't determine the rank of the man riding in front, but his uniform was decorated to leave no doubt that he was the leader.

Joe pulled the hammer back, took careful aim, stopped breathing and pulled the trigger. The leader fell from his horse, and ten other rifles fired almost as one. More than half the unit of solders fell or slumped over, and the others retreated as fast as they could ride. Only three Mexican soldiers managed to turn and ride out of the line of fire without being killed or wounded.

There had been no shots from the other side of the canyon, so Buck and the Double J men had not made it to their position. The thought that something might have happened to Dave, meaning Buck didn't get the message, sent a chill through Joe. He reloaded his rifle and signaled Roberto to come join him.

"Roberto, do you think I made the right decision to kill those men?"

"Those men are Pancho Villa's soldiers, not rustlers. I think they came to rob and kill, perhaps worse."

Before Joe could digest the answer, a man on horseback, waving a stick with a white flag on the end, appeared in the floor of the canyon. Roberto said, "He doesn't carry a gun. They wish to remove their dead comrades and give them a proper burial."

"If you think this is not some sort of trap, you can signal that we will allow them to remove the dead and wounded," Joe told him.

After handing Joe his rifle, Roberto climbed onto the rock Joe had used as a rifle rest. He motioned Joe to hand him his rifle. He held it over his head with one hand as he motioned to the men behind other rocks not to shoot. Then he slowly turned to face the soldier with the flag. He lay the rifle down on the rock he was standing on.

After observing the activity in the canyon floor a few minutes, Joe spoke to Roberto, who was still standing on the rock. "They handle the bodies with reverence," he said. "Before reaching to pick up a body, each soldier makes the sign of the cross."

Roberto's voice was sad as he said, "For some reason my people respect a dead person more than they respect life. To get the graves away from the traffic on the floor of the canyon, they'll take them to a plateau up on the mountain south of where they are now. There they'll make a proper cemetery, with a cross for each dead man."

Roberto spoke with such sadness it caused a chill to pass through Joe's entire body.

"Roberto, this is causing you pain," he said. "If you wish to go back to the ranch instead of continuing this fight, I'll not hold it against you."

The young Mexican ranch foreman remained quiet as he watched the men in the floor of the canyon finish their job and disappear. He handed his rifle to Joe and climbed down from the rock.

"We are fighting to defend your ranch and those who live there, including my wife and children," Roberto said. "South of the river there are two armies, both led by men who are greedy. If I were living in Mexico, I'd be killing my countrymen, because I'd be

311

forced to fight for one of those armies. Today, I kill my countrymen, but you do not force me to. I fight beside you because I choose to.

"You noticed there were over sixty men moving bodies, and there may be many more we didn't see. There are eleven of us, and they know where we are. When they come back, we'll have a real fight on our hands."

When Roberto and Joe walked back to make sure everyone was prepared for the next attack, they noticed John was nowhere in sight. Dan, who had been sharing a large rock with the black Indian, said, "I don't know where he is. I don't see how he could leave without me knowing. All of a sudden he was just gone. He must be planning to come back, because he left one of his rifles."

By the time Joe and Roberto got back to their rock, they saw John running toward them from the south. When he stopped near them, he was breathing hard but talking fast. "They're right behind me. This time they plan to have men on each side of the canyon as well as in the canyon, to draw our fire as the main force comes up this ridge."

"Good work, John," Joe said. "You and Roberto go tell the men what you just told us, so some of them can get in position to shoot across the canyon. Wait!

The Mexicans can't advance on us from across the canyon! Tell the men to try to have cover on their left side as well as in front. That way we can concentrate our fire on the main force coming up this ridge and not be distracted by fire from the canyon or the east ridge."

Roberto and John left immediately to get the men in position. Joe, who had been lying on his stomach near the top of his rock, moved to a position behind the west side of the rock.

He had just settled in place when a bullet slammed into the ground close to him. He surprised himself with the quick thought that this was the first time in his life anyone had fired a gun at him. He took careful aim and made sure the man who fired at him never fired at anyone again.

The volume of rifle fire, coming from both sides, soon became constant. The Mexican soldiers were pinned down about seventy-five yards away from the J bar C crew. For about twenty minutes, they made no progress. Rifle reports from across the canyon told Joe that Buck and his men were in place.

After a short lull in fire coming from the Mexicans, a rapid volume of fire kept Joe's head down for a few minutes. He looked up briefly to see soldiers taking position about forty yards in front of him. He fired two shots and ducked behind the rock, just as the volume of incoming fire increased again. Obviously, the soldiers had decided to use the tactic of laying down a volume of fire to keep the rancher and his men behind their rocks so other Mexican soldiers could move closer.

Bullets slamming continuously into the rock sent pieces of rock flying in every direction. Joe knew showing his head would be committing suicide. The only thing he could think to do, as he stayed on his knees on the north side of the rock, was reach for his pistol. Not knowing if the first Mexican soldier would come from the right, left or over the top, he knew he would need to react fast in order to kill one or more of the attackers before they killed him.

The few seconds he waited behind the rock felt like hours. He thought about his wife and unborn child, about Miriam, about Itza, about his brother and ranch hands who would lose their lives because they had followed him.

As he waited for someone to come over the rock, he realized the rifle fire from the north was increasing, and the volume from the south was decreasing. He looked behind him to witness so much rapid rifle fire it was almost like a continuous roll of lightning and thunder coming from each rock.

As the sun went down, Pancho Villa's men fell back. Joe discovered that men from other ranches had joined the fight on both sides and in the floor of Panther Canyon.

They were late, because the horse Dave was riding to the Double J in the dark stepped into a hole and fell. In the fall, the horse's leg and Dave's collarbone were broken. Dave finished the run on foot and arrived in such bad shape, it took a while for Buck to understand the message. The following morning, all soldiers from Mexico were gone.

CHAPTER 40

West of West,
Birds are singing —
From the mountains,
Strange sounds ringing.

The young general in charge of the invading army
had decided to use the headquarters of the J bar C
as his command post. When he was told his army
was on the run for the river, he chose to make his run
south in Dan's Ford automobile. About fourteen miles
south of the headquarters, the Ford stopped running.
Precious time was lost trying to make the car run,
because the general didn't like the idea of walking.
Men from the J H Ranch, east of Joe's, found him, and
he surrendered without a fight.

The next day, soldiers from Fort Davis arrived
to interrogate him and other captives. They learned

Pancho Villa intended for this army to travel to the north as far as possible in Panther Canyon, then the remaining few miles to the town of Marathon, Texas. Their orders were to clean out the banks and return to Mexico with anything of value, after burning the town.

The force Joe discovered, that he and the other ranchers turned back, was an advance party assigned to control the high ground on both sides of the canyon and to protect the main army traveling on the floor of the canyon. The colonel leading the U.S. Cavalry from Fort Davis told the ranchers, "You men cut off the head of the snake."

The citizens of Marathon now hold an annual celebration in honor of the local ranchers to show their appreciation and to thank the ranchers for defeating an army and preventing the destruction of their town.

Dave almost died from his wounds that were complicated by his gallant run to the Double J. Dan almost died from exposure in the mountains, because he was not dressed for cold weather. "That's the first time in my life I laid eyes on a mountain, much less spent the night on one. When we left the ranch headquarters to go to the mountain, I didn't know you guys were all wearing long wool underwear, and you didn't know I wasn't."

The sight of a team of mules pulling the Ford back to the ranch house caused him to comment, "After using that damn car for the trip out here, I just don't think they'll ever catch on. They won't ever be used much for cross-country travel. I tell you one thing — I plan to go back to Mississippi on the train! By the way, I plan to go through New Orleans on the way home, to visit with Betty Sue." Both men felt sadness, thinking about their sister. They had not seen her in over eighteen years.

Joe enjoyed bringing Dan up to date on the many things that had happened during the last ten years and telling about the people who were so important. He told of how much respect he had for Walter and Judy Ragsdale, and how their good opinion of Josh and Dan had influenced them to enter into the business deal with him for nearly two hundred mares.

"Dan," said Joe, "you've been doing business with Walter ever since our paw died, and never met him. Why don't you make plans to come to the Fat Stock Show in Fort Worth next year? I can promise you it'll be the damnedest show you ever will see. They now have most of the stock show and the rodeo inside a huge building.

"I've been so busy here," he continued, "I haven't been back since I passed through on my way out here. But I do plan to go next year and make a run at the cutting, before my bay horse gets too old. Last year the roping was won by a man riding a full brother to my bay. He'd bought him from William Anson.

"I was second in the cutting in San Angelo last year. Got beat by Henry. But that's okay, because he was riding one of my horses. We sold the one Henry was riding, after the cutting, for top dollar."

"Well you can just send Henry to Fort Worth," Dan said with a smile.

"You can bet that I'll take him along, and my money'll be on him."

Joe talked about William Anson, his Head-Of-The-River Ranch and his horses. About Korus Korus, the dentist from Alpine, who taught him about the plants on his ranch, and the neighboring ranchers. They talked of horses and why people were coming from miles away to buy breeding stock and trained horses and mules from the J bar C.

It took some time to review the activities of the man who drove horses for their father when he was only ten years old. "It seems that the longer Coat works on the train, the more rumors we hear. The last I heard, he was suspended for running a crooked crap game on the train. Whether that's true or rumor, I don't know. On any given day he may show up here looking like he's been drug through hell backwards, and the next time we see him, he'll be wearing a fine suit and tie with his detective badge showing.

"Not the last, but time before last, when he came through, he had a man with him that was presented to us as a prisoner. They were both about dead from exhaustion and dehydration. The horses they rode in on were used so hard, one lay down and never got up. The other one foundered and never got over it. Later Coat told me that guy he described as a prisoner was a Texas Ranger who had been undercover in Mexico and has since been killed.

"I sent him a letter letting him know you were here, in hopes he can stop by before you head home.

"Some folks around here think he may be providing information to some of the rustlers. I just can't bring myself to believe he would do such a thing.

"I hope you can stay, at least until the baby comes. Vergie says it'll be about a month. She says Itza is only a few days from having hers. This'll be their third."

"I left Judge McCool's son, Gary, looking after things back home," Dan said, beginning to think about what his schedule could allow. "When I told him I would be back in about six weeks, I had no idea it would take me three weeks to get here in my new Ford. I'd love to see your son or daughter, but I better head home in about a week or ten days.

"I plan to make you a present of that automobile. Someday it may have great historical value. I can picture it in a museum with a sign above it saying, 'The Mexican general leading an invading army was captured because this automobile broke down.'"

Both men laughed, and Joe said, "Part of the exhibit needs to be a photograph of the car being pulled by my team of mules.

"I don't want to forget to tell you about Calvin, John and Miriam's youngest son. It might surprise you to know that I am not the best hunter on this place. Fact is, I may be the third or fourth best. John and his boys are unbelievable. The young one, Calvin, is probably the best of all. He and I love to spend time together talking about hunting. Some men work for years on a ranch around here and never see a mountain lion. Those cats usually move only at night and are good at staying out of sight. Calvin has killed ten or twelve — two of them with his bow and arrow. I sure take a lot of pleasure in time spent with that boy, talking about hunting."

With Roberto to supervise the work on the ranch, Joe's main job was to check the livestock and keep an eye on any activity in Panther Canyon. The two brothers enjoyed several days of riding together, talking about the Big Bend country of Texas and about things that happened in or near West, Mississippi.

One day they found a Hereford cow having trouble giving birth to a calf. Joe said, "These cows bring more money than longhorns, but they sure are more work. We only have this one pasture of white face cattle, but most of my neighbors have lots of them. They spend most of their time pulling calves and doctoring Hereford cattle."

After the brothers had pulled the calf, and it was nursing, Dan picked up the afterbirth to carry it to a gully some distance from the newborn. When coyotes came to claim it during the night, it was always better if the newborn calf was not close.

After a few minutes Joe heard Dan call and went running to find his brother sitting on the ground holding his leg. "I was paying attention to some mule deer down in the gully and not looking where I was stepping. I stepped in a hole full of rattlesnakes. One got me just above my boot."

After tightening a belt around his brother's leg and cutting across the fang marks, Joe sucked the blood from the wound. He managed to get Dan back to the ranch headquarters. Once there, he yelled for a rider to go for Dr. Green, in Alpine, even as he was carrying Dan into the house.

John and Miriam Thomas's oldest son, Harry, had recently moved into the bunkhouse. When he heard that Dan had been snake bit, he turned to the other hands and gave a direct order. "Hook the buckboard up, go to the cave and bring my parents here — and hurry!" He jumped on the nearest horse and sprinted toward his parents' home. The men were in shock, because this was more than he had spoken since moving into the bunkhouse. They didn't know why he'd said all he did, but they knew he must have a good reason. They immediately hooked a team to the buckboard, and Henry drove to the cave.

When John and Miriam Thomas arrived at the house, Dan's leg was swollen and red. His entire body was hot with fever. Miriam began pouring a foul-smelling liquid down his throat, while John began covering the entire leg with an even more foul-smelling salve. After about an hour, Dan fell into a coma-like sleep.

When Dr. Green arrived the next day and examined the patient he said, "I don't know if the Indians saved your leg and your life or just your leg. I've seen, or should I say smelled, this treatment before, and it always gets better results than any medication in my bag or in the books in my office." He looked with respect to the Seminole Indian and his wife. "Can you read and write?" he asked them.

"In Spanish and English," John answered.

"I wish to compliment you on what you have done to save this man, and I have a request. Please write down the ingredients and procedure used to make the tonic and the poultice. If you know more than one name for the plants, please give me both names. In the past the people whom I observed using this or similar medication didn't know how to write down the ingredients or how they were mixed. If you do this, there's a dentist in town who will help me find the correct plants. Perhaps we can share your medicine with the rest of the world."

CHAPTER 41

West of West,
When things look right,
Terror can strike
With all its might.

A week later there was joy on the J bar C. Dan was walking with the aid of a crutch, and Itza had given birth to another healthy baby girl, the Arridondos' third child.

After Sunday morning breakfast, Dan and Joe each rolled a cigarette to enjoy on the porch of the rock house. The bright sun rising in the East made it more comfortable for the brothers to turn facing the mountains, west of the house. A shout from Russell Allsup, as he came from the bunkhouse, alarmed them — "SMOKE TO THE EAST!"

Without orders being given, every man on the ranch, except Dan with his crippled leg, ran to saddle a horse. As they left the barn, Dan handed each man several burlap feed sacks.

After nearly an hour of hard riding they came to a fence joining the J H Ranch.

It was common to construct wire gaps in fences between ranches. This made it easy to move stray cattle to the ranch they strayed from. Also, if a rider saw his neighbor's livestock needing immediate attention, he could let the gap down, ride onto the neighbor's ranch, throw a rope on the cow and tend to the problem.

Joe arrived to throw the gap down and then hurry to a water tank near a windmill on his neighbor's ranch. He soaked the burlap sacks he'd carried with him just in time to pass them to the next man in exchange for the dry ones he was carrying. He repeated this process until every hand from the J bar C was riding to the fire armed with wet feed sacks. They quickly crossed the burned area and joined the crew from the J H Ranch. After an hour, men using shovels, wet saddle blankets and feed sacks beat the fire down to a fraction of the size it was when Joe and his men arrived.

Joe had heard a gun shot but paid little attention until a J H hand rode up dragging the charred remains of a yearling heifer. "She was staggering around just about dead, so I put her out of her misery. I drug her up here, so you men could see her tail."

Jed, the owner of the J H, examined his dead, burned heifer carefully.

"There's wire wrapped around her tail," he said. "It looks and smells like someone used wire to tie feed sacks soaked in oil to her tail, then set them on fire and turn her loose. Why in the world would someone want to set fire to my range?"

"I can't think of but one reason," Joe answered, "and I hope I'm wrong. I think maybe they wanted us to come help fight fire so that rustlers could move my livestock into Panther Canyon."

"The wind is beginning to lay, so I think we can gain control of this fire," said Jed, " if we don't stand around talking too long. You better take your men and see to your livestock."

The most valuable livestock on the J bar C were the horses in a pasture on the northeast corner of the ranch, as far from Mexico and Panther Canyon as possible to still be on the ranch. Instinct and thoughts about how well planned this attack was caused Joe to lead his men to this pasture. When they arrived, his worst fears were confirmed. Fences had been cut.

Over three hundred of the best horses in Texas were missing.

It was easy to follow tracks, but tracks were unnecessary, because everyone knew to ride to Panther Canyon. An empty pasture and one holding longhorn cattle had been between the horses and the canyon. The fences had been cut and the cattle ignored. The rustlers had come for Joe's best horses.

As bad as feelings were over the loss of the horses, a much more horrible sight awaited Joe and his men when they reached the foot of the mountain and the trail leading up the mountain into the canyon. In the middle of the trail, mangled by the hooves of the horses, lay the body of Calvin Thomas, the youngest son of John and Miriam. His rifle lay beside him — trampled, like its owner.

Calvin had left his home before daylight with plans to return with one or two mule deer. He loved to hunt mule deer, and everyone liked bragging on the meat he brought to the cookhouse. Everyone knew that when Calvin pulled a trigger, something died. It was obvious Calvin had stood in the middle of the trail to attempt to turn the horses. More than likely he'd been shot before the horses trampled his body, but the damage to the body was so great, no one could tell. His father and brother did not cry out loud, but their pain and sorrow were obvious as they removed their shirts and wrapped Calvin's remains to be carried back to the only home he had ever known. Henry had a slicker behind his saddle. He brought it forward to complete the terrible task.

After helping them secure Calvin's body behind his older brother's saddle, Joe asked his men to gather around. "I plan to follow the men who did this and kill every one of them," he said. "As much as we'd like to go after them now, we're not equipped. Most of us don't even have a gun. We must ride to headquarters to get guns, ammunition, food and fresh horses. The bastards got a head start and will be in Mexico before we catch up to them. That may be a good thing, because we can kill them in Mexico and not violate United States law.

"I plan to cross the river and kill every last one of them. If any of them survive the gunfight that's probably going to happen, they'll be hanged. Fort Davis is over a hundred miles away, Austin is over three hundred miles away, and Washington is thousands of miles away. We are the only people who can get this done. I vow to kill them or die trying. If any man doesn't want to cross the river, I can understand. If you choose not to ride with us, I'll not hold it against you."

John rode up beside him and said, "I'll meet you at the river and tell you where they are. I know that if something should happen to me, you'll keep your word to kill them all." Without waiting for an answer the sad, black Indian rode up the mountain and disappeared.

Back at headquarters, Vergie had trouble understanding John's action. "I would think John would come home to be with his wife and family during time of grief," she said.

"I turned this over in my mind on the way back here," Joe said. "For many generations his ancestors have been fighting to survive. I suspect, in most cases, there was no time to grieve. I suspect there are more of them buried in unmarked graves, along the trails, than in cemeteries. More times than not they had to bury a loved one and ride on, or sometimes just ride on."

"Yes, like we did when my mother was killed." Vergie trembled as she replied.

Joe recalled that sad morning, years ago, when he could not comfort Vergie. This time he did hold her, as he knew she would hold Calvin's mother while she grieved.

Dan was leaning on his crutch in front of the barn waiting for his brother. Before stepping onto his horse, Joe asked, "Will you stay to look after things until I get back?"

"I'll be here," Dan said, knowing his brother might not come back.

"Roberto's oldest daughter, Maria, can ride like the wind. If you need to send for the doctor, you can count on her to get the job done. If you need to send for me, tell her to get in the canyon and ride to the river. Tell her not to cross the river. If we're not there, she's to hide and wait for us on this side." Joe rode the length of two horses before stopping to add, "If we don't show up in twenty-four hours, she's to ride back here."

CHAPTER 42

West of West,
Go slow and wait.
Hell itself
Is through that gate.

The ride to the river was calculated to cover ground as fast at possible without killing their horses. Joe planned on the rustlers slowing down after crossing the river — thinking they would not be followed. Every man had at least one handgun and a rifle. Joe also carried his twelve-gauge shotgun.

Riding made conversation almost impossible, but thoughts flowed through Joe's mind in a steady stream. Roberto's brother had been with the rustlers who stole mares and colts. If another of Roberto's family was with these rustlers, would Roberto kill him? Would Roberto kill his own kin?

It was obvious that someone who knew their way around the J bar C had planned this attack. Coat Calcoat had helped plan the fencing layout, and he would know how to use it in such a well planned raid. After agonizing over this possibility, Joe tried to dismiss the idea that his old friend could be involved is such a horrible crime. The question that continued to go through Joe's mind was what he'd do if he found himself in a showdown with his longtime friend.

Counting John, Joe's crew consisted of three black men, three brown men and four white men. John and his son, Harry, were also Indians. Joe knew that, like the vision of Vergie's mother's body, he would live with visions of young Calvin Thomas' mangled body for the remainder of his life.

John was not at the river when Joe and his men arrived. About sunset they found John's horse grazing peacefully along the riverbank. Not wanting to start a fire, they set up a cold camp and waited. Joe knew the horses and men needed some rest, and he was confident John would show up before too long. About two hours after dark, John appeared at Joe's side. No one saw him come into camp. He was just there.

His sudden presence startled Joe. "John, I'm sure glad you are on our side," Joe said.

Not being in the mood for small talk, the Seminole began to explain the situation. "They crossed the river and turned east. About four miles east and about a mile south there's an abandoned ranch headquarters. They have the horses in a pasture to the south, and they are inside the barn and ranch house. They left one man on a high lookout about two miles from here to watch their back trail. A lot of whisky was waiting for them. Come daylight, we can catch them asleep and get in close."

"John, you know the layout best. What do you think our plan should be?" Joe asked.

"There's probably a plan to change the lookout man in three or four hours. We want the man who is being relieved to report, to whoever is in charge, that there's no sign they are being followed. I'll go watch and wait until the change is made, then I'll kill the one who is left. I can drop down on this side of the lookout point and build a fire without the snakes in the house and barn seeing it. Have a man on the hill yonder, and when he sees the fire, move out along the trail, due east. I'll meet you about two miles from here. If we move fast after the lookout's gone — and with some luck — we can take up position around the house and barn before daylight. If something happens to me, please remember you promised to kill them all."

John's only remaining son, Harry, seldom spoke, but he did now. "I will not sleep until the men who killed my brother are dead," he said. "I'll take up position on the hill and watch for my father's fire."

Joe nodded approval. The two black Indians, still without shirts, walked away.

"I'm with you, Joe — sure am glad those two are on our side," Henry said.

Joe said, "Yeah, the colonel over at Fort Davis told me that in years passed, when Comanches would come down from the Indian territory and Apaches were coming from Mexico to raid in The Bend, things were really bad around here. But the army had a black Seminole scout, and more often than not the Seminole would put the army in a position to kill the Comanche and Apache or put them on the run.

"Even if we build a big fire out in the open, no one will see it. So, I vote we be extra cautious and build a small one on the west side of that big rock and boil some coffee," Henry said.

"I always thought I'd have liked to have been here a hundred years ago," he continued, "but if things were bad then compared to now, I ain't so sure,"

Russell Allsup couldn't resist saying, "Don't be trying to bullshit us, Henry. We all know you *was* here over a hundred years ago."

The wait was longer than expected. It was several hours past midnight when they heard the whistle from Harry Thomas signaling them to ride. The moon was not bright, but the stars provided enough light for them to move at a good steady pace. When they arrived at the abandoned ranch where the rustlers were holed up, it was still dark, but soon the sun would light up the eastern sky.

An oil lamp was burning in the house. It gave credit to the idea of burning the buildings to run the rustlers out.

There was a rise on two sides of the house that provided Joe's men good cover. In contrast, the area around the barn was open, and provided no cover. John Thomas signaled for everyone to remain in place as he moved across the yard and looked in a window of the house. He quickly returned to the cover of the rise, where the others were lying on their stomachs, rifles ready in case the rustlers spotted John.

"I think there are more men here than when I was here last time. The house is made from logs. It has a dirt floor but a thatch roof. It'll burn but not so easy."

He stopped talking as someone came from the front door of the house. The starlight silhouetted the man as he stood on the porch of the house to relieve himself. The sun was not up, but light was showing in the eastern sky before the man was back inside and everything was quiet again.

John whispered, "There are whiskey jugs on the table near where the oil lamp is burning. I think I can take a position just to the side of that window and hit the oil lamp and a whisky jug with one shot. The oil and whisky should cause a pretty good fire. I've got to move to the window now before they wake up. When another man comes outside, shoot him. That'll be my signal to shoot the lamp — and one less snake to deal with." Without waiting for an answer, he stood erect, walked across the yard and took a position, against the wall, on the side of the window.

Roberto had remained quiet as he lay on his stomach with rifle ready. Now he whispered, "There's someone in the barn. I heard them cough."

Without waiting, Joe backed away from the rise and answered, "You men have the house covered, and you know the plan. I'll take two men to the barn and try to keep whoever's there pinned down." He motioned for Henry and Russell to follow him as he used the rise for cover and moved away from the house.

"You men do your best to get to the front of the barn without being seen. Swing wide and stay low.

I'll go to the back and try to set the hay in the loft on fire to drive whoever is in there out."

The door to the hayloft was missing. When he got to the back of the barn, he could see some old hay in the loft. While he waited for action to start at the house, he used his knife to cut the tail off his shirt. Then he used the shirttail to tie some dry grass into a bundle. Before he could move to the barn, a rifle shot from the area of the house startled him. Knowing he had to move fast, he ran to the door of the barn, struck a match to the bundle of dry grass, and threw the torch into the loft of the old barn.

Shots were coming from the house and from the men on the rise near the house. He could see smoke coming from the house, but it appeared to be burning slowly. In contrast, the old dry hay and lumber caused the barn to go up in flames almost as soon as Joe's torch landed in the loft. He heard shots coming from the house and the front of the barn and knew he must get away from the burning building. As he raced across the open area, a shot from the barn knocked his right leg from under him and sent him tumbling. As he was falling, he started the process of removing his shotgun from his shoulder. By the time he stopped rolling he was lying on the ground with the shotgun pointing in the general direction of the barn door. A rifle muzzle sticking out from behind the heavy barn door let him know where the shot that put him on the ground came from. With the barn burning fast, he knew the door would soon open, and he and the rifleman would try to kill each other.

He cocked the mule-ear hammer that fired the right barrel, and while he used his thumb to hold the hammer back, he held the trigger down tight with his trigger finger. Then he jammed his middle finger, tight, into position in front of this trigger finger to insure the trigger would stay in the back position. Now, even if the man behind the door shot Joe, the hammer would drop, and the person behind the door would also die. He was sitting on the ground, without any cover, waiting.

He didn't wait long. The door swung open. Joe's shotgun sounded like a cannon. Without firing his rifle, the man dropped it as he fell.

With tears already in his eyes, Joe left his shotgun and crawled to the man he had just shot. The man was not dead, but with a full load of double-ought buckshot in his chest, he soon would be.

"Why?" Joe asked him. "Why would you rob from me and your daughter, and your grandchildren?"

"I didn't. I told them not to go to your ranch. I didn't know about the boy getting killed until they came back here. I always wait on them here. I didn't know it was you running from the barn." Carson Finley took one more tortured breath, and it was his last.

Joe asked the dying man, "Why didn't you shoot when you opened the barn door? Did you recognize me?"

No answer came.

Joe felt hands clamp around his arms, and he realized someone was dragging him away from the burning barn. He lay on the ground, thinking about his father-in-law. He knew Carson hated the government, the railroad, and anyone who was more successful than he. Now he began to understand how twisted Carson's hate was.

CHAPTER 43

Men of the mountains,
High in the sky,
Men of the mountains,
Your ghosts came by.

When Henry cut the mangled boot off Joe's right foot, he found a badly bruised, bloody foot, but no serious damage. Apparently the bullet had hit the heel of the boot. Fragments had only made cuts and bruises.

In a gully east of the burned barn, they found Carson Finley's wagon and team. As the bodies of the dead men were being placed in the wagon, Henry told Joe, "It would be better for you to ride in the wagon and keep your foot elevated."

"Henry, riding in a wagon full of dead men may be better for my foot, but it would be hard on me otherwise. After you bandaged it, one of the men brought me a large boot off one of the dead men. It has room for my swollen foot and the bandage. Bad enough wearing a dead man's boot. I'll make it all right horseback."

With the wagon full of bodies leading the way, followed by the stolen horses, the drive back to the mouth of Panther Canyon was underway by noon. The rustlers involved in the gun battle at the house had given Roberto and John information, but now they were all dead. Joe didn't ask if they were killed after they talked, or talked while they were dying, like Carson. They'd learned that Carson, who had furnished fence posts for just about every ranch in The Bend, exchanged information for stolen livestock. Joe was wishing he didn't have the job of telling his wife about her father. The realization came to him that when he saw someone die, something inside him died as well.

He wanted to be with his wife so desperately, but he so dreaded facing her and telling her that he had killed her father, who was part of a gang of bandits.

He and Roberto rode behind the others. They discussed the plans the two of them had made the night before while waiting on the signal from John Thomas. They had found picks, shovels and axes around the abandoned ranch and in Carson's wagon.

Handles had been replaced on those that had handles burned away.

Near the mouth of the canyon, on the United States side of the river, they would bury the bodies. Each grave would have a cross. There would be a fence around the cemetery leaving just enough space for someone on horseback to pass, into and out of the canyon. No one could drive a herd of cattle or horses out of the canyon and across the river without desecrating the burial ground. A large cross would be placed over the gateway into the cemetery, and each corner post would support a cross.

All the men were exhausted by the time the horses had been moved across the river into the canyon. Between exhaustion and his throbbing foot, Joe felt he had never in his life been so anxious to get off a horse. After Henry helped him dismount, Joe insisted he would boil some coffee and prepare supper. While he performed this task, the men settled the horses. Then they started cutting poles for the cemetery fence and digging graves.

That night he gave thanks that he and the men who rode with him had all returned with only minor wounds.

***

Roberto and Joe had no way to know how well their plan would work. Whether it was because they killed off the main rustling gang, or because of the cemetery at the mouth of the canyon, or both, no one knew, but the members of The Cattlemen's Association *did* know that the raids and rustling through the canyon stopped.

Over time, though mountain lions continued to travel the mountains and canyons, the name of Panther Canyon evolved to become known as "Ghost Canyon." The mountains on each side of the canyon that held the bodies of Indians from ancient times, Spaniards that were buried before Plymouth Rock had a name, Comanche and Apache from more recent years, along with Pancho Villa's soldiers, became known as 'Ghost Mountains.'

The next morning all the men were busy by daylight. The desire to get the unpleasant task behind them and return to the ranch was strong. As the men came back to camp for a breakfast of beans, tortillas and coffee, Joe noticed Roberto. Roberto was standing alone, looking up to the mountaintop where his brother had been wounded and J. W. had been murdered, by a band of rustlers. As Roberto shifted his attention to the river and found a rock to sit on, Joe knew his ranch foreman was dealing with heavy thoughts. He gave his friend some extra time for private thoughts before taking his own seat on a rock just a few feet from where Roberto sat. Joe didn't speak. He waited.

Finally, Roberto said, "You know it feels like so long ago when I first crossed this river, just a few miles to the east. I don't know if it was luck or fate that I walked on to William Anson's ranch and got a job there that lead to a job on your ranch. I've been thinking about all the men and women who wade or swim across, going in both directions. I hear they even have a bridge, over near Ojinaga.

"It's like trying to sort those longhorn cattle by color. We found out there were good ones and the other kind in all colors. Same for people who cross this river going in both directions, and those who stay home. There are many good ones and, unfortunately, many of the other kind. Sometimes, I think we don't understand each other, because we don't know where we are. People from this land where I grew up think this is North. Those from where you come from think this is West."

As they rose and walked to the camp, Joe asked, "Roberto, do you think you'll ever move back to Mexico?"

"I don't think so, but I don't know. I'll take my family there to visit. One thing I know is, children change a person. Now that we have children all the things that happened before are less important. Our love for family and friends is still as strong as ever, but now the love for our children dominates. The decisions Itsa and I make now are much more important, because they influence the lives of our children."

Just before noon, Joe looked up when he heard the shouts, "Rider coming!"

Roberto's oldest daughter, Maria, rode in on a horse that was so overheated and tired it was covered with foam and could barely stand. She immediately began to breathlessly apologize for riding the horse so hard. Her father interrupted her, asking, "Why are you here, Maria?"

"Señor Joe's brother told me to come tell Señor Joe the bambino is coming, and he should come home pronto. He told me to ride hard and not let the horse rest."

"Get me two good horses!" Joe shouted. "Thank you for coming, Maria. Was the doctor there?"

Within minutes he was riding north on a sorrel mare and leading a sorrel gelding. He planned to use them as hard as the young messenger had used the gelding she rode in on. Maria's report about the doctor being there yesterday and still there this morning didn't sound good. He rode north on the rocky canyon floor and up the mountain on the east side before jumping to the ground. He fell as he came off his horse because his damaged right foot would not support him. He got up, pulled the bridle off the mare and let it fall to the ground. He climbed on the gelding, and rode east to his home and wife — and perhaps a son or daughter. With every hoof beat he dreaded telling his wife that her father was dead, by his hand.

When he arrived, he found his brother and the doctor sitting on the porch waiting for him. The expression on their faces told Joe the news was bad.

He climbed down from his horse and limped onto the porch. Dr. Green stepped forward and put his hand on Joe's shoulder. "Your baby girl is fine. Your wife will be gone within the hour. I did everything I could. I am so sorry."

Joe almost fell off the porch. Dan caught him by the arm and held onto it to help Joe enter his home.

The door to the bedroom was open. They could see Vergie lying in bed. Joe walked to their bed, sat down, slipped his hand under her head and spoke her name.

From the bedroom doorway, Dan could see her lips move, so he knew she said one word to her husband before she passed on. He couldn't hear what the word was. It was obvious that the dying wife and mother had saved her strength to speak her last word to her husband.

Joe sobbed as Doctor Green pulled the bed sheet over her face. His heart broken, his dreams shattered, he rose and walked to the main room where Itza was seated in a rocking chair. Itza sat with tears on her face and a white baby sucking on her brown breast.

Joe walked to them and knelt down. Through his tears he looked at the baby girl. Then, talking very slowly, his voice weak, he said, "Vergie always said she wished her name was Virginia instead of Vergie. This is Virginia Collins."

Dan felt as helpless as he had when his mother and father died. He watched as his brother, who looked old beyond his years, limped to a cabinet, removed a bottle of whiskey, limped to his horse, climbed up and rode off into the night — much like their father had done years ago.

After Joe disappeared, Dan began a shout of "YOU...," but didn't finish it. He knew his younger brother could not hear anything outside the world in his brain. He knew his brother had never grieved the loss of their father. Now that Joe knew how his father must have felt, he would have the grief of his father's death added to grief for the loss of his beloved wife. It was more grief than anyone should have to take on. And Dan didn't know about the pain his brother felt from having had to kill his father-in-law.

They both could hear their aunt's shrill voice saying, "All Collins men die drunk, and they don't live to be old men."

The exhausted doctor, knowing that Itza would take care of Virginia, went to the bunkhouse to get some sleep.

Dan went to the cabinet to see if there was another bottle of whiskey. There was none, so he simply walked to the front porch and sat in a rocking chair. He didn't rock. He just sat and stared out into the night, listening to Blue, Vergie's dog, howling the mournful sound that hound dogs make when there's death in the family.

At dawn, Miriam Thomas and Itza Arridondo cleaned and dressed their white sister's body for burial. They also cleaned the house and cared for the babies. Dan moved from the porch into the house, picked up his niece, and began to walk the floor, looking at her and loving her as she slept. After a while he heard some shuffling on the porch.

Joe came through the door. He limped over to the cabinet to replace the whiskey bottle, unopened. He sat in the rocking chair and motioned for his brother to hand Virginia to him. After holding her and rocking a few minutes, he said, "School! I'm going to build a school."

Dan now knew the word that Vergie, who had never been inside a schoolhouse, spoke with her last breath. "School."

And he knew Joe would live because his wife's dream had become his dream. Dan also knew his brother, who had a strong will to make dreams come true, would build a damn good school.

> *West of West,*
> *I dream of you today,*
> *And your dreams*
> *Will never fade away.*

ABOUT THE AUTHOR

Jim and his wife Shirley both started riding horses at a young age and continue to consider it important to have good horses and a good dog on their place near Seguin, Texas. They both love to ride and talk about horses. He promises more books will follow with stories about people and horses.

Printed in the United States
87416LV00001B/85-249/A